Yeager's Getaway

An Abel Yeager Thriller

Scott Bell

Yeager's Getaway
An Abel Yeager™ Thriller
Red Adept Publishing, LLC
104 Bugenfield Court
Garner, NC 27529
http://RedAdeptPublishing.com/

CHAPTER ONE

D*iamond Head, Oahu, Hawaii*
Saturday, 8 May
1340 Local Time

Kanoa Ino had chosen the meeting place to serve a purpose. Diamond Head Lookout presented a panoramic vista of Honolulu and Waikiki Beach and, by extension, modern Hawaii. Used in countless scene-setting shots for televisions and movies, the view represented an iconic image, instantly recognizable. High-rise condos, hotels, and offices. Smog and exhaust fumes. Blue ocean to the left. Rolling surf.

He could picture the scene in those distant resort hotels lining the beach: groups of island women in fake grass shorts swishing their asses to the sound of a tinny ukulele, mocking the spiritual *hula kahiko* dance, while fat, lobster-broiled mainlanders gawped at them... and men in anklets of grass, whirling lit torches, as if the Samoan fire dance was of Hawaiian origin instead of imported shtick canned and repurposed for the titillation of tourists.

Bobby Palakiko leaned his crossed arms on the rail next to him. "Aloha, Kanoa. You are looking massive as always."

"Aloha."

A stiff breeze off the ocean fluttered Palakiko's Born Hawaiian T-shirt and flattened his cargo shorts against his spindly legs. Salty black hair whipped away from his comb-over. Next to Kanoa's towering height and powerful physique, the diminutive old man seemed to be a different species. Tourists milled around the two of them like a constant flow of brightly colored beetles, oohing and aahing at the view or screeching at their hyperactive children. Adult *haoles* and their offspring bumped into Kanoa, heedless and unapologetic as they huffed along the concrete path.

An Asian tourist in a white, short-sleeved shirt stood slightly apart from the crowd. A pair of binoculars dangled from his neck. Kanoa kept his gaze away from the prim little Asian so as not to draw attention to him.

Sunlight glinted off Palakiko's Ray-Bans. "A beautiful day."

Kanoa shaded his watch with a palm, checking the time. He let the silence linger. The old man waited. A faint permanent-press smile creased his lips, as if everything in this world—including Kanoa—amused him.

He won't smile for long.

"Did you hear about the Akaka bill?" Bobby offered at last. "It has a chance this time, I think."

"It will fail. Again."

"We will achieve the same status as Native Americans. You'll see."

"And earn the right to live on a reservation? Maybe sell beads to the haole?"

"Always such a downer, Kanoa. You should learn to relax. Aloha, brah."

"This"—Kanoa spread a broad palm to include the world around them—"is what one hundred twenty-three years of *aloha* have wrought—a world full of haole, white Americans, yellow Japanese, black Africans, and sheet-wearing Muslims—massed on the beaches, bobbing in the waves, oiling themselves with suntan lotion. Snapping selfies, eating, drinking, puking, and pissing. Taking everything of value. Leaving nothing but trash... trash and money. Always money. And we're complicit in our own degradation, prostituting ourselves for the price of a color TV and a case of Miller Lite—Hawaiian culture whored out three times daily with a matinee on Sunday. No, *brah...*" He sneered the word. "The time for aloha has long passed. It is time for Kūka'ilimoku."

Kanoa tracked the old man's expression with his peripheral vision.

Palakiko sighed. "We are a people of peace—"

"And peace has killed us, old man!" A gaggle of Japanese ceased their chattering and gave Kanoa sideways looks at they edged past. Kanoa glared, and they hurried on. *Time to show some fire.* "Our language, dead. Our people, slaves. Our culture, gone. The imperialist conquest is complete, and all your hand-wringing does is salt the wound with a little more white-man guilt, which they will appease by offering us platitudes and half-measures, as always."

"Why again with this argument, my bruddah?"

"We are tired of waiting." Kanoa glanced at his watch. "My men are ready to do battle. Hawaii for Hawaiians, now and forever."

"Your men?" Palakiko smirked. "What is the name these days? The Niho Niuhi—Teeth of the Tiger Shark? Whatever. Listen, my giant friend. The movement won't allow you to tear us apart with violence."

"I don't need your blessing, Bobby. My men are ready, and Ku will bless our struggle with victory."

The old man tilted his head back to match Kanoa's stare. The crow's feet radiating out from around his sunglasses deepened. "What do you mean?"

"The Anglos have not listened to us. They annexed the islands illegally, by force, for the benefit of the sugar barons. They have ignored us ever since. Raped our land. Destroyed our people. Beguiled us with bullshit promises. For too long, we have waged peace and begged for scraps. No more. Kūka'ilimoku demands blood. The Niho Niuhi will honor him with it."

"An ancient Tiki god demands blood? Did he send a text or what? You been smoking some primo weed, brah."

"We are tired of waiting. Bumpy promised us things would change, yet even he sits and talks instead of doing things. Nothing changes through peace. Nothing. Aloha!" Kanoa spat over the railing. He checked his watch again.

As if to punctuate his expectoration, a fiery flash blew out from the side of a beachside skyscraper, followed by a dirty-white billow of smoke. Seconds later, a flat *crack* traveled up the coast. A rumble followed, vibrating the air. On the heels of the first explosion, a sequence of four more blasts shook the distant skyline.

"The targets just hit," Kanoa stated, "were the Marriott Resort, the Hilton Hawaiian Village, the Ala Moana Mall, the Outrigger Reef Resort, and the Hyatt Regency Waikiki."

Tourists crammed the guardrails of the overlook. They shouted and pointed. Many held up cell phones to record the wounded buildings as they were wreathed in brown fog. It was too far away to hear the screams of the injured, although the wail of alarms drifted to Kanoa's ears, thin and remote. Bobby Palakiko gripped the rail, more to keep himself upright than anything else, Kanoa suspected. The old man seemed frail enough to blow away on the wind.

"Those were the first shots fired," Kanoa continued. "The Niho Niuhi will rain blood throughout these islands, and we will keep bringing the pain until all the haoles have gone. Hawai'i will again be ours."

Palakiko's head cranked around as if on rusty bearings. Gape-mouthed and pale, the old man regarded Kanoa and, without a word, collapsed in a dead faint.

Kanoa spared a quick glance at the Asian tourist dressed in white. They exchanged minuscule nods. *Phase One, complete.*

VILLAGE OF LA MANZANA, Chiapas, Mexico

Friday, 7 May

1650 Local

Approximately Twenty-Three Hours before the Honolulu Bombing

Victor's Law *Numero Uno*: Get too happy, bad shit happens.

Case in point: there he was, sitting under the lifted rear hatch of the green Ford Explorer, his feet dangling over the sandy asphalt main street of La Manzana, Mexico—population 601 people, fourteen goats, and enough chickens to stock a KFC franchise—enjoying the warm, satiny breeze off the ocean and really getting into a game of Toss the Pebble into a Pothole. He was about as happy as he'd ever been, if he wanted to be really honest with himself.

The village was La Manzana—the Apple. Victor thought they should name it La Manzana Podrida—the Rotten Apple. Dr. Alexandra Lopez, aka Dr. Hot Stuff, was inside the *clínica*, doing medical stuff with stethoscopes and probes and wicked hypodermic needles. Soon she would come out of the one-room building and jump in the Explorer with him. They would zoom off to a rented beach condo with a postcard view of the Pacific Ocean. After cocktails and before dinner, they would engage in profound and spiritually moving carnal knowledge of the vigorous and sweaty variety.

Maybe twice, if we skip the appetizer.

After a warm night of post-dinner cuddling—and maybe more belly bumping, if he could recharge in time—they would get up, have breakfast, zoom to the airport for a series of flights out of the ass end of Mexico, and enjoy a weekend in Hawaii with their friends, Abel and Charlotte Yeager.

"Why exchange a cheap ocean view for a wildly expensive one?" he had asked.

"Because I've never been to Hawaii," Alex had told him.

If she wanted something, Victor would eat broken glass to see she got it. She was that kind of woman. "And now look," he said to himself. "Extreme buzzkill, incoming."

Three young men swaggered up the hill with the gangsta-cool strut that was stamped into the DNA of amateur thugs everywhere. T-shirts stamped Bangers 'R' Us would have been less obvious. Instead, they wore the uniform of every Mexican male under twenty—shiny football jerseys over sloppy pants. They sported all of the national team's colors—green, white, and red—as if a flag had decided to go for a walk dressed as three punks.

Not punks, Dr. Alexandra Lopez would say. *Misguided youths.*

Victor shook the half-dozen pebbles in his hand like dice and waited for the wayward youngsters to make their approach. The youth in the middle stopped a few feet away, out of arm's reach, and his amigos spread out in a flanking maneuver. A splattering of orange soda stains decorated the white jersey of the guy in the middle, who smiled and revealed the most disgusting teeth Victor had seen on a human.

Victor cringed. *Orange soda must not cut plaque.*

"You with the doctor?" said Teeth.

"Yes."

"She treats the people? For free?"

"Yes."

"*Mi madre...*" Teeth spoke without inflection, not even trying to sell the lie. "She has a headache. You have some drugs for that?"

"You sure you're not looking for the dentist?"

"What?"

"I mean, shit, *hombre*. Have you been eating dirt all your life, or you just start lately?"

Teeth traded glances with Green Shirt, to his right, and jacked up his belligerence a notch by edging closer and practicing his baby-faced intimidating loom. The open hatchback of the Explorer forced the kid to dip his head, negating some of the loom's effectiveness. The pull strap dangled in the kid's face, and he ducked around it.

Victor stifled a smile. He'd been loomed over by the best, and this kid had a long way to go before he could call himself a quality loomer. Assuming he lived long enough.

"Give us the drugs, cocksucker," Teeth growled.

"All the drugs," Green Shirt chimed in. Red Shirt said nothing, but then again, Victor supposed that was only natural—Red Shirts weren't important anyway, and the kid's slack expression made him look as if he had some kind of mental impairment on top of that.

Victor squinted and cocked his head to one side. "You boys need to go home. Play with your *narcotrafficante* action figures or with the PS4. This is not a game for you to be playing."

"You think I'm playing?" Teeth pulled up his soda-stained shirt to show off the butt of a revolver tucked in his waistband. "This is not a ga—*ahh!*"

Victor's hand snapped out, whipping pea gravel into the kid's face like shrapnel. Teeth jerked back, flinging up a belated forearm block. Victor powered off the SUV's back deck in a fullback rush, driving his shoulder into the kid's midriff. His hand snaked out and tugged the revolver free of the punk's waistband.

When Victor stopped, the kid didn't. Teeth hit the street on his back, head cracking against the pavement with an audible smack. Victor spun and leveled the revolver at Green Shirt, whose hand had disappeared into his back pocket.

"Don't do it, amigo."

Green Shirt froze. Red Shirt frowned as though vaguely confused.

Victor sidestepped to keep Teeth in his peripheral vision. "You *pendejos* are lucky. I have a friend, this Marine? He would have chopsockyed all you pricks to oatmeal and fed you to the hogs. He does not have restraint. Not like me. Lucky for you, he is on vacation."

Victor waggled the pistol. "Now, pick up your friend, and don't let me see you outside of Sunday school again. *¿Entiendes?*"

He backed up and let the two would-be henchmen gather their dazed and fallen leader. As they slunk away. Green Shirt scowled as if to say, *We'll be back to kick your ass*—a look common to dick-punched thugs everywhere.

After they'd gone, Victor resumed his seat, his happy mood tarnished. He inspected the weapon, a vintage Smith & Wesson Model 10—something Humphrey Bogart might have carried in one of his old black-and-white gangster movies. The bluing had worn off to bare metal on the cylinder and barrel, and the wooden grips shone from a hundred sweaty palms handling it. Victor flipped open the cylinder and discovered three cartridges, the brass shells tinged with green corrosion.

"Damn thing. Blow my hand off if I shoot it." Victor punched the ejector and pocketed the shells. He tossed the gun into a milk crate loaded with boxes of Johnson & Johnson gauze, tongue depressors, and tape. "Throwing you in the ocean, Mr. Smith & Wesson." The happy mood oozed back into his soul, and a grin tugged at his cheeks. "After sex, of course."

Victor's Law *Numero Dos*: "Make love as soon as possible." He'd made that one up on the spot.

All of Victor's clouds were lined with silver, unlike that doofus Yeager, who carried the whole world on his shoulders. Although come to think of it, the big, dumb jarhead had gotten almost goofy with happiness since he'd hooked up with Charlie. Victor could roger that. Alexandra Lopez injected pure joy right to his heart with just a smile and wink. Not even a trio of knuckleheads like the tricolor-shirt gang could put off Victor's happy state for long.

One of a million of La Manzana's ubiquitous chickens clucked her way across the road, keeping a wary eye on him as though he might fancy a chicken dinner. "Go on, *el pollo*. You're safe for now."

The hen didn't look convinced.

CHAPTER TWO

Fair Breezes **Cruise Ship, Off the Coast of Molokai, Hawaii**
Saturday, 8 May
0840 Local Time
Five Hours before the Honolulu Bombing

An epic hangover cracked Abel Yeager's head like an egg. His yolk of good cheer dribbled out, leaving nothing but an empty shell of misery. A bowling ball squatted atop his shoulders, heavy and hard, while chimpanzees trampolined off his stomach lining.

The pocket-sized cruise ship, *Fair Breezes,* bobbed more than a cork on a fishing line, and the only thing keeping Yeager's insides from erupting in a volcanic expulsion of stale beer and pretzels was the uncertainty of making it to the head without falling over from dizziness. The stateroom bed embraced him in sweat-damp sheets and held him in a plush cocoon. He planned to stay under the blankets until paramedics arrived.

A larger-than-normal wave rolled the ship. Yeager groaned and covered his eyes in the crook of an elbow.

"Serves you right." With an e-reader braced on her belly, Charlie reclined near the balcony doorway, sunlight streaming through her coppery hair and a breeze ruffling the collar of the cotton cover-up she wore over her one-piece swimsuit. Her long legs were propped on the corner of the bed, crossed at the ankles, treating Yeager to a view of the soles of her feet. "How late did you stay up drinking with your new best friends?"

"I don't know," Yeager mumbled. "One o'clock, I think."

"No, you came in at three."

If you knew, why'd you ask? He kept his mouth shut.

"Reeking of beer, I might add."

You just did. That, too, he kept to himself. The warning flags were out: Charlie was pissed off and didn't need any nitrous oxide injections to get her fired off the starting line. Normally, Charlotte Buchanan Yeager was a joy to live with—smart, funny, and naturally happy. Like Victor. On the rare occasions when she did lose it, Yeager found it best to lock up the breakables and hunker down for a storm. His bleary-eyed reading of that day's weather indicated a squall approaching, and it could either blow over or brew up to hurricane force.

"Just my luck," Charlie said without looking up from her reader. "I finally ditch the kids and go on a much-delayed honeymoon cruise with my husband, who used to be a Marine. And guess what? The ship is packed with Marines."

"Three is hardly *packed*. And those guys were salty."

All three of them were Vietnam vets, telling tales of the Rockpile, Ca Lu, and Hill 881. Hue City... Khe Sanh. Who wouldn't want to hear those war stories?

"And while you're out swapping lies with the Leatherneck Legends, your wife is waiting up for you in her brand-new nightie. See-through, like you like it." Charlie stabbed her reader with a finger and flipped an electronic page.

Yeager could almost hear the page snap. He lifted his pounding head with ponderous effort. "I'm sorry I missed that." And he meant it. She could make his heart race when she was wearing a spacesuit and face cream. Charlie in sexy lingerie made him lose his mind. He groaned again and flopped back. "I really, really am."

She must have taken pity on him, because she got up and brought him a bottle of water from the minifridge. "Here. Rehydrate, caveman. You're going to need it today."

"Why's that—" A memory clawed its way up through the corpses of dead brain cells. "Wait. Oh, hell no."

"Oh, hell yes, Staff Sergeant Yeager." Charlie stood by the bed with her hands on her hips and a smug expression. "We hike the nature reserve today. Three hours of exercise should sweat all the beer right out of you."

"God hates me," Yeager groaned.

"God will forgive you. I, on the other hand..."

PUERTO ARISTA, CHIAPAS, Mexico
Friday, 7 May
2210 Local
Approximately Eighteen Hours before Honolulu Bombing

Dr. Alexandra Lopez stalked into the bedroom, muttering curses. One towel wrapped her figure, while another rode her head like a downy-white turban. Blood trickled a thin line along her thigh. She breezed by the bed, where Victor was nursing a full tummy and savoring the comfort of clean sheets and foam-filled pillows.

"What's wrong?" he asked, though truth be told, his attention was arrested by the sight of Alex's butt as she bent over and rooted around in the boxes of medical supplies lining one wall of the condo's bedroom. The towel rode up the back of her thighs the way a super-short miniskirt would. *Just a little more...*

"I cut myself shaving my legs. You Americans and your damned fetish for shaving." Alex opened a second box. "Where's the box with the bandages?"

"Hmm? Oh. Next one over, I think. Deep in the box... no, really deep."

"Aie! What's this?" Alex popped upright with the old Smith & Wesson dangling from a finger by the trigger guard.

"*Una pistola.*"

His flippancy earned him a cocked eyebrow and a pursed lip. Alex crossed her free arm and propped the elbow of the one holding the firearm.

"It was Surrender Your Gun Day in Armlick, Mexico," Victor said in English. "How lucky for us."

"Mm-hmm," Alex said, which Victor translated as *Bullshit.*

"Some kids trying to be tough," he said with a shrug. "Set it by the door so I don't forget to throw it in the ocean." Victor let his eyes drift closed as he listened to Alex bustle around, getting herself ready for bed. Her soft sounds had a domesticated feel that left him... content. Was this how Yeager felt with Charlie? It was really nice.

Not for the first time, the word *marriage* crept into his unguarded mind.

Shit, dude. Get a grip.

Alexandra was a doctor, with more degrees than a thermometer, brilliant and beautiful and accomplished. As for Victor, ever since his antique Huey had blown its engine, he was a helicopter pilot with no helicopter and a former United States Marine—Bronze Star, Purple Heart. He was also a part-time smuggler—of contraband only, not drugs or people—and occasional soldier of fortune.

And of course, don't forget: galactic-class heartbreaker and lovemaker.

But hell, Yeager was a big, dumb jarhead without enough nickels in his pocket to buy a pack of gum, and he'd hooked a woman almost—*almost*—as pretty as Alex.

The bed sagged as she slipped under the covers. Her warm, very naked body cuddled up next to him, sending wakey-wakey signals to his sleepy pecker. Alex hooked a leg over his, and the heat from her sex warmed his thigh.

"Who were the kids?" she murmured.

"Huh? What?"

"You said some kids were trying to be tough. Who were they?"

Victor blinked and tried to focus. Punks with guns were about the last thing he wanted to talk about with two firm boobs pressed against his side. "Ahh. Just some misguided youths. I spanked them and sent them to bed without supper."

Alex lifted up to look him in the eye. "You could have been shot. Again."

"Not me. I'm bulletproof."

"Bool shit." She traced a ragged scar on his ribcage. "You almost didn't make it last time, *mi hermoso*."

"I had motivation." Victor grinned and twisted around, pulling Alex tight to his chest.

"Mmm," Alex hummed. "I feel your motivation poking me in the belly."

"What can I say? You are extremely motivational."

Much later, Victor sank into the fog of sleep, cocooned in cottony bliss. The only sound in the darkened room came from the ocean breeze buffeting the windowpanes, and the very faint *shush* of breakers rolling in from the west. His consciousness floated on a lazy stream, thoughts dissipating before forming, and his awareness ebbing on the outgoing tide of the ocean of sleep. In that state of near-unconsciousness, he thought he heard Alex whisper so softly that the puffs of air from her words tickled his shoulder, and her tiny voice came from a distance, so he wasn't sure whether he actually heard her or only dreamed of her speaking: "*Te amo.*"

I love you.

MOLOKAI FOREST RESERVE, Molokai
Saturday, 8 May
1355 Local

Ten Minutes after the Honolulu Bombing

The combination of steamy heat and brilliant spears of sunlight stabbing his eyes treated Yeager's head to a drum line of painful throbbing. He counted himself lucky to have managed a quiet morning of upchucking his toenails before Charlie dragged him from the cabin to join the platoon of tourists for the boat ride to the shore of Molokai. The brochure had represented Molokai as "emerald mountains lofting over blue diamond seas," and Yeager could find no fault with the description. They landed at a boat ramp next to a white-sand beach. A bus idled in a nearby parking lot.

Soon after a drive in air-conditioned comfort, the hardier and more adventurous passengers of the *Fair Breezes* had piled out into the tropical heat and transferred to a trio of four-wheel-drive vehicles. After the gut-crunching drive, they reached an overlook to a deep gorge, where everyone supplied their *ooh*s and *aah*s. Venturing past that point required permission, which the tour company had obtained, so the passengers shouldered their packs and followed their petite guide up a steep trail, heading eastward into the Molokai Forest Reserve. To their right, the mile-high tip of Kamakou and the East Molokai shield volcano dominated the skyline. To their left were trees and trees and more trees.

Wayward Ventures, the tour company that operated the *Fair Breezes,* billed their Hawaiian cruise as an "off the beaten path" experience. As a small ship that carried about forty passengers, the *Breezes* catered to a demographic that spanned middle-aged people to hardy seniors. The passengers tended to be younger and in better shape than the average cruise ship tourist. The three Vietnam vets and their wives were the oldest by far, whereas Yeager and Charlie fit near the other end of the age bracket. A vegan couple from Mountain View, California—who checked all the appropriate boxes on the social-awareness questionnaire—won the youth prize, clocking in somewhere under thirty.

Only nine passengers, including the Leatherneck Legends—as Charlie called them—had opted in for this hike. As hikes went, it could make a Boy Scout cry. "Vigorous" was how the pamphlet described it.

Fucking miserable was how Yeager labeled it.

By the middle of the six-mile hike, even the California vegans were starting to flag. The tour leader called a halt, and everyone milled to a stop on a shaded section of narrow trail. Yeager parked his butt on a boulder bordering the path and mopped sweat with the back of his sleeve. He flexed his left hand, which had started tingling again. After taking a partial blow from a machete to the forearm, the hand had never really been right again. Of course, whenever Charlie asked about it, he claimed there was no numbness at all.

He drained his sixth bottle of water. Winston Pettigrew appeared at Yeager's elbow. At an age when most men wanted a rocking chair and a nap, Winston—one of the three Leatherneck Legends—had the energy of a hyperactive four-year-old. He reminded Yeager of a brisket left on the grill too long: lean, black, hard, and gnarly. He wore a too-big cap with "Vietnam Vet" stitched in yellow on the forehead, and he huddled inside an ancient Members Only windbreaker despite the heat.

"That's your wife, right?" Pettigrew hitched his chin to where Charlie stood next to the couple from California. All three heads were together, looking at Charlie's phone. By the couple's rapt expressions, Yeager gathered his wife was showing baby pictures of John Riley Yeager, seven pounds, four ounces. Charlie couldn't get enough of showing off the kid to anyone who would hold still long enough. To Yeager, the boy resembled a miniature Edgar G. Robinson—pissed off and scowling.

"Yes, it is," Yeager said.

"Shee-it, boy. I had her back in my cabin, I'd never come out."

Yeager snorted. "I wish I'd thought of that before this here Bataan Death March."

"Whaddya think's going on?" Pettigrew had a gravel-mixer voice from a fifty-year Marlboro habit.

"With what?"

"Lu Kim. She took a call on her sat phone, and now look at her."

The activity director from the cruise line, Lu Kim was as chipper a person as he'd had ever met. He suspected the tiny Korean woman's blood could be used to cure hatred in the Middle East. Yeager leaned out and craned his neck to find Lu at the front of the pack, distancing herself from the rest by hunching over her phone with a finger in the other ear. Her posture resembled that of someone sucker punched in the gut.

His scalp prickled. "I don't know. Bad news, looks like."

Danny Osterchuk wandered within range, waving a hand in front of his nose. "Hoowee. That heat don't halfway leave a man drooping, don't she?" A Minnesota-bred farm boy, Osterchuk was Winston Pettigrew's genetic opposite. Six-two with the girth of a polar bear, Osterchuk hadn't missed a buffet since mustering out in 1971. Sweat slicked his ruddy face and soaked the collar of his XXXL Hawaiian shirt. Early on, Yeager had voted him most likely to collapse of a heart attack. "I can't believe we're paying good money for this. Uncle Sam used to pay *me* to hike in the damned jungle. I should have stayed on the ship with my wife."

"Look on the bright side," Winston said. "Ain't nobody shooting at you. No malaria, no booby traps, no crotch rot. No two-dollar hoes with the ten-dollar clap."

"But enough sweat to drown an alligator." Yeager squeegeed his forehead with a finger and flicked the droplets away. "Fair warning, Osterchuk: you fall out, ain't nobody doing CPR."

"If I fall in a combat zone," Osterchuk chanted, "box me up and ship me home."

Pettigrew broke into a greasy cough, bending double and holding his knees. "Need a butt," he wheezed after the spasm passed.

"No smoking here in God's garden, ol' buddy." Osterchuk thumped a meaty palm on Pettigrew's back. "We can't fuck up that volcanic tang with yucky cigarette smoke."

"Uh-oh. Check this out," Pettigrew said.

Lu Kim was waving her arms for everybody to gather around. In cuffed shorts and a tan work shirt over a tank top, Kim stood at a whopping five foot one.

"There's been a terrorist attack in Honolulu," Kim announced. Though pale and shaky, she spoke with a firm voice and appeared to have her wits gathered. A stir passed through the passengers as she continued. "Several bombs exploded at Waikiki locations. An unknown number of dead or injured." She held up a hand to halt the first sputtering questions. "If you have friends or family in the Honolulu area, transportation will be made available to you immediately. And of course, we should have cellular phone coverage and Wi-Fi once we return to the ship."

"Who did it?" asked a passenger Yeager didn't know.

"I don't have that information at this time."

"Fucking ragheads," muttered Pettigrew.

"What if we want to go home?" That question came from a Rhode Island insurance salesman named Tom or John or something. "Do we get a refund?"

Yeager tuned out the answer and found Charlie then put his arm around her shoulder. She leaned in, resting her head on his chest. Yeager sighed and held his wife close. "Honolulu's two, three hundred miles away. We're safe here. And should be even safer on the ship."

"I know." Charlie hugged him. "More random violence. And for what?"

"No good reason, I'm sure."

"How can we keep going? Can we have our honeymoon and enjoy ourselves when America's been attacked? I don't feel like having fun, knowing what those people are going through."

"We don't let the terrorists win, for one thing," Yeager said. "We've planned this trip for months. I'll be damned if I'll cut it short because some fanatic is killing people to make his sick point."

Charlie searched his face with her clear blue eyes. "Are you sure?"

"Absolutely." Yeager grinned and planted a wet kiss on her forehead. "No terrorist is going to spoil our honeymoon. Besides, Por Que and Alex are coming. I'd hate to miss seeing them."

CHAPTER THREE

Lu Kim asked for a show of hands, and the hikers unanimously agreed to continue their trek. Charlie noticed Abel's hand didn't exactly leap up with enthusiasm, which she chalked up to his hangover. The man was a hurting puppy. Sweat saturated his short-sleeved button-down work shirt—the same shirt she was positive she'd thrown out at least once. *And good God, the jeans.* The man refused to wear shorts, so his legs had to be sweltering in a pair of Wranglers that were worn to a frazzle around the back hem and bleached out to a blue so light it was almost white. A striation of chalky sweat lines marked his inevitable gimme cap in a historical record of previous sweaty days.

Charlie studied her husband as he unlimbered his backpack and retrieved yet another bottle of water. His eyes had a natural cant that made him appear a little sad and world-weary and as dangerous as a fuzzy stuffed otter.

But she'd seen the other Abel—the one who came out when bad things happened. It was spooky, the way Abel transformed from an amiable, warm, sincere human male into a... war beast. His skin tightened, and his eyes turned hard, glittering, and soulless. The predator surfaced, dominating his features and attitude in a way she found both disturbing and exhilarating. And she was even more disturbed to find it so exhilarating.

A primal force lurked behind her husband's thin mask of civilization. Charlie sensed it when they made love. She teased it, the way one would court mortality by walking along the parapet of a skyscraper or toying with the lock on a tiger's cage, testing her control of a dangerous power that could snuff out her life in the blink of an eye—though knowing he never would. Feeling that potency, that barely contained violence held in check by his utter commitment to her, humbled and exalted her in equal measure.

It's like making love with a werewolf.

People stirred, gathering their packs and retying hiking boots. Ted Pyle, the third of the Leatherneck Legends, joined the group around Yeager. Pyle's wife, Betty, hovered at his shoulder. Of the trio, unmarried Pettigrew was the fifth wheel. Betty had volunteered to hike the wilderness trail, while Jan Osterchuk had remained aboard the ship for a "mai-tais-and-trashy-romance-novel afternoon."

"We ready to do this thing?" Pyle asked in the overloud voice of the nearly deaf. Ted had earned the inevitable nickname Gomer while serving in 'Nam during the same era as the television show with Jim Nabors. Gomer had a bald, liver-spotted head surrounded by a fringe of white hair that tufted over both ears. He hunched a little, carried a bowling-ball belly, and regarded the world through watery blue eyes. Two dumbbell-sized hearing aids weighed down his ears and did little to improve his colossal deafness. Betty, a sparrow of a woman with infinite patience, mother-henned him around the ship—a helicopter wife. Charlie had been surprised Gomer had slipped her leash long enough to get drunk with Abel and the other Marines.

Betty patted her husband's arm. "No need to shout."

"I'm not shouting!"

Osterchuk, looking like a red-faced polar bear, had parked his considerable butt on the boulder in the spot recently vacated by Abel. He didn't look well either. "I think I need to sit a bit longer."

That prompted a visit from Lu Kim, and Charlie tuned out the discussion. She'd known at the outset that the big Minnesotan wasn't in shape for a hard wilderness hike. Betty Pyle must have had the same opinion. Charlie met the older woman's eyes and shared a knowing look.

"You guys go on," Osterchuk said to the activity director. "I'll catch up. Or if not, I can find my way back to the overlook."

"I can't leave you alone, Mr. Osterchuk." Lu Kim reached for her sat phone. "Let me call the rangers."

"No, no. It's okay, really."

Charlie caught Yeager looking at her. They'd been married less than a year, and they could already read each other's minds as reliably as two telepaths. She nodded. He winked. Communication sent, received, acknowledged.

"I'll stay with him," Abel said. "No need to drag a ranger up here."

"But—"

"We got this," Abel said in his staff sergeant voice.

Lu hesitated but hung in there. "The trail is not well marked."

"If two ex-Marines can't follow a gaggle of tourists through the woods, we deserve to get lost."

"In fact, all us geezers will hang here a bit," Winston announced. He snagged Gomer by the sleeve and tugged him closer to the rail. "Betty, you go on with them others and leave Gomer here with me."

Betty's eyes narrowed. "You didn't bring any beer, did you, Winston Pettigrew?"

"No, ma'am, not a drop. Swore off the stuff."

"Bullshit." The profanity from the prim white-haired old lady triggered a bark of laughter from Charlie. The two women shared another look, this one roughly translating as, *If men didn't kill spiders, what use would they be?* "Let's go, Charlie Yeager," Betty said. "Leave these boys to their mischief. Come on, Lu. You're better off not arguing with them."

Charlie hugged her husband and found it surprisingly hard to let go. His warm, solid bulk felt so... strong. When she was wrapped in his arms, nothing would get to her. Nothing could harm her. The extended contact set off the familiar tingle below her waistline, and the urge to drag him into the bushes and claim him right there surged up from her belly. She wanted to feel him inside her—to ride the lightning and unleash the thunder.

She shook off her fancy and pulled away. Charlie smiled at the smolder in his eyes. Not only did they read each other's minds, but they read each other's bodies as well. It was obvious the same feelings had sparked in him, and his eyes pledged some major fireworks. Later. When they were alone.

A mini-shiver ran up her back. *How long is this damn hike supposed to take?*

THE LAST OF HIKERS trailed out of sight, and Pettigrew fished into the pocket of his windbreaker for a pack of cigarettes and a lighter. He scorched the tip of a fresh Marlboro faster than Yeager could have triggered off a shot from a single-action revolver. Pettigrew's nostrils vacuumed up every wisp of smoke, letting none escape until he sighed it out in one long stream.

"Give you credit," Yeager said. "You waited a whole thirty seconds before firing one up."

"Twenty-nine seconds too long," Winston said through another stream of smoke.

That far inland, away from the beach, the air stuck to Yeager's skin like Scotch tape. Midges raved in clouds of black spots, and party-colored birds played tag through the trees. Wind stirred the upper branches, only occasionally penetrating deep enough into the jungle to breathe across his sweat-soaked shirt and provide a little relief from the muggy warmth. Lu Kim claimed the temperature was unseasonally warm for this altitude.

From another pocket of his jacket, Pettigrew produced a silver flask, sloshing the contents for emphasis. "I didn't lie a bit. I didn't bring no beer, but I brought a little hair of the dog, for sure."

"Gimme that," Osterchuk said.

Pyle grinned and held out his hand when the big man finished a long pull.

Yeager's stomach clenched at the thought of more alcohol. He waved it away when Pyle made to hand it to him. "No, thanks."

Pettigrew snagged his flask out of Pyle's hand. "Did I ever tell y'all about this little camp whore, turned out to be a Victor Charlie in-*feel*-traitor?"

Osterchuk groaned. "Not again."

"She shows up at Firebase Henderson at the cross streets of Fuckall and Jackshit. Middle of the boonies. No pimp. That right there should have been a clue. Not having any better sense, these boys snuck her inside the wire and got her set up inside a tent. Turns out she had a grenade stuffed up her cootch. Three white boys took a turn without noticing a thing, but the first brother that stuck it in snagged that pull ring with his dick." Pettigrew wagged his head from side to side in pure sadness. "Man, talk about a blow job..."

The groans only seemed to encourage Pettigrew, who proceeded to roll out one dirty story after another. Uncouth, politically incorrect, racist, and in every other way inappropriate for polite company, Pettigrew's tales always happened to somebody he knew, and he swore they were true, no matter how unlikely.

"I can't listen to more of this," Osterchuk groused after a fable that featured a mule and a mildly nearsighted private first class near Da Nang. "I'd rather die on the trail. Let's move."

Pyle forged ahead, walking point as if he was born to it, while Yeager stuck close to the big man, who seemed to have recovered his wind. Yeager made Pettigrew take the drag position so he wouldn't have to eat the man's smoke. The four of them fell into the rhythm of the march, as natural and smooth as any four-man patrol. No talking. No excess noise at all, for that matter. Walking and breathing, breathing and walking. Yeager let his mind go blank and opened up senses that had been dulled by domestic living for too long.

Because his warrior brain was switched on, he recognized the faint *tock-tock-tock* of small-arms fire several seconds before his companions. Pyle walked on, oblivious. Osterchuk took several steps before he noticed Yeager had frozen in place and was rotating his head to fine-tune the sound.

Pettigrew approached from the rear. "Who's shooting? Hunters?"

"Shhh!" Yeager hissed.

The group had been warned not to stray from the trail, as hunters roved the forest for wild pigs and axis deer. But this was no hunter. Unless deer and pigs had armed themselves, hunters would not be shooting at them on semiauto.

Pyle must have noticed everyone had stopped. He wandered back, eyes scrunched in a question. Osterchuk held up a hand to keep him quiet.

"We're out in the open here," Pettigrew said, "standing around like a bunch of dweebs. Let's get off the trail."

Yeager nodded absentmindedly, his senses dialed up to the max. He led the way into the forest, going right by instinct, in the direction of higher ground. Yeager approved of the way Pettigrew and the others fanned out and advanced in a near-silent heel-to-toe stalking stride.

He froze. From far ahead, attenuated by distance, a very high-pitched, very female scream filtered through the jungle. Yeager broke into run.

LANAI RESORT, LANAI, Hawaii
   Saturday, 8 May
   1201 Local
   One Hour, Forty Minutes before Honolulu Bombing

Dave Draper paced the plush carpet of the Lanai Four Seasons ocean-view suite and listened to Ron Gonsalves make excuses. The phone grew warm against his ear, but that was nothing compared to the heat building up from his collar as the manager of his Tustin BMW dealership continued to enumerate the reasons he was a grade-A fuckup.

"And, you know," Ron said, continuing his litany, "with the construction on I-5, the traffic's just down, man. We just aren't getting the walk-in traffic like we used to."

"You forgot to mention the Orange County economy," Dave prompted.

"Yeah, you're right. The economy's been in the tank for the last three quarters here." Gonsalves rambled on about all the reasons he wasn't making his numbers, and Dave listened, more for tone than substance, until his general manager ran out of gas.

He took a breath then let it out. He owned twelve dealerships in and around Orange County, and the Tustin BMW location caused more trouble than the other eleven combined. Sarah Rae had told him Gonsalves was the problem, and though Dave didn't want to believe it at first, he had to admit his wife was probably right.

Whatever. He was supposed to be on vacation, not listening to this crap. He needed a Pepcid.

"We'll talk when I get back," Dave said and disconnected.

Sarah Rae's voice came from the suite's bathroom, muffled by the closed door. "Dave? Can you call down to the desk and get some more towels?"

"Sure," he yelled back then muttered to himself, "Thirteen hundred dollars a night. You'd think they'd have enough fucking towels."

A commotion in the hallway interrupted him halfway to the room's phone. Some assholes out there were yelling and banging stuff around. A bunch of fricking college kids, no doubt, though how they could afford the place was beyond him. "You'd think thirteen hundred dollars a night would keep out the trash. Like staying in a goddamn truck stop, this place."

A banging at the door caught him with the phone still in his hand. He frowned at the distraction, considering whether to go ahead and call or answer the door. The banging repeated with even greater intensity. The solid door rattled in its frame.

"What the everlasting fuck?" Dave growled. "This is too much."

"Someone's at the door," Sarah Rae called out.

"No shit, Sarah Rae. What gave it away?" Dave said under his breath. Crossing the suite, he yelled, "Who is it?"

"Hotel manager," came a muted voice. "There's been an emergency."

Dave swung the security hook off and opened the door... to find a gun barrel stuck up his nose. A broad man with more tattoos than a 38th Street banger shoved his way inside, propelling Dave by the front sight of a semiauto hooked in his nostril. A second man, smaller and wearing a hotel uniform, followed close behind, carrying, of all things, a clipboard and a pen.

"Draper, David C.?" the clipboard holder asked, pen poised in the air. "And Sarah Rae Draper?"

"Wha—w-what do you want?" Dave experienced a sudden and powerful need to empty his bladder. He squeezed down and somehow managed not to piss himself. The pistol-poking Samoan spun Dave around with his free hand and kicked his feet out from under him. Dave's face ground against the fine-pile carpeting of the Four Seasons. His hands were jerked back and zip-tied together. Sarah Rae was yelling something from inside the bathroom, but Dave couldn't make it out. His brain was stuck in WTF drive.

Clipboard said, "We want you and your wife to join us for a short stay in the jungle, Mr. Draper. Get the woman." The last bit, Dave was pretty sure, was addressed to the big man.

"Sarah!" Dave twisted on the floor like a landed fish. "Stay in the—"

Bam! The crash of the giant's foot into the bathroom door shattered the lock and broke it open. Sarah screamed.

Dave goggled up at Clipboard. "Don't hurt her!" He meant it to sound tough, but it so whiny and scared it humiliated him.

"Nobody will get hurt," Clipboard said as the Samoan dragged Sarah Rae into the room. His wife had her pants on but no blouse. Her frothy white bra contrasted with the tan she'd been working on for the last three days. Clipboard continued speaking over Sarah Rae's blubbering. "No, Mr. Draper, everything will be fine. Cooperate, and everyone will go home safe and sound."

The Samoan grunted a derisive laugh.

CHAPTER FOUR

Molokai Forest Reserve, Molokai
Saturday, 8 May
1410 Local Time

To Charlie, the mood of the hike had turned from happy to funereal. Expressions of delight at the natural wonder and beauty of the island paradise had all but died off, and reactions from the hikers seemed subdued, contained. It felt wrong, somehow, to celebrate and enjoy their time here while others were suffering the shock and agony of brutal, unprovoked attacks.

Yeager had said terrorists wouldn't ruin their honeymoon, but truly, they'd already done so. And so many people had had more than their vacations ruined. Guilt knifed her heart. How shallow was it to complain about her mild unhappiness when others were dealing with the loss of loved ones? She couldn't even imagine the horror they were enduring.

The trail pinched to single file and wound through a series of switchbacks. No one had spoken in the last few minutes, and Charlie noted with surprise that she and Betty Pyle had fallen behind. Lu Kim, Tom from Rhode Island, and the California vegans had disappeared ahead of them, lost around a bend in the trail.

They separated further when Betty Pyle stopped to tie her shoes—a serviceable pair of Magellan hiking shoes, Charlie noted. She'd looked at that exact style before upgrading to a pair of Merrells prior to the trip. The older woman also wore a pair of unflattering desert-brown shorts and a tan cotton T-shirt under a green Eddie Bauer short-sleeved shirt that had seen better days.

Betty squinted up at Charlie as she tightened her laces. "Abel seems a little under the weather today."

Charlie smirked. "War wounds from last night's stories."

"Hah! Well phrased."

"I've never actually seen him drunk, so this was a first for me. And hopefully a last. It wouldn't bother me except for the whole *romantic honeymoon* thing."

"He seems to dote on you, so I doubt you need worry." Betty finished with her shoes and straightened, brushing out her shorts. "Besides, we have to give our Marines a little slack. They have a bond you and I will never understand. Ted recognizes a kindred spirit in your Mr. Yeager. It's like they can smell each other—smell the death and bloodshed and sense the weight of the shield they bear to protect the rest of us from harm."

"I know, I just—"

Pop-pop-pop!

Gunshots. Loud and close. Charlie was an instant behind Betty Pyle in hurling herself to the earth. She scrambled after the spry old lady as both of them sought cover off the trail. Screams laced the forest where Lu Kim and the others had disappeared. Charlie squeezed into a dense growth of ferns, pushing past Betty, who had her cell phone out, peering at the face of it.

"Signal?" Charlie whispered.

"Nothing," Betty said equally quietly.

"Damn."

"Damn is right."

"What happened?"

Betty nudged her shoulder, pointing out a natural tunnel through the brush that led in the direction of the yelling, angry voices. "Let's go find out."

Before Charlie could voice a protest, the older woman belly-crawled forward. Charlie watched the soles of her Magellans worm past and disappear into the undergrowth. Swishing brush marked the older woman's path as she crawled off the trail and up an incline toward the deadfall.

Charlie hesitated. Heading toward the sound of gunfire had never seemed the wisest course of action. Hunkering down and staying invisible seemed more prudent, considering they were unarmed.

The voices had gone quiet, but the trees rattled with the squawks of disturbed birds. The scent of loamy earth tickled Charlie's nostrils, and she wiggled her nose to stifle a sneeze. The soil was soft and deep, and staying put seemed like a really, really good idea.

Charlie huffed out a frustrated breath. She wiggled forward, following Betty Pyle's crawl marks. She found Betty hiding under the remains of a dead tree that lay at a forty-five-degree angle and was held up by its neighbors like a drunk at a party. It overlooked the hiking trail, and the gap under the vine-covered tree proved an excellent vantage as matted brush packed the triangular space under it and allowed a green-filtered view of the scene below. Charlie wormed her way up next to the older woman, who patted the air, gesturing for her to stay down.

As if she needed to be told.

Charlie winced at the variety of crawly things motoring around the earth under the dead tree. Steadfastly refusing to look at a beetle the size of a walnut that waddled past her nose, she peered through the foliage at the leaders from their hiking group. She spotted Lu Kim and the two vegans sitting hunched together, hands laced over their heads. A trio of Asian gunmen hovered nearby, index fingers alongside their trigger guards. They wore black tactical clothing and black berets, and they carried stubby carbines that were either automatic or semiauto. Unlike Abel, Charlie wasn't into gun porn, so she couldn't tell what they were by sight alone.

The trio became a crowd when six more appeared from the surrounding forest, including one brutally ugly specimen with a face as harsh as an Easter Island statue. That one appeared to be in charge. He issued a string of orders in a singsong language that—to Charlie's untrained ear—could have been anything from Mandarin Chinese to Korean to High Klingon. One thing it didn't sound like was Hawaiian.

At his direction, two men forced Lu Kim and the California couple to their feet. With pushes and prods, they marched the three captives away, heading north, perpendicular to the marked trail. The leader moved a few steps farther away.

Only when he toed the unresponsive foot of someone lying prone did Charlie take a closer look. Tom from Rhode Island lay sprawled in the ferns. Clearly dead.

She bit back a gasp.

The ugly giant barked more orders, and two more gunmen hustled over and dragged Tom off the trail. His head lolled on slack muscles, confirming her snap judgment. *Dead.* The leader dispatched two others back down the trail—toward Abel!

"Dammit," she hissed under her breath. Charlie and Betty exchanged glances, sharing a silent communication. The guys would be walking right into a trap. No, correct that: Abel had undoubtedly heard the shots. He would be *running* directly into a trap.

"We need to draw them off," Charlie said into the older woman's ear. "Are you up for it?"

Click.

The tiny metallic sound from directly behind her froze the blood in Charlie's veins. Somebody kicked her foot, and a guttural voice said, "Up. Up. On feet."

Charlie risked a look over her shoulder. A black-clad soldier stood behind them, holding a rifle against his shoulder, his cheek pressed to the wire-frame stock. His finger was inside the trigger guard.

"Well," Betty said. "Hell and damnation."

AT A HUNDRED YARDS, Yeager was already feeling it—legs straining, breath coming hard. He hated running—always had—and the last few years of avoiding it had exacted a toll. As a boot, he'd come in dead last on company runs time and again, as the DIs had frequently reminded him. *Speed it up, Yeager. Get your ass in gear, you maggot.*

That had been many years ago in a body younger, stronger—*and let's face it, leaner*—than the one he hauled up this narrow, humid trail at an altitude where it was already hard to breathe.

Running parallel to the trail, dodging, ducking, and twisting through heavy foliage, low-hanging limbs, and clinging vines was its own special edition of hell on earth. And he couldn't just blunder through the brush. He had to remain somewhat quiet so as to not alert the shooters. If they heard him coming, it would be game over in a heartbeat.

Speed it up, Yeager.

With an application of will power, Yeager managed to hold his pace—slower than a jog, faster than a walk. Any more speed was out of the question. The grade angled uphill, adding to his misery. It canted steeply enough that at times he was digging in with his fingers to keep moving forward. The trail roughly followed the contour of a ridge as it switchbacked up to its highest elevation. On his right, the brow of the ridge topped out and angled sharply downward to the depth of a canyon below, while to the left, the grade sloped away more gradually.

The vegetation was a green blur.

Yeager topped out on a lip overlooking a wide spot in the trail. He stumbled to a halt and braced a hand against a fallen tree. Spent brass cartridge cases littered the soil. Churned and trampled earth marked the trail.

The shooters, whoever they were, had departed the scene. Yeager remained still and tried to control the heaving gulps of air his lungs clamored for.

No bodies. Whoever fired had either missed or—*no, check that.*

A pair of hiking boots, toes up, poked from the weeds beside the trail. Yeager clenched his galloping heart with a steel fist and side-stepped down the incline, moving slowly so as to not draw attention. The booted feet came into view, followed by hairy legs and men's hiking shorts. John. Or Tom. From Rhode Island.

Yeager allowed his heart to start again. Tom was no longer going back to Rhode Island, except in a box. Three entrance wounds, clustered center mass, made sure of that.

Yeager conducted a careful sweep of the area, staying out of the soft soil where many tracks crisscrossed the trail. *Save those for later.* At the moment, it was more important to determine if there were any other casualties.

When he could safely say that no one else from the group—including Charlie—remained in the vicinity, Yeager worked on calming his breathing and reading the scene laid out before him. The footprints varied in number, size, and quality. He picked out several heavy-tread patterns that he classified as military-grade boots.

A dozen cartridge casings littered the scene—a lot of brass for only one victim. Who were they shooting at, and more importantly, did their targets get away?

Where is my wife? Yeager checked his phone. No service.

Think, Yeager. Think. He clubbed his forehead with a palm, trying to knock loose the frozen gears. He started a circuit of the trail, staying in the grass along the sides, trying to read the profusion of tracks. An imprint of Lu Kim's tiny footprint led him to a spot where clearly three people had sat together for a time. Round impressions of butts—along with deeper angled divots where heels dug into the soil—suggested as much, anyway. He was no Apache tracker, but he believed the trio had been escorted away to the left of the trail, down the easy slope of the ridge.

That accounted for four of six people, leaving two…

"Yeager!" Pettigrew and Pyle stumbled into view and stomped over part of the tracks before Yeager could signal them to stop.

"What the hell?" Pettigrew wheezed, holding his chest, bent at the waist.

"Ambush of some kind. Best guess. Or our people ran into some bad guys up here. Tom's dead," Yeager said with a gesture to the corpse. "But I can't find any other bodies or blood trail." That he'd dispassionately described the lack-of-blood situation with Charlie at peril surprised even him. The warrior brain was waking up, taking over operations from the gibbering husband without a clue. Yeager welcomed the change, allowing his emotions to recede into the background, feeling the coldness steal through his mind and shunt any negative thoughts into a box to be opened later.

"We have three of our people moving that way"—he pointed with a bladed hand—"under escort of two. Four to eight OPFOR total. Disposition of remaining enemy unknown."

At Pyle's baffled look, Pettigrew transferred the message, cupping a hand close to the man's ear. He concluded with, "We don't know where Betty is." By then, Osterchuk had appeared, red-faced and blowing hard, so Pettigrew repeated the message.

"Listen up," Osterchuk wheezed. "I saw a couple of guys with AKs headed back down the trail. They didn't see me."

Yeager nodded and continued sweeping the area in slow passes, moving in a wider and wider spiral from the point of contact—which he identified as the pile of brass.

Osterchuk picked up one of the casings and examined it. "Seven-six-two by three-nine. From one of the AKs, I imagine."

"That helps not one damn bit," Pettigrew griped. "Every ass-lickin' commie and terrorist on the planet uses AKs."

"I know that," Osterchuk countered. "I was just making an observation."

"Your observation ain't helpful."

Yeager reached the pair in two long strides, caught them each by the shirt collar, and jerked them together. "Stow it, both of you. We have people missing, and y'all are acting like this is a picnic."

"Yes, Staff Sergeant," they chorused.

Pyle looked on, squinting in concentration. He nodded his understanding.

"The three of you, haul ass off this mountain." Yeager released the two men. "Hump the trail as fast as you can without dying. Get some help. I'm gonna see if I can track down where they took our people."

"Aye, aye, Staff Sergeant," Osterchuk said.

"I tracked Victor Charles back in the day," Winston said. "Like an injun, only of the darker variety. I'd rather come with you if it's all the same."

Yeager hesitated.

"Take him," Osterchuk said. "That way, when you find our people, you can send him back with the coordinates."

"All right." Yeager nodded. "That makes some kind of sense. Let's—"

Voices. They came from the top of the ridge, speaking in a foreign language.

"Scatter," Yeager hissed. "Get Pyle. Go to ground."

CHAPTER FIVE

Puerto Arista, Chiapas, Mexico
Saturday, 8 May
0950 Local Time
Eight Hours before Honolulu Bombing

Victor and Alex had left at the condo before dawn with the property manager's son, who would be driving them over the mountains to Ángel Corzo International Airport. The transportation for this ride was a VW Beetle, of which Mexico seemed to have an abundant supply. They strapped their luggage to the top and piled inside the vehicle as the sun flared over the horizon. The 1970-model car rattled and fumed, and the gearbox made a noise like a Transformer eating breakfast. The two-hundred-kilometer journey, much of it on two-lane almost roads, took three hours—including one stop to change a flat and one stop at a gas station with a reeking toilet that Alex claimed had bacteria big enough to eat her whole.

"I'd rather pee in the bushes next time," she told him with a shudder.

They had raced to the gate in time to grab a seat on an Interjet flight to Mexico City, which arrived late, cutting their one-and-a-half-hour layover to eighteen minutes. A couple of ticks before the attendant closed the cabin door on their flight to Los Angeles, Victor and Alex slipped through the portal, sweating, panting, and hungry. Alex claimed the window while Victor stuffed their bags into the overhead. He flopped into the middle seat next to a sweaty man in a worn-out shirt and tie.

The jet lifted into a sapphire-blue sky, and Victor entwined his hand with Alex's.

"Did you mean that last night?" he asked.

"Mean what?"

"What you said. You know."

Her brow dipped in a frown. "I don't know what you are talking about."

"You know..." A small bead of sweat trickled down his neck. *I should have kept my mouth shut.* "Right before we went to sleep."

Alex shook her head. "I didn't say anything."

"Oh. Okay."

Victor listened to the roar of the jet engines for a time without saying anything. The *ding* indicating they'd passed ten thousand feet came and went, along with the obligatory announcement that it was okay to use laptops.

"Me too," Victor said.

Alex's lips curled in a smile, and she held his hand tighter.

MOLOKAI FOREST RESERVE, Molokai
Saturday, May 8
1422 Local

The Vietnam vets moved with speed and purpose once properly motivated. Yeager waited for the three of them to clear the trail and fade into the brush before he slunk off to the side. Thick ferns banked each side of the trail, providing decent concealment, though the secret to remaining invisible was not only blending into the surrounding ecosystem but also achieving a state of near motionlessness. Movement attracted the eye. Unfortunately, so did color, though there was nothing he could do about the bright tourist clothes worn by Osterchuk and the others—or his own lack of camouflage.

He froze when a duo of paramilitary types in black fatigues appeared from the east, walking the trail downslope in the opposite direction from the tour group. The pair stopped to examine the dead body, and one stooped to rifle through Tom's shorts, removing his wallet and cell phone.

They spoke in a language that Yeager was embarrassed to say he couldn't identify. *Asian* was the best he could do—sing-song with lots of vowel sounds and probably not Japanese, though even that was a best guess. It wasn't the border Spanish of his upbringing, for damn sure.

Yeager peered through the fronds of a particularly large fern with leaves the size of hand towels. The two men seemed content to stay in place, overlooking the trail, and as long as they stayed there, Yeager and the other Marines were pinned down. Movement would attract attention, and attention would draw fire.

Osterchuk's assessment of the cartridge proved accurate—the men carried AK variants with folding stocks and extended banana magazines. *AKM-74s?* Whatever the number stamped on the side, they were definitely enough gun to chop the four Americans to dog meat.

In their black clothing and tactical gear, these guys appeared more professional than the spray-and-pray jihadi with whom he was familiar. Yeager couldn't count on them having poor fire discipline and a lack of understanding of the front sight.

Tactical problem. Regress into the forest while under surveillance from armed opponents. Coordinate movement with the Leatherneck Legends to evade and escape. Notify armed responders of threat. Locate OPFOR base camp.

Oh, and find Charlie before I completely lose my shit.

Yeager gathered himself to move, only to settle back when two more gunmen appeared from the direction of the tracks leading into the forest. They met up with the first pair, and there followed a lot of atonal discussion that involved arm waving and gesturing. One of the newcomers stood apart from the others, both in size and demeanor. Big enough to be classified as a planet, the guy had a gravity all his own, and the body language of the others demonstrated this one was in charge. His moon-scarred face emitted danger, death, and destruction the way a Soviet-era plutonium reactor leeched life-killing radiation into the surrounding soil.

Moonface made a chopping gesture with one hand and barked a command. Yeager didn't need a translator to understand that he was saying, "Enough." He pointed downslope and issued a series of orders. The three soldiers acknowledged with their equivalent of "Yes, sir. Right away, sir" and straightened up. They formed a loose skirmish line and disappeared—down the trail toward the base, effectively blocking Osterchuk and Pyle from following the easy route back to the trailhead.

Damn.

The leader reversed course and returned the way he had come, headed roughly northeast. He moved with the lethal grace of a warrior, nearly silent, his weapon at port arms. Yeager held his breath, convinced Moonface would trip over Pettigrew and the guys.

Seconds dragged by and compiled into a full minute. Nothing happened. Yeager waited. Watched.

Birdsong dialed back up slowly as quiet returned to the trail. Yeager became aware of his own sweat smell, harsh and pungent, over the earthy scents of the forest. One good thing: at least his hangover was gone.

The far brush stirred with movement. Yeager focused and, a second later, registered Osterchuk's big body sliding from cover, followed by Pyle. Pettigrew appeared like a jack-in-the-box, popping up from a cluster of flowered vines. Yeager snorted at the white blossom that clung to the black man's hair.

Yeager slid out from his hiding spot and motioned the others closer. When they were gathered, he kept his voice pitched low but didn't whisper. The sibilant sounds of whispering tended to carry farther than a normal voice. "Anybody recognize the OPFOR?"

"North Korean," Pettigrew said.

"You sure about that?"

"Ah... no," Pettigrew admitted. "Just a guess."

"Sounded like Chinese," Osterchuk put in.

"North Korean sounds like Chinese," Pettigrew said.

"No, it don't."

"Stow it," Yeager ordered. "We have a force of six-plus bandits armed with AKs, sidearms, and field gear consistent with a light patrol. We have to assume they have a base of operations relatively close. They could be anything from dope runners to part of the terrorist crew that hit the big island today. It was our bad luck to run across a group of them."

"Especially Tom's bad luck," Pettigrew said.

"Asshole," Osterchuk muttered. "Yeager and Pyle's wives are missing."

"Fuck, you're right. Sorry."

"The situation has changed, but the mission remains the same." Yeager gripped the back of Osterchuk's neck and pulled him close. Speaking almost nose to nose, he said, "Marine, listen up. If you stay on the trail, you'll hit that patrol sooner or later. Are you good to find a way downhill without following the trail?"

Osterchuk nodded and shot him a thumbs-up. "We got this."

Yeager held the older man's eyes for a count of ten. "You're Marines. There ain't an ounce of back-up in you. It comes down to it, you're gonna want to fight, but I need you to be sneaky motherfuckers and get past the bad guys. Don't engage. Don't get caught. Bring help."

Pyle had somehow caught enough of the conversation or understood the tone. He echoed Osterchuk. "We got this, Staff Sergeant."

Yeager nodded once. "Me and Pettigrew will follow the trail, locate the hostages. Maybe find their base. We'll set this spot on the trail, right here, as a rendezvous point. I can't time it out, but one or both of us will return to this location and either leave a message or report in person." Yeager polled the faces around him and noted nothing but grim determination. "Okay, gentlemen. Let's get moving."

YEAGER AND PETTIGREW caught up with the enemy rear guard faster than Yeager expected. The group of enemy combatants moved through the woods with the fluid ease of professionals, causing Yeager to revise his estimate of their capabilities. Their rear guard would spin around without warning or freeze in place and go to ground, which was how Yeager's plan nearly fell apart inside the first hour. Had Pettigrew not grabbed his shoulder and pulled him off the path, Yeager would have walked right into their gun sights. Minutes later, the two-man rear guard had ghosted away, their passage marked by unobtrusive flashes of black swishing through ferns like a malignant breeze.

Their diligence forced Yeager to back off farther than he wanted, losing sight altogether, and move forward at a slow crawl, checking every leaf and bush before resuming movement.

Exotic birds provided background music, their calls strange and unsettling. At a half mile above sea level, the air contained slightly less oxygen than Yeager breathed in Texas, and a headache bloomed over his right eye in response. Adjustment to the altitude would take time. Yeager prayed silently it would take hours and not days to find Charlie and get the hell off of Molokai.

Pettigrew followed without sound or complaint. Yeager would barely have known he was there if not for the burnt-tobacco reek that clung to the man. The old man had grit to spare.

The slow pace meant noon had long come and gone... and Yeager's belly was telling him he'd skipped breakfast and lunch after expelling whatever remained from the previous night. His grumbling stomach threatened to alert all the bad guys in the neighborhood to come and kill him. He needed Charlie's backpack with its supply of water and trail-mix bars. The woman made a better Boy Scout than he. "Be prepared" was more akin to a religion than a motto to her. He promised himself to never again gripe about the size of the diaper bag she packed for John Riley. The pang of missing her stole his breath.

Pettigrew touched his back, and Yeager paused and looked over his shoulder. "What?"

"You're moving too fast again."

Yeager gritted his teeth and acknowledged the truth of Pettigrew's words, as much as they annoyed him.

"Look," Pettigrew murmured, "these boys are leaving a trail a blind duck could follow. We need to hang back until it gets dark and injun up on 'em."

Yeager studied the man's tea-colored eyes. "You can find their trail in the dark?"

"I can find their trail in the dark on a moonless night with a blindfold on. I done told you, I tracked some gook bastards—excuse me for my heathen ways. I don't mean to say *gook*. I mean some *Viet*-nam-ese *sol*diers. I was a black Daniel Boone back in the day. I could follow those pajama-wearing motherfuckers across a swamp in a monsoon."

Jaw clenched, Yeager studied the skinny man in the too-big cap and Members Only jacket.

"It won't do no good," Pettigrew continued, "to get yourself shot. Then where will your wife be?"

"All right," Yeager said after studying the faint trail. So far, the soldiers had maintained a nearly straight path running downhill and almost due north. Following their trail would be simple. "Let's find a place to hunker down. We'll give them an hour."

"It won't be dark in—"

"An hour. Period."

"You know," Pettigrew said, hands on hips, "I had a sergeant like you once. Best goddamn sergeant ever. Right up until he stepped on a landmine and blew his leg off."

Yeager squinted one eye. "Are you trying to tell me something?"

"Naw. I know better than that."

CHAPTER SIX

Ted "Gomer" Pyle used the compass built into his wonder phone—he called it that because he wondered how it worked—to get a bearing of 280 degrees, almost due west. Osterchuk said something, and Gomer nodded as if he'd heard. Very few sounds penetrated the stiff and unresponsive membranes in his ears. Most of the time, it wasn't worth the effort to ask for a say-again. He lived in a cocoon world of dull silence and had learned to fake comprehension long ago.

They hiked off at an oblique angle, keeping the marked trail on their left, and cut across country into a dense growth of jungle vegetation. If he tilted his head and squinted just right, Gomer could almost imagine himself back in Vietnam. Hawaii was similar but different. Not as hot. Not as buggy. Not as yellow. The yellow clay of Vietnam would stick to everything, not the least being a man's soul. There were not as many people trying to kill him in Hawaii. Of course, after Hill 881, there would never be as many people trying to kill him, so maybe that didn't count as an official "not."

Gomer felt himself switching on—achieving a state of awareness in which every sensory input was amped up to max and he became a human radar, seeking threats, assessing the trail for booby traps and ambush points, and cataloging the flight of birds and how they reacted to their environment. Without his hearing, Gomer's other senses worked overtime to supply information, which his brain sorted, weighed, and filed.

The first hundred yards passed easily enough, then the brush grew tighter, and picking through the gaps became more of a chore.

Moving fronds out of the way, dripping sweat... yeah, this was almost a trip down memory lane. If not for his dulled hearing, bad knees, bad hips, and corrosive heartburn, Gomer was back *there*. All he needed was some Johnny Rivers or Tom Jones playing on a plastic transistor radio, and it could be Khe Sanh Combat Base all over again.

Stay focused, old man. No time to freeze up.

It didn't happen as much these days as it once had, but the so-called episodes would strike when a certain smell or sight or combination of outside stimuli ganged up to cause a freeze-up. He would go into a catatonic state that would last for a minute or an hour. Betty said it was as if he turned to stone, and his expression scared her witless.

The conditions were ripe for an episode. *Maybe a full season of episodes.*

Osterchuk grunted, and Gomer—surprise, surprise—heard the sound. He checked over his shoulder. The big man was struggling to keep his balance over uneven ground. He'd slipped on a green rock and left a gash in the mossy covering. Osterchuk caught him looking and waved Gomer on with a gesture that said, *I'm okay.*

Khe Sanh Combat Base. A patch of red dirt slashed out of the verdant greenery of South Vietnam, pinched between Laos and the DMZ, covered with tents, sandbag revetments, and wood huts and crisscrossed by trenches. It stank of latrines, aviation fuel, diesel, and unwashed boys in sagging fatigues. Dominated by an airstrip long enough to take C-130s, the base provided overwatch of the Ho Chi Minh trail, which was heavily used by the North Vietnamese Army as a primary route to invade the south.

Gomer hadn't thought of the place in... oh, at least four hours. Rarely would an entire day pass without one memory or another popping up. The most frequent recording on the playlist?

On 24 April, 1967, six months past his senior prom, eighteen-year-old Private First Class Ted "Gomer" Pyle had squatted in a firebase atop Hill 700, northwest of KSCB, with two of his squad members, Jimmy Dearborn and Jon Paul Riddeau. All three were with the 1st Battalion, 9th Marine Regiment, nicknamed the Walking Dead for the horrendous percentage of casualties they'd taken in the previous two years of combat. Most of the guys' names Gomer didn't know and didn't want to know. *FNGs now and for always.*

Hill 700 was one of several that dominated the landscape and commanded the approach to the base. First and Third Platoon had established a mortar emplacement on 700 and were eyeballing 861 and 881 to the north. Pyle and his buddies were shirtless, smoking cigarettes, scratching bug bites, and talking either about girls or cars—because that was all they ever talked about. Pyle's bare feet stuck out in front of him, covered in foot powder to counter the red, peeling fungus that threatened to crawl all the way up past his ankles and eat his balls.

Riddeau's dissertation on the qualities of Holley carburetors was interrupted by distant sounds: *Pop-pop-pop. Dah-dah-dah-dah-dah.*

"What de fock?" said Riddeau, the Cajun.

Pyle twisted around, staring off to the north. "Firefight. Up there on 861."

A five-man patrol had gone out to scout the hill earlier that morning. It sounded like they were in the shit. The captain sent a squad to check it out.

The squad tripped over swarms of NVA regulars—gobs and gobs of the hard little motherfuckers, as it turned out. The hills were riddled with bunkers and spider holes and jam-packed with enemy soldiers. The anthill had most definitely been kicked over.

A favorite tactic of the NVA was to ambush a patrol then fade back into the jungle before reinforcements could arrive, so Captain Sayers sent 1st and 3rd platoons—which included Pyle, Riddeau, and Dearborn—to cut off any NVA retreat and hit the North Viet-namese in the rear. Except the NVA weren't in a retreating mood. Division 325C had been laying in supplies for a concerted thrust at KSCB and the Special Operations camp at Lang Vei, an effort inter-rupted by five unlucky-as-shit Marines scouting the hill.

Within hours, Pyle and the rest of the 1/9 were cut off at the base of Hill 861 and surrounded. Blistering fire pounded them from all directions. Riddeau caught a round in the throat that blew his neck in half. A mortar round landed on top of Dearborn's helmet. Pyle fired his M16 until the action jammed, grabbed up a dead Marine's M60 and kept shooting. He pissed himself at one point, partly in ab-ject terror and partly because there was no time to take a leak.

The PAVN regulars wore green uniforms. Only their pith hel-mets distinguished them from Pyle's fellow marines, and he prayed every minute that his bullets would find only the enemy. There was no way to know for sure.

For three days and three nights, PFC Pyle fought up and down that miserable rock. Cut off and with their airlift choppers ham-mered by mortars and unable to land, Company B absorbed too many casualties to move without leaving their men behind. They hugged the ground and called in artillery strikes so close to their own positions that Pyle ate dirt from the explosions. The brutal, mind-crushing, head-splitting roar of sound—cracking M16s and AKs, hammering M60s, thumping mortars, body-slamming crumps of ar-tillery rounds—blew out Pyle's eardrums and permanently ruined his hearing. He wore hearing aids at thirty and was 80 percent deaf at fifty.

Company K of the 3/3 relieved the Walking Dead on day four. The 1/9 had pushed the enemy back far enough that trucks were brought up to carry them away.

"Fuck that," Pyle said, and the rest of the regiment agreed. They refused the trucks and marched out of that combat zone holding their heads up. The 1st of the 9th had stood toe-to-toe with a division of Vietnamese regulars and backed them right the fuck off. No way did they need a ride out of the combat zone.

In the days following his withdrawal from KSCB to the USNS *Comfort*, other Marines took Hills 861 and 881 away from the goddamn commies and killed a whole bucketload of them in the process.

When the Marines were finally done kicking the enemy's ass, they were airlifted away from the top of that stinking hill, not the bottom. They had pushed the Vietnamese back into Laos and were not allowed to continue the chase.

Later, in 1968, the NVA came back and laid siege to the hill complex and Khe Sanh for three months. The Marines refused to budge, and the Vietnamese gave it up... which amounted to nothing in the end. The geniuses in MACV decided the strategic advantage of KSCB wasn't worth the effort and pulled out. The NVA had marched into Khe Sanh unopposed and hoisted their flag. A great victory for the People's Army.

Gomer was marching down a different hill today. In the jungle. On a mission.

Deja vu. If he tilted his head and squinted, he could picture Riddeau and Dearborn *just over there*, sitting on ammo crates and shooting the shit, smiling and laughing and dragging on their cigarettes on a foggy day in April, 1967... about to die for ground that didn't matter, in a war that most people had forgotten and everyone else said was nothing but a waste.

"Semper Fi, boys," he whispered.

FAIR BREEZES Cruise Ship, off the Coast of Molokai
    Saturday, 8 May
    1615 Local

Jan Osterchuk lounged on the sundeck of the *Fair Breezes* and sipped from her frozen—now slushy—margarita, enjoying the breeze, the sea, the slight buzz that tickled her nose, and a romance novel featuring kilted Scotsmen and English noblewomen.

The highest of the three decks on the pocket cruise ship, the sundeck seated twenty people max, but that afternoon, she had it to herself—under an umbrella, of course. Her blinding-white Minnesota body would burn to the color of a ripe tomato within minutes of exposure to the sun. A waiter magically appeared when her drink ran dry, but otherwise, she was left alone to read and doze as the mood struck her.

In other words, it was a perfect afternoon. If she chose to look, she'd see the green gem of Molokai rising from the ocean to her left, two miles or more away, while the sapphire of the Pacific stretched to the horizon on her right. Her book lay tented on her bosom while she sipped her drink. She set the glass on the table next to her, aiming carefully so as not to miss the coaster, and returned to the dozing phase of her quiet afternoon.

The sound of a small boat engine buzzed closer. It was too early for Danny and the others to get back from their hike, so she didn't bother opening her eyes. A tiny needle of unease pricked her: maybe the party was returning early because her husband had suffered a stroke or a heart attack. The idiot seemed determined to prove that he was still a vigorous young man in his prime instead of a grandfather shaped like a department-store Santa.

The boat engine cut out. By the sound of it, the craft had docked in the ship's boat well, which allowed the *Fair Breezes*'s rubber excursion boats to arrive and depart with minimum effort by the passengers. Someone had docked with the cruise liner. From the sundeck, she could not see the well, so she had no clue who it was.

Jan sighed and moved her book to the table in preparation for getting up. She really needed to check and see if everything was all right with Danny. Even when he wasn't here, the man could try her patience worse than their four-year-old grandson. He could certainly find more trouble in a shorter amount of time, which was saying something.

Gunfire rattled from below. People screamed.

Knowing the world's propensity for terrorism and active shooters massacring crowds of helpless innocents, Jan instantly recognized the situation: someone had boarded the ship with the intention of shooting people on board.

She and Danny held concealed-carry licenses and practiced at the range frequently to maintain their proficiency. Of course, they couldn't travel with their firearms on a commercial airline, so her Ruger P85 rested snug in their gun safe in St. Cloud. Based on the woodpecker sounds of weapons on full auto, even if she were armed, she would be outgunned and outnumbered.

Which left one option. Jan stripped off her cover-up. She kicked off her flip-flops and tossed her wide-brimmed hat to the side—sunglasses too. In 1972, Jan had gone to the University of Minnesota on a swimming scholarship. She had set no records in the four years of her college, but she had a killer breaststroke. Of course, that was fifty pounds—well, sixty pounds—ago.

She was wearing nothing but her best-looking one-piece. Two miles of open ocean lay between her and the island, including some wicked rip currents and powerful tides. And sharks.

Gunshots ripped the decks below. In only a matter of seconds, they'd reach the top deck. *Swim or get shot.*

Jan Osterchuk ran to the edge of the deck and dove off.

CHAPTER SEVEN

Māmala Bay, off the Coast of Oahu, Hawaii
Saturday, 8 May
1730 Local Time

Hawaii for Hawaiians, now and forever.

Kamahalo Makani braced one foot on the gunwale of the thirty-foot sport fisher. The boat bobbed in the light chop of Māmala Bay, drifting with the current half a kilometer from the tip of runway 8R/26L—also known as the Reef Runway—of the Honolulu International Airport. To Makani's surprise, Homeland Security and FAA officials had halted flight operations into and out of the airport—commonly referred to as HNL—for only two hours, despite the attacks in nearby Waikiki. With more than seven hundred daily takeoffs and landings, HNL was small by global standards, not even making it into the top fifty of the world's busiest airports. It was, however, the top tourist gateway to the islands, handling an approximate twenty-five thousand tourists per day on four runways. News reports showed the terminals jammed with people fleeing the islands. Lines for security screening extended outside and along the sidewalks. Shutting down the airport would have meant mass chaos and pandemonium.

Had they closed the airport, Makani would have had to abort his mission. They had not, so he would have to go through with it. Makani examined the kernel of unease in his gut and was surprised—but not surprised—to find that it was dread. He had never killed anything bigger than a cockroach, yet that night, he would kill several hundred people.

A string of twinkling lights hung in the evening sky, indicating a steady stream of incoming air traffic on approach from the east. As Makani watched, a 777 with Delta markings roared into the setting sun, climbing for altitude and banking out over the ocean. The thunderous rumble of the twin GE90 turbofan engines vibrated Makani's chest, adding to the near-panic thudding of his heart.

The time had come. He had to act. *Hawaii for Hawaiians.*

Kanoa had said, "Makani, you will be the sole person in strike team four. You will be on your own. Alone. Harden your heart to the necessities of the mission."

Instead of being hardened, his heart threatened to blow out of his chest. The salty spray of the ocean mixed with sweat beading his face, and the breeze sent shivers through his cold, damp flesh. He wished he'd had a teammate, someone to share the pressure. *And the blame.*

He believed in the cause. Hawaii should be free. The unlawful annexation of the island kingdom by the rapacious, greedy whites had been facilitated by the peaceful nature of the rightful inhabitants. Well, no more peace. No more aloha. It was time for war.

Makani lifted the North Korean copy of the Russian-made 9K38 Igla, man-portable air-defense missile system to his shoulder. The Igla used a heat-seeking warhead to track and kill its prey, zeroing in on the hot exhaust of rotary or fixed-wing aircraft. The detachable trigger mechanism was already assembled to the blocky, breadbox-sized control seated at the front of the weapon. The launcher tube extended backward over his shoulder. A simple sight and even simpler trigger made it usable by the most illiterate peasant soldier, and the missile itself was truly a fire-and-forget device. The operator merely had to point it toward the target, achieve a lock tone, and shoot. Then he'd drop the launcher, crank up the boat's twin 250s, and scoot for safety the second the missile exited the tube on its plume of fire.

The instructor had explained in broken English that Makani would probably only be able to strike one aircraft, incoming or outgoing. For outbound air traffic, due to wake-turbulence separation minimums, a jetliner would not depart until the preceding aircraft had reached at least four nautical miles and perhaps as many as eight. The heavier the preceding aircraft, the longer the next flight needed to wait before departing, to avoid any risk of hitting the wingtip vortices of the previous plane. Wake turbulence had been cited as a cause of the crash of American Airlines Flight 587 into Belle Harbor, Queens, in 2001, and ever since, ATC had been scrupulous about minimum separation distances. Four nautical miles was about thirty percent beyond the Igla's fifty-two-hundred-meter range, meaning jet A would be out of the engagement envelope before jet B left the runway. If Makani chose inbound traffic, the line of approaching aircraft would see the strike and veer off before getting into range. In any event, the first exploding aircraft would no doubt disrupt traffic and divert all aircraft out of the kill zone.

Meaning one shot, one kill.

Truthfully, even if more planes were within range, Makani knew in his heart that he wouldn't have the guts to reload, aim, and fire a second missile. Shivers racked his body and he urgently needed to urinate. Though there were many targets to choose from, he would have the strength for one shot and one shot only.

"So pick one," Makani said to himself.

AIRBORNE, ON APPROACH to Honolulu International Airport

Saturday, 8 May

1745 Hours Local

After an unexpected layover at LAX due to the hotel-bombing disruption in Hawaii's inbound traffic, Victor Ruiz was getting goddamn sick and tired of sitting on planes. At LAX, they had watched the news of the attacks along with the other passengers. The airline allowed people the option to change tickets to alternate destinations without a fee, and the check-in desk was mobbed in minutes.

"You promised me Hawaii," Alex said when he asked her if she wanted to abort.

"It'll be nuts there."

"You'll fit right in."

Somehow, he had the middle seat again. This time, an obese woman had claimed the armrest and part of his seat and seemed determined to keep both. Her flesh pressed into his side like a squishy pillow. Immediately after takeoff, the woman had popped in earbuds, turned on the seat-back movie system, and reclined her seat as far as it would go.

Victor had emptied two tall bottles of water while waiting then switched to beer after they were airborne, and now he was back on water. All the liquid had the predictable impact on his bladder, meaning he had to disturb the sack of pudding in the aisle seat and stand in line for the head every hour or so. The last time he'd interrupted the woman's movie marathon, her glare had been so cold it should have frozen the pee inside his bladder.

Make it a pee-sicle.

The shuffling and bumping of his return woke Alex from her latest nap. When not working, she could sleep more than a house cat. She wiped her mouth with a grimace and looked at him with puffy eyes. "Are we there yet?"

Her question was punctuated by a ding and the captain's announcement that they were beginning their descent. Through the porthole, Victor saw nothing but black ocean and a faint indigo smear of horizon. The wing's flashing light strobed the darkness.

"Finally." He checked his watch. "A hundred or so hours since we woke up in Mexico."

"Funny." Alex stretched her hands straight up as if surrendering. Her shirt tightened across her chest in a way that Victor found distracting. "But I'm not tired at all."

"Amazing."

She leaned close and whispered, "Can you ask the lady on the end to get up? I need the toilet."

WEST COAST OF MAUI, Hawaii
Saturday, 8 May
1745 Hours

On the western edge of the island of Maui, dozens of resort hotels lined the beaches from Lahaina to Honokowai Point in a near-solid line of luxury development stretching more than five miles. The properties were designed to pamper tourists with pineapple-flavored drinks and white-sand beaches, offer them fluffy towels and turn-down service, feast them with luaus, and adorn them with leis.

The man known as Manu Ho began the slaughter at the sliding-glass entrance doors of the Hyatt Regency Spa and Resort. He led two other supposed Niho soldiers toward the lobby of the hotel overlooking Kā'anapali Beach. His men followed him toward the valet-parking apron in front of the Hyatt. The members of the strike team wore black pants and T-shirts and covered their faces with black ski masks. They each carried a Type 88-1 automatic rifle with a thirty-round banana-shaped magazine, along with a Baek-Du San copy of the CZ 75 pistol and their blade of personal choice. Manu Ho's choice was a pineapple-harvesting machete with a plain wooden handle and a fifteen-inch blade that thickened toward the tip.

His group was one of four teams striking targets all along the Maui coastline.

An overweight white woman and a teenager lingered to the left of the Hyatt entry, gazing into their phones. Ho triggered a burst from the hip, ripping the woman from her stretch pants to her colorful headband. A tiny swivel brought the Type 88-1 in line with the daughter. Ho stitched a compressed burst of fire into the younger woman, punching holes through the phone she held and slamming her into the portico's support column. She slid to her butt, painting a streak of crimson on the white stucco.

His men fired in controlled bursts. More tourists dropped. The screams began.

The team split around a Cadillac Escalade parked in the drive. A native Hawaiian valet, not old enough to shave, froze halfway out of the SUV's door, dark eyes bulging wide. Ho twitched his head. *Go!* He bypassed the black vehicle and led the way into the lobby.

"Hawaii for Hawaiians," Ho shouted. "Now and forever."

AIRBORNE, ON APPROACH to Honolulu International Airport
Saturday, 8 May
1750 Hours Local
Victor pinched his nose and cleared the pressure on his ears. The attendants roved up and down the aisles with trash bags, admonishing those with laptops to power down and put them away. The aircraft engines whined, and the flaps groaned. Victor caught glimpses through the porthole of sparkling lights set against a velvet-dark sea.

Alex took his hand and grinned. "This is going to be so much fun!"

MĀMALA BAY, OFF THE Coast of Oahu
Saturday, 8 May
1754 Local

Makani eyed the traffic and made his choice. He sighted on an inbound Delta flight, but his hands were shaking so badly that, by the time he'd gotten a lock, the plane was on the ground. He gingerly set the launcher on a bench seat and hunched over to light a cigarette. He had never smoked... until the day he was selected for this mission. The instructor had handed him a smoke right after his first successful training session. Despite his hacking and coughing, the nicotine had seemed to soothe his jittery nerves.

He decided to have another and see if that helped with the shakes.

AIRBORNE, ON APPROACH to Honolulu International Airport
Saturday, 8 May
1800 Hours Local

They landed with a double-thump, and Victor breathed out a sigh. Not for the first time, he wished he could sleep on a plane. Being airborne with someone else at the wheel left him edgy and paranoid.

Victor creaked off the jet bridge with sweat patches under his arms and two carry-on bags under his eyes. Alexandra, in contrast, was fresh-faced and chipper. They wheeled their luggage into the terminal a little after six o'clock in the evening. Two pretty girls in flower-print dresses handed out leis. Their smiles seemed brittle and forced.

The airport teemed with extra security. Police officers in full SWAT gear patrolled the concourses, dogs at their heels, M4s slung across their body armor. The lines at the TSA checkpoints meandered through mazes of black stanchions, hundreds of people deep—tired parents with fractious children and couples holding hands. Conversation was muted, the eyes of the departing passengers haunted. The buzz of tension was so strong that it vibrated on the back of Victor's tongue.

"Looks like everyone else is leaving," Alex said.

"Should mean a good deal on a hotel," Victor muttered through a yawn.

"That's awful!"

After a stop at the rental counter, they drove to a chain hotel near the airport and checked into a room with a king bed. Victor changed into shorts and a T-shirt, found the hotel's gym, and used the elliptical. He followed that with a few sets of curls, flies, push-ups, and crunches. By the time he showered and changed clothes, he'd shaken off travel-induced zombie-ism.

Too tired to go out, they ate an overpriced meal at the hotel's restaurant. On the television over the bar, a newscaster standing at an airport lobby was speaking into a microphone, looking grave. People were running around in the background. The screen showed a video of the night sky, shaky and out of focus. The sound was muted and the TV too far away for Victor to read the crawl. It looked like bad news anyway, and he wasn't in the mood for bad news.

"I tried calling Charlie," Alexandra said as they waited for their order.

"Anything?"

"No answer."

"Probably out of range." Victor sipped a cold Modelo. "Or, you know, they're dancing at a fancy-dress ball on their cruise ship."

"Can you see Abel dancing at a ball?"

"Hah!" Victor added in English, "Only if somebody was chooting at his feets."

Alex pulled a face. "Will you stop with the Chicano gang-banger accent? You know I hate it when you speak like a moron."

"Is how I talk. Besides, I thought you liked that I was a not as es-mart as choo." Victor winked. "Anyway, we'll see the Yeagers tomorrow morning sometime. I'm sure they're just busy partying and whatnot."

"You're right, I know." Alex glanced at her watch. "We should go to bed."

"What? You slept, like, a hundred hours on the plane!"

"You really aren't very bright, are you? I said go to bed, not go to sleep."

MĀMALA BAY, OFF THE coast of Oahu
Saturday, 8 May
1830 Local

Makani was ready. This time for sure.

A whining roar cut the night as an Aloha Airlines 757 spooled up on the tarmac. Makani sighted on the jetliner and steadied his breathing, which was coming in fast gulps. He blocked out the line of portholes, refusing to picture the passengers in their seats, heads bowed over magazines or engaged in conversation with their neighbors.

The 757 started its takeoff roll, gaining speed from a walk to a jog to a run then to a full-out sprint. Thrust from the engines powered out in twin shimmers of overheated air, driving the airframe down the runway in a thunderous crescendo of percussion. At V1, the jet's nose tilted up, followed in seconds by V2, whereupon the twelve-thousand-ton monster lifted from the earth.

Makani pressed the first stage of the trigger, panning the missile tube from left to right to keep the Aloha Airlines Boeing framed in the optical sights. With a squeal, the missile locked. A spasm of terror clutched his heart. Doubt swept through him. The lives of at least two hundred people hung by the weight of his trigger finger. Once done, there would be nothing left of the old Kamahalo Makani. There would only be the mass killer Kamahalo Makani. His jaw trembled, and he forgot how to breathe. His insides clenched, and his bowels threatened to flood his shorts with shit.

Hawaii for Hawaiians. Makani clenched his eyes closed. And fired.

CHAPTER EIGHT

Pearl City, Oahu, Hawaii
Saturday, May 8
1906 Local Time

The man known as Pete Kaneholani rode in the lead of three extended-cab pickup trucks cruising on the Kamehameha Highway. The driver of his vehicle signaled, pulled off at Hekaha Street, and turned toward the water. The second and third trucks followed. At eleven o'clock, the Bradley Shopping Center was quiet though not deserted. The shops and offices were closed, a few cars remained, and a group of youngsters skateboarded outside a thrift store. Their wheels washboarded across the pavement, echoing in the dark, nearly empty lot.

The lead truck stopped for a pair of late-night bicyclers to whip past before continuing deeper into the parking lot. Both extended-cab pickups rolled *very gently* over the speed bumps before they stopped in the middle of a small parking lot, secluded behind the last of the four rows of long, narrow buildings. Twenty meters away, a fringe of greenery bordered the waterfront of East Loch, Pearl Harbor. The lights of the Ford Island Bridge glittered over the dark water, backlit by the glow from Joint Base Pearl Harbor-Hickam.

The drivers turned their trucks toward the building, their rear beds facing the water. They lined up their vehicles with yellow marks that had been spray-painted the previous day by the advance team, on the concrete. Lights switched off. All six doors popped open. Kaneholani and eight other men scrambled out. Two, armed with automatic rifles, jogged back the way they'd come, to set perimeter security. Men from each vehicle pulled the cover off the beds, the snaps coming loose with muted pops. They leaped into their assigned truck beds and lifted the tubes of the two 81mm mortars into their prepared bases. The third truck carried crates of ammunition, which were removed, opened, and stacked next to the mortar tubes. Each weapon was nestled in a bed of sandbags, the base spot-welded to the truck bed. The weapons' ski-pole forelegs fitted into an arc of holes drilled in one-centimeter increments. The "best guess" positions were circled in red tape and aligned the weapon along the truck bed's center axis. The extra holes would allow for crude deflection adjustments. Once the trucks were parked at the designated positions and the bipods set, the gun tubes would supposedly be as ready as the trainers could make them without firing them. Presighting was well and good, but it was a rare mortar that could hit accurately on the first shot.

Time from parking to basic setup was eight seconds—slower than they'd done it in training but faster than the team leader had planned. His false identity of "Pete Kaneholani" would pass a cursory inspection and not much more, though the authorities would have no other trail to follow. Unless he broke under interrogation, they would never learn Kaneholani's true identity. Even his DNA would leave a false trail.

Kaneholani waited while his crews finished their final adjustments. Waves sloshed against the piled stones of the shoreline, and the fitful breeze carried the oily-fishy smell of the inner harbor. He listened to and cataloged the suburban noises: a car stereo's thumping bass from the Kamehameha, a distant—very distant—siren, and an unseen boat puddling through the harbor at just above idling speed.

"Ready," Tommy Chin said. As mission commander and the leader of mortar team one, it was his job to issue fire orders to the team leaders as well as call out adjustments from the distant spotters. He stood between the two trucks, where he could speak to both crews easily. He checked the leader of Mortar Two, who indicated that his tube was ready as well.

Kaneholani pressed a speed dial on his disposable cell.

"Yo," Don Akiona, one of the idiot *terrorists*, said.

"Stand by."

Kaneholani held the phone to his chest and said to Tommy Chin, "One round, smoke."

"One round, smoke."

Mal Ka'uhane, another of the native Hawaiian idiots on the team and the ammunition bearer, selected the round from a foam-padded box. The propellant increments had been installed and the safety wires removed prior to leaving their staging area, which had made Kaneholani's balls crawl up into his belly every time the truck dipped into a pothole. These Hawaiians were too untrained to properly load and fuse the rounds on sight, in the heat of battle. *What will be, will be.*

"Hang," Chin said.

The gunner, one of his and not a Hawaiian, took the round from Mal Ka'uhane and slid the tail into the tube the proper distance. On Chin's command of "Fire," Morris dropped the round and twisted away.

Thud!

The concussion of the small rocket firing slugged Kaneholani in the chest. At a little over two kilometers, the target was well within range, and the round impacted seconds later, out of sight and sound from Kaneholani's position. He held the phone to his ear.

"Shot out."

"Splash," the idiot said. "Ahh... one hundred meters long... uh-hh... fifty meters left."

Kaneholani consulted a laminated table taped to his sleeve and called out corrections.

"Ready," Chin said.

"One round, smoke."

Thud!

"On line," the idiot on the phone said. "Fifty short." After the next smoke round hit, Don Akiona reported. "Oh man, wow. Dead ringer, brah. Ahh... target hit. Fire for effect."

Success ignited a warm blaze in Kaneholani's chest. Even working with barbarian numbskulls, his mission would be a success.

"Round, HE," he told Tommy Chin. "Fire until you run dry."

By his informal count, mortar one had fired eight rounds during the time it took him to lay in mortar two. Both mortars engaged until they ran out of ammunition. In twelve minutes, fifty rounds of high-explosive shells had rained on the targets.

"Pack it up," Kaneholani told the crews. Into the phone he said, "Report."

"Oh, dude," Akiona crowed. "You should see this!"

"Idiot. Tell me the result."

"The Arizona Memorial is a crater in the water. It is fucking gone, man! And on the Missouri... uhh... I see fire aboard the ship."

During the planning of the strikes, the dapper spook—the true mission leader, no matter what the Hawaiians thought—had pulled Kaneholani aside and said, "You know what this will mean, right?"

"What?"

"You, my honored comrade, will go down in history as the man who conducted the second attack on Pearl Harbor."

Kaneholani sneered at the glow over the water. Just like Americans, to memorialize a defeat. Now they would know that taste again, and Kaneholani was only too happy to be the instrument of his country's will. In truth, he was honored to be the one to deliver it.

"Come," he ordered the team. "Secure the weapons, and return to base. We have more to do. Move!"

HIDDEN CAMP, MOLOKAI
Saturday, 8 May
1910 Local

The gunmen marched Charlie and the other captives through the forest, following no discernible trail that she could see. The first time she had tried marking their passage by snapping a green branch of a leafy vine, one of their captors screamed at her and threatened to strike her in the face with the butt of his gun. From then on, Charlie stepped hard into every soft spot she could find, trying to leave footprints for Abel to follow.

They hiked for over an hour. Late-afternoon shafts of sunlight speared the forest by the time they crossed a rippling stream and entered a clearing under the trees. Netting laced the trees overhead, woven through with green patches. *Camouflage cover.* Four buildings huddled under the netting—long, narrow cabins of raw timber that resembled National Park Service buildings. Thick mounds of earth were piled on the roof of each cabin, held in place by more netting.

Charlie leaned close to Betty, whose arm she held to steady the old lady. "Why the dirt roofs?"

Betty glanced up with watery eyes. Red-faced and sweating, Betty Pyle didn't look well. The forced hike and the tension of captivity had worn on the older woman's stamina. "Blocks infrared," she whispered back. "From drones and aircraft. Satellites—"

"Stop talking!" snapped the slab-faced leader of the soldiers. Charlie had nicknamed him Kong for both his size and the undercurrent of violence that bubbled close to the surface. "Move!"

One of the guards unlocked a door in the second cabin from the left, and the other gunmen chivied the hostages into the dim interior. Lu Kim went first, followed by the California couple, Austin and

Melissa. Charlie led Betty inside last. The door slammed shut, followed by the sound of a padlock clicking into place.

As her eyes adjusted, Charlie made out a row of eight cots lining each wall, reminiscent of every barracks in every military movie she'd ever seen. People occupied thirteen of the sixteen beds spread out on each side.

"Welcome to the Molokai Ritz," the man closest to the door said. "Room service is a bitch, and don't expect a mint on your pillow."

KIMO EKEWAKA GOT THE five new hostages locked away and dismissed the patrol to their barracks. He crossed to the command hut and entered, finding three of his people inside, all Hawaiian. *None of that mercenary trash.*

"Ho, boys! Look who's home."

Kenny Po glanced up from his computer. "Let me guess. A butt-ugly troll?"

Kimo settled by the table that served as a desk in the camp's command hut. The chair groaned under his bulk. He propped his feet on the table, cracked a water bottle, and slugged down half of it in one long pull. It had been a long hike on a warm day, and he needed to rehydrate.

He used the half-drained bottle as a pointer, stabbing it at the skinny little punk, Keola Alapai. "You make the videos yet, College Boy?"

Alapai's lips pinched, reminding Kimo of a baboon's anus. The kid hooked his own bottle of water from the minifridge and took his time twisting off the top. The interior lights flickered brighter as the puny generator—hidden out back—kicked on. At another desk, Kenny Po kept his eyes fixed on a streaming news service that played on a tiny Toughbook propped in front of him. The always-sweaty

Hambone Kaleka found something interesting to pick at on the bottom of his shoe. The other men—the "outside contractors," as Kanoa called them—had gone back to their duties or retired to their barracks. The command hut contained only Kimo and Kanoa's people at the moment.

"Why'd you bring the hikers?" Alapai asked.

Kimo sneered. "What's wrong, brah? Getting squishy on us?"

Alapai stiffened, almost as if he had a backbone. *Fat chance of that.* "No. I'll do what needs to be done. Just seems like a lot of extra effort for nothing."

"I don't throw nothin' away that can be used." Kimo grinned with fake humor. His face was made from the stuff of nightmares—he had no illusions otherwise—and his grin was particularly nasty. Wild pigs would scream for their mamas when Kimo grinned at them.

"And the ship they came from? What happens when the tour doesn't come back?"

"Da fuck, brah? You think I'm stupid? I sent a squad to waste ever'body on board. All hands lost." Kimo glared at the little prick, who looked away, unable to hold his gaze. "Why haven't you made them videos yet?"

"Are you kidding? We just got here an hour ago with the Lanai bunch."

"Better get your ass in gear, bruddah." Kimo slapped his thigh again and stood. He stretched and twisted, feeling the joints in his back pop. "I had to shoot one already—tried to run away. A waste of haole. Go make us a motion picture. Get it done now. I gots an itch I need to scratch." Kimo grabbed his crotch. "Right here."

"Excuse me?" Alapai pushed his glasses up with one finger.

"We're gonna shoot 'em all anyway. Might as well get some—what's the word?—entertainment value."

The kid looked as if he'd swallowed a caterpillar and the fuzzy thing wanted to crawl back up his throat. "You're a twisted fuck, Kimo."

"Dude!" Kimo clapped Alapai on the shoulder. He squeezed, and the kid's thin bones grated. "Grow a pair. I need to liven this party up. Get on that camera quickie-quick. Sooner we put the word out, sooner we have some insurance."

Alapai winced and squirmed. Kimo dug his fingers in, and the kid gasped, his knees buckling. "Stop it, Kimo."

"Don't cry, boy." With a toothy grin and a final squeeze, Kimo released the scrawny brat. "Get busy. I'm in a bad mood. I need to go relax." Kimo laughed at Alapai's expression. The boy slunk away, shaking his head, and Kimo sneered. "Don't worry. I'll save you some, little man. Now, gimme the satellite thingie. I need to call in the status to Kanoa."

CHAPTER NINE

W*elcome to the Molokai Ritz.*

"All things being equal," Betty said, "I'd rather be in Philadelphia."

"Dave Draper." The man stood and extended his hand. He was pudgy around the middle with blondish hair going gray, the top of his head reaching Charlie's collarbone. He wore only pants, no shirt. He pointed to a man on the left-hand side. "That guy is Montelle, no last name. You might recognize him if you listen to the same music your kids do. Those two folks are Japanese. I can't make out a word they say. And this is my wife, Sarah Rae."

Sarah Rae was a poster child for misery. Wearing stained white trousers and a Hawaiian shirt that was clearly too small for her, straining over surgically enhanced breasts stuffed into a frilly brassiere, Sarah Rae resembled a poorly dressed Barbie doll. Charlie noted Dave's bare upper body, and it wasn't hard to connect the two.

Draper continued, "We haven't gotten around to everybody, so I don't know the others."

Several of their fellow captives left their bunks and introduced themselves. Seconds later, Charlie was at a loss to remember a single name. The Japanese pair drifted up and attempted greetings of their own. The elder of the two called himself Goro, and the younger man was Haru, if Charlie understood them correctly. The singer, Montelle, slipped over and perched on the cot near Draper. Charlie vaguely recognized him from the covers of grocery-store rags.

"I think they're father and son," Draper supplied, indicating the Japanese.

A prehistoric cockroach skittered across the floor, eliciting a shriek from Lu Kim. The group from the cruise ship stayed clumped near the door as if afraid that moving into the building would mean admitting defeat.

Charlie breathed deeply to settle her nerves. "Okay, Mr. Draper—"

"Call me Dave."

"Okay, Dave," Charlie said. "Do you know what's going on here?"

Draper told his story in staccato bursts, with frequent interjections by Montelle and the other hostages. Kidnapped at gunpoint from Lanai and dragged to a waiting boat, thirteen hostages were zipped across the water to Molokai and marched through the jungle to the Terrorist Resort and Spa. They had been informed by a skinny young man with a clipboard that they would be staying here until the "insurgent action" was concluded. And then they'd been shoved into barracks and left alone for the last few hours.

"How many bad guys?"

"At least twelve," Montelle said. "They come and go, so it's hard to tell."

"Add that to the guys who came with us, that makes sixteen," Betty said.

Voices sounded from outside, followed by approaching footsteps.

"Somebody's coming," Charlie said.

Draper made a face. "This can't be good."

HOLIDAY INN, HONOLULU, Oahu
    Saturday, 8 May
    1930 Local

Victor couldn't sleep, which was not natural. His time sense was all whacked out of shape, sure, and sirens whooped like crazy from the streets outside, near and far, but damn... he could normally sleep anywhere, anytime, and without a twinge of worry. Cuddling with a warm and naked Alexandra Lopez wasn't helping, despite their having fooled around earlier. A shower and a snack and the drone of the hotel room AC should have knocked him out like a bullet to the head.

But no, being awake while spooning up to Alexandra's backside and cupping a full breast while dozing resulted in an inevitable reaction. Soon his cupping turned into stroking and fondling, which turned into nuzzling and kissing, which resulted in more swelling and some gentle prodding.

"Hey," he whispered. "You wanna play doctor?"

"Do you never get tired of that joke?" She reached back and took him in hand, guiding him. Her bottom ground against him, and he slipped inside her moist heat as if it was the most natural thing in the world.

"Mmm," he hummed into her neck. "You were ready for me. I like that."

"I'm always ready for you, *mi cielo*."

Afterward, Alex went to clean up. Victor dug around for the remote, propped himself up in bed, and turned on the television. Punching off the free movie advertisement, he hit a news station, and his finger paused on the channel button. He blinked, his brain refusing to match the image to anything he could comprehend. Was that the Arizona Memorial? The white concrete of the bridge structure was broken into jagged shards, and the top appeared completely ripped away. Holes gaped where windows once stood. Fireboats sprayed high arcs of water into the smoking ruins. The pole from which the American flag waved had been knocked askew, bent like a flexible drinking straw, and the Stars and Stripes sloshed in the turgid water.

Victor's mouth gaped, and his belly clenched as though he'd taken a punch to the gut. "*Madre de Dios*. Alexandra! Come here!"

The news went downhill from there. Active shooters on Maui. A jetliner downed. A huge cruise liner brutally sabotaged. Tourists kidnapped. Hundreds dead.

Wrapped in a towel, Alex hurried from the bathroom and perched on the edge of the bed. She watched with him in silence as the extent of the destruction was laid out between commercial breaks. They remained spellbound throughout segment after segment.

"It's 9/11 all over again." Alex turned to him, her eyes glassy wet. "Abel and Charlie? You think they're okay?"

"Yeager. Pssshhh!" Victor waved his hands as though overhanding a throw in from the sidelines. "I'd be more worried about the terrorists. Yeager, he don't get mad fast, but when he does... ai-yi-yi."

"You think they'll come to port with all this going on?"

"Good question," Victor said, hopping off the bed and digging in his discarded pants for his phone. "Let me see what I can find out."

OPEN SEA, NORTH OF Molokai
Saturday, 8 May
1945 Hours

Anxiety. Exhilaration. The sense of falling without a parachute. All these feelings had racked Kanoa for hours. As the leader of the Niho Niuhi, the responsibility for success or failure lay with him, and the stakes came no higher than those on the table now. Ever since his meeting at Diamond Head with Palakiko, where they had witnessed the hotel bombings, he had been wracked with doubt.

And not a little guilt. Many true Hawaiians had died that day. Was it worth it? Only time would tell.

Sweat slicked the plastic cover of the scrambled satellite phone he gripped in one hand. He braced the other hand on the instrument console of the *Kekepi* as it pitched through moderate seas twenty miles off the coast of Molokai. They were running without lights, and the reflected glow of the instruments blocked any view through the bridge windows. Matty Abbado, one of the few nonnative Hawaiians in the Niho Niuhi, stood to his left, keeping an eye on the radar while holding the helm.

The sat phone beeped. Kanoa keyed the sequence to accept a scrambled call.

"Strike Leader."

"Strike Leader, Strike Two. Objective Poha. No casualties, no problems."

"Acknowledged. Charlie Mike. Leader out."

"Strike Two out."

Kanoa ended the call from Kimo Ekewaka, and the belt of tension around his chest eased a notch. The team taking VIP hostages from the resort hotels of Lanai to the hidden camp deep in the forest on the neighboring island of Molokai had reached their destination without incident. More than twelve wealthy and influential haoles would be locked in barracks constructed under a shroud of heavy foliage and heat-shielding materials. They would provide human shields to prevent aerial attack on the camp.

The brooding figure in a white suit—the Korean known as Mr. L—stirred and queried him with a look.

"All is well," Kanoa said. "Only one strike team unaccounted for."

"Team three." Mr. L pursed his lips. "They had the most difficult objective."

"News reports would seem to indicate they were successful."

Team three's mission: infiltrate the six-thousand-plus passengers aboard the mega-cruise liner *Delphinus Oceanus.* The nine-man team would disable the massive ship's watertight compartment doors, sabotage the lifeboats, and blow gaping holes in the liner's hull, using containers of smuggled C4 explosives. Once the ship was gutted and sinking, the team would abandon ship in an inflatable raft and rendezvous with Makani in his sport fisher off the coast of Oahu.

The news had not run any reports of the men who attacked the cruise liner having been captured, and he didn't know if they were merely delayed in reporting through some malfunction or the authorities were keeping quiet to avoid tipping their hand.

Makani's strike on the jet liner had succeeded, but that was the last message Kanoa had received from the man. All other attacks had been a complete success. No casualties taken. Maximum damage inflicted—just as his "advisers" had predicted.

"It's crazy out there," Kelly Pajela said. He'd been monitoring the news feed via a tablet computer while seated in the captain's chair. He met Kanoa's eyes. "Like an anthill. The governor's called out the National Guard. Police and firemen are swamped. Riots at food stores. Tourists running around in circles, demanding to get off the islands." He grinned. "Looks like we got their attention."

Tension knotted in Kanoa's chest again, tighter than before. "They'll be after us now."

"I expect so."

They had prepared for this day. Five years of dreaming had been followed by two years of planning, training, and making contacts with the right people to supply weapons and personnel, including trainers and experienced soldiers—contract killers, really—to bolster the ranks of his followers.

Kanoa had no illusions that they would succeed in overturning the United States's enslavement of Hawaii. The beast was too big, too powerful. He'd seen firsthand, while serving in Iraq as a private, what the US military could do once it set its mind to accomplishing something. With one misstep, his remaining time on this earth would be measured in days, if not hours. Liberty for Hawaii would come, but he would probably not live to see it.

The trick would be to prolong the ordeal, to bring attention to the Hawaiians' cause by focusing the media and the eyes of the world on their tiny group of islands in the middle of the Pacific Ocean. The average US citizen had no clue that native Hawaiians hadn't asked to become a state but had been annexed because a small group of sugar barons wanted to consolidate their hold and control the market without compensating the natives. It was the ultimate westward expansion of *manifest destiny*, which translated to white men stealing all the land they could grab and hold.

America, overreaching as usual. Well, they would learn a very painful, long overdue lesson.

CHAPTER TEN

Molokai Forest Reserve
Saturday, 8 May
1955 Local Time

True to his word, Winston Pettigrew led Yeager along the path taken by the captors and their hostages. Occasionally, the older man would use the flashlight feature on his phone—shielded and filtered through his fingers—to point out a footprint or a broken branch, proving he was still on the trail. The man seemed to have a sixth sense for terrain and moved more quietly than anyone Yeager had ever hunted with. Yeager was, in short, impressed all to hell.

The trail crossed a fast but shallow stream, the water running knee-high at its deepest point and colder than Yeager expected. He sloshed through after Pettigrew, soaking his hiking boots and the bottom of his jeans. When they climbed the far bank, Pettigrew froze. He held up a barely visible fist, and Yeager turned to stone.

His nostrils flared at the smell of cooking food. Pettigrew's eyes gleamed in the dark, expressing a silent question. Yeager nodded and motioned to go low. The skinny man eased down into a belly crawl, and Yeager mimicked his action. They oozed up the embankment at a pace that would put a snail into a coma. Pettigrew led the way, laboriously moving loose brush out of their path to avoid cracking branches or snapping twigs. Yeager inched along behind, senses itching for any input that would add data to his knowledge of the enemy's position or condition.

Spotting sentries first would be a good thing.

Yeager and Pettigrew edged forward until they came to the edge of the undergrowth, where the vegetation had been chopped back with weed whackers to create a clearing between the trees. Yeager had a rabbit's-eye view of four wooden huts that resembled the pre-fabricated buildings used for extra classrooms at overcrowded schools—or for barracks, come to think of it.

All four buildings were concealed under the spreading limbs of the surrounding trees, and above them, the night sky was blocked by a splotchy thicket of darkness that Yeager suspected was camouflage netting. Each building had a door at the narrow end that faced inward toward the center of the cleared space. More recon would be required to determine if back doors existed. High, narrow slots provided some cross ventilation, which would not be nearly enough to cool the interior.

Illumination came from a shielded amber light over the door of the nearest hut. The puddle of light spread in a narrow arc and was so dim that Yeager doubted it could be seen above the trees... assuming anybody was looking to begin with.

A hidden generator kicked on with a rattle. The amber light glowed a tad stronger, and the outline of a sentry materialized between the hut on their left and the next one over. The man leaned with his back against a tree, immobile and nearly invisible. He might as well have been a statue.

Professional soldier. Well trained.

Yeager tapped Pettigrew and pointed to the guard. Pettigrew tapped him back and pointed to the gap between the middle hut and the lighted one. At first, Yeager couldn't see what Pettigrew was showing him—the amber light was blinding him to anything in that direction. Cold washed over him when another sentry moved, just beyond the light, and began patrolling a slow circuit around the two middle huts.

Was Charlie in one of the huts? He had no way of knowing.

He tugged Pettigrew's sleeve, and they backed away from the clearing with all the breakneck speed of a landlocked glacier. Yeager led the way back across the stream and picked up the pace, moving another five hundred yards to a patch of ground covered in upthrust boulders and leaf-scattered soil. He eased down, rested his back against a boulder, and let the tension drain from his muscles.

Pettigrew hunkered beside him. He lit a cigarette, keeping the flame cupped behind his hand. The breeze blew at a slant, away from the campsite, so Yeager didn't say anything. Pettigrew spoke in a barely audible tone. "Well, we found 'em. Not sure who we found, but that's got to be their base camp."

Yeager grunted. *What the hell do I do now?*

THE DOOR SHOVED CHARLIE in the back and forced her to step away as it swung open. Kong the Giant filled the doorframe. No exaggeration. His shoulders brushed the jamb on either side, and the tips of his spiky hair tickled the top of the frame. He ducked and entered the room, which had gone silent at his appearance. A collectively held breath seized all the women simultaneously. Charlie included herself in that suspended moment of dread, but she forced herself to exhale even though she wanted to crawl under a cot and curl up in a ball. The man's piggish eyes roamed across the room, brushing over Charlie and leaving an oily stain on her nerve endings before moving on.

"You." Kong pointed at Lu Kim. "Come with me."

Charlie experienced a tiny flutter of relief that the thug wasn't interested in her. Shame, followed by anger, broiled her face. She knew that if she looked in a mirror, her neck and cheeks would be cherry red.

Lu Kim shrank back. Betty Pyle stood with her, chin lifted in defiance. The other captives exchanged looks of fear and dread—and outrage, in some cases. It was too sudden, the reality of violence too foreign to many of the hostages. They didn't know how to react, and no one wanted to take the lead. The crowd dithered.

Charlie swallowed sandpaper. "Leave..." The word came out as a whisper. She sucked in a deep breath and tried again. "Leave her alone!"

Kong barely glanced her way. His backhand whipped at her face so fast it blurred. He hit her with the speed of a whip snapping. *Crack!*

Charlie was on her butt on the floor, with no memory of falling. Her lips blossomed with acid pain. Her teeth ached. Migraine-strength bolts of purple agony rocketed through her skull. When the lights stopped flaring behind her eyes, Kong was pulling Lu Kim through the door. He held her by the wrist and hauled her along like a reluctant child. Betty held her other arm, dragging back in a one-sided tug of war. Kong barked a threat and jerked the small woman loose from the older lady's grip.

Betty screamed at the top of her lungs. Others were shouting. The sounds rang hollow in Charlie's ears.

The door slammed, leaving the hut murky with shadows.

Blood dripped off Charlie's chin. It left bright red blotches on her yellow blouse.

A hand touched her shoulder. Betty Pyle. "Are you all right, sweetheart?"

"No," Charlie said, looking up through shimmering vision. It hurt to speak. It hurt worse to think of Lu Kim in that monster's clutches. "I'm not all right. Not at all."

YEAGER VOICED HIS THOUGHTS aloud, testing his theories with Pettigrew. "Those middle barracks... the hostages are probably in the middle barracks." His mind skittered away from the image of Charlie locked in a hot, stinking cabin. "The two guards seemed to be hanging close to the middle one."

"And at least one is the barracks for the... what the fuck are they? Terrorists? Chickenshit North Koreans invading Hawaii?"

"Let's go with *terrorists* for now. I'm thinking there has to be a connection with the attacks in Honolulu." Yeager grimaced when his stomach grumbled. "What do we know about them so far? At least five, probably more, individuals. How many could they house in one of those barracks?"

"Eight, maybe twelve. More if they stack the bunks."

"Worse case, forty-eight. Probably less, but we can't count on that until we know. Armaments include AKs and sidearms. Men professionally trained, with good discipline."

"Asian for sure. Not Vietnamese, and that's a fact. I know me some Cong, and these ain't them."

"At least one guy was Polynesian," Yeager said. "Probably native Hawaiian."

"Strange mix."

"Objectives?"

"Unknown."

"And why take hostages from the *Breezes*? It would have been easier to shoot them all, like they did Tom." Yeager ignored the clutch in his chest. He had to compartmentalize—put Charlie in a mental box, lock it, and bury the box down deep. Otherwise, he'd be incapable of acting—damn near incapable of thinking.

"We don't have enough intel," Pettigrew said.

"And we got shit for resources. No food, no weapons, no comms."

"And lookie here—I'm damn near outta butts."

"We're fucked," Yeager said.

"Roger that."

For a time, Yeager did nothing. The rock scuffed his back when he shifted, and the sourness of his own sweat wafted up to him. Night birds he'd never heard before called to one another. Smells he couldn't identify drifted on the breeze. It was as dark as only a place far away from modern electrical service could get.

He felt alone in a dream universe that he didn't understand and didn't like. The last time he'd felt this way, he'd been a boot in Butt-fuckistan, wide-eyed and near peeing himself at every owl hoot and goat fart.

Charlie had used a good word the other day when they were touring that damn volcano on the big island, Mount Waka-waka or whatever Hawaiian vowel-job name it was. "Surreal," she'd called it. Well, this was for damn sure a big can of surreal, opened up and poured over his head. Surreal as shit.

Yeager's head snapped up.

"Did you hear that?" Pettigrew asked. "Sounded like—"

"Screams. Coming from the camp."

OPEN SEA, LOCATION Unknown
Saturday, 8 May
2147 Hours

For longer than she believed possible, Jan Osterchuk had stroked toward Molokai. For every yard forward, the current carried her a foot sideways. She rested after every hundred strokes, floating on her back and closing her eyes against the intense sun. The rest periods carried her even farther away from the island, but it couldn't be helped. She needed to catch her breath.

The salt water was colder than she'd expected, and it drained her strength faster than the exercise of swimming, which was bad enough. Spitting seawater and blinking her burning eyes, Jan fought through bouts of shivering.

At last sighting, the island had been nothing but a blob on the far horizon.

As the sun sank into the west and darkness swallowed her, Jan admitted to herself for the first time that she wasn't going to make it. She was tired. So very tired. And she could no longer fight the current or tell which direction to swim.

Jan rolled over on her back and gazed at the blanket of stars covering the night sky. She felt at peace. God was there, waiting for her. The beauty of the night sky provided more than ample evidence of that, if one knew how to see with the heart instead of the eyes. The vastness of space and the tiny mote of her own existence convinced her she had nothing to fear from death. Who else but God could have created such wonder?

But Danny. Poor Danny. What will he do without me?

Jan wept at the pain he would experience at losing her. The man could barely find his shoes and socks without help. How could cope without her being there to keep him safe and well? Their youngest daughter, Cindy, lived close by. She would check on her dad from time to time. Hopefully, it would be enough.

"Goodbye, Danny," she said to the stars. "I love you with all my heart."

AFTER KONG HAD LEFT, their captors recorded videos of each of the captives. A scrawny boy barely out of his teens had used a compact digital camera with a light grip attached to record each person giving his or her name and place of residence. Two stoic guards with automatic rifles flanked him throughout the process. *He needs the protection*, Charlie thought. *Even I could knock this kid out flat with a solid right cross.*

That was two hours earlier, and three hours since the brutally ugly man had taken Lu Kim. Charlie had no illusions about what the man intended. Her lips flattened into a grim line, and goose bumps prickled her skin.

I've seen that movie up close and personal. Don't want a sequel.

The long shadows had swallowed the room as night fell. Two dim LED lanterns provided enough light to navigate the interior of the barrack. Charlie leaned her back against the closed door and surveyed the room.

Sixteen cots. Seventeen people. One five-gallon pee bucket. No paper.

"Fricking awesome," she muttered.

A memory popped into her head: the dinner table back at their home in Texas, deep in the Hill Country. She had been just starting to show her baby bump. Abel was still having difficulty with his left hand, having survived his latest venture into Mexico by the skin of his teeth and with the sacrifice of a few good men. Charlie cut his meat, listening as Abel told David a story about being cut off in Afghanistan and how he'd made it out alive.

"What would you do," Abel had asked David, "if you were walking in the woods out back of the house here, and it came up a storm? A big mother—a big whopper of a storm. Gobs of rain. Lightning. Winds like to tear your hair off."

David frowned. "I'd run for home?"

"It's dark as hehhh—heck. You can't see nothin'. Anything. You can't find your way home, and you get lost."

"Umm. Find shelter?"

"That's good. Yep. But what do you do first?"

David's eyebrows drew together. Charlie smiled, liking how Abel was letting David find the answer on his own. "I don't know. I'd have to think about it."

"That's right," Abel told the boy. "You think first. Take a minute, no matter how much noise and light and scary sh—stuff is happening around you. Stop and think it through. Make a plan. Work on your plan. If things change, change your plan."

The discussion had continued throughout the meal, Abel coaching David on how to survive in adverse circumstances. Her boy—*their* boy now, as Abel had adopted her son—had soaked up the lessons, coming up with the right answer more often than not.

Now it was her turn. She had to think, plan, survive—just as she'd done in that cooler in the convenience store when the maniac, Skeeter, had come for her. There she'd created a plan of pure desperation. She had dug down deep and tapped into a fiery core of strength she didn't know she possessed. Armed with nothing but a box cutter, Charlotte had fought the dragon. *And won.*

"Now," she said to herself, "if only I had a box cutter."

CHAPTER ELEVEN

An exposed root reminded Yeager that running flat out through the jungle on a moonless night was a stupid idea. He scrambled upright and proceeded at a more cautious pace, ducking and weaving around barely seen obstacles. Pettigrew caught up and stayed close behind.

They crossed the stream again and dropped belly down to worm the last few feet to the same observation point they had previously occupied, and they saw... nothing.

Whatever had caused the commotion had passed, and the camp was quiet again. The two guards remained as before, one circling, one stationary. The generator kicked on and burbled in the background.

Yeager put his lips next to Pettigrew's ear. "What the hell happened?"

He got a shrug in response.

Using hand signals, Yeager directed the old vet to scout the perimeter in a clockwise rotation while Yeager moved counterclockwise.

"Use the generator to mask your movement," he murmured.

Pettigrew shot him a look that said, *Teach your grandma to suck eggs.* Yeager patted the older man's shoulder and oozed away to his right, moving like a stop-motion film of the world's slowest lizard. Stones roughed up his belly, and vegetation scratched his cheeks. Insects skittered across his hands and wriggled under his shirt. Damp earth soaked him from collar to cuff. Yeager ignored all of it.

Moving silently through the jungle did not mean never making a sound. It meant making only small, natural noises easily dismissed by the human ear. Creatures moved at night—wild pigs, deer, rodents. Leaves rustled with the breeze. Twigs and acorns fell from trees and plopped on the ground. Keeping movement small, slow, and random allowed a stalker to blend in with the sounds of the night.

In Afghanistan, Yeager had been a master stalker. In the woods, at night, with or without NVGs, he feasted on sentries and observation teams. Many a Taliban had gone to hell with a surprised look and a hole under one ear from six inches of double-edged Gerber steel. The piss stink of their last minutes on earth haunted some of Yeager's deep-night, sweaty wake-up moments, filling his nostrils with a ghost scent that he'd never quite forgotten.

The generator cut off, and Yeager froze in place. He had traveled less than twenty yards from his starting point, which had been about the five o'clock position relative to the camp. The building with the light over the door loomed closest, and Yeager detected the glow of interior lights—very dim ones—through the ventilation slots near the eaves. *Either some low-light lanterns or electronic screens.*

The urge to move, to do *something*, ate at Yeager's nerves. He forced himself to hold in place. The guards were no longer visible from his position, but abrupt movement might bring them running, alert and ready. Half-formed plans to kill the roving guard—bash his head in with a rock, maybe—and take the man's weapons flitted around the edges of Yeager's thoughts. In order for such a plan to work, he needed the guards bored, complacent, and tired of staring at nothing, rather than agitated by strange noises.

And then what? He would have a single automatic rifle against a platoon-strength cadre of trained soldiers. Rambo lived on the movie screen, not in real life. Aimed fire from the bad guys would not miss the way it did for the action heroes, and he had no sequels for which his survival was required. A sustained firefight would get him dead quicker than telling Martina, his ex-wife, that yes, those slacks did make her ass look fat.

The generator kicked back on, and Yeager allowed his joints to unlock. He resumed his slow crawl, looking for anything, hoping for a miracle.

DANNY OSTERCHUK AND Gomer Pyle hoped to make it back to the overlook before night fell, and they further hoped the four-wheeled vehicles that had brought them up from the embarkation point would still be there.

They failed in the first objective, so there was no way to judge the second. Night descended like a drawn curtain, plunging them into a groping, gasping forward progress measured in feet per minute rather than miles per hour.

Osterchuk blamed their tardiness on a combination of extreme caution and a need to stay off the main trail that forced them into a cross-country hike through some really shitty terrain. More than once, they'd had to backtrack out of a dead-end path to find another route forward. Add to that the fact they were both old as Moses's Little League coach and could only move as fast as their geriatric muscles allowed.

Not that I ever moved fast to begin with, you betcha.

When true night fell and they began flailing through unseen vines and tripping over invisible obstacles, he and Pyle made a command decision to sit the fuck down and wait for some light. They hunkered together at the base of an enormous tree and shared the rations they'd packed for the hike. *Bottled water and energy bars. Yum.*

Osterchuk kept his griping to himself. Having a conversation with Gomer was out of the question. For one thing, he'd have to damn near shout, thereby revealing their position to any lurking terrorists, and for another, the responses from Pyle would often be unrelated to the subject under discussion. The man heard about half of what you said, and half of that he heard wrong. *No, best to stay quiet. Try to get some rest. So sayeth Osterchuk.*

Only a few thin, high clouds whispered across a night sky so brilliant with a wash of stars that Osterchuk felt the impact of his insignificant existence on the galactic stage deep in his belly. That was saying something, since one thing Osterchuk could do was hide a Ford Explorer—with room left over for a Jeep Wrangler—inside his belly. Only the most profound revelation could register deep inside his gut.

He grunted a short laugh at his own expense, and Gomer looked a question at him.

"Nothing," Osterchuk said with a shake of his head. "Pay me no mind."

The day's exercise claimed its toll. A deep ache stole into his muscles and throbbed with every heartbeat. Tiredness pulled at his eyes. Osterchuk let his head flop forward and felt sleep lurking just around the corner. One thing he could do was sleep at the drop of a hat. That he could do. *Oh my, yes—*

NEAR PHU BAI, SOUTH Vietnam
24 December, 1967
Danny's Story

On 31 January, 1968, the North Vietnamese launched a surprise attack on several targets in the South, including Hue City, located six miles from the coast and sixty miles from the DMZ. The NVA called this undertaking General Offensive-General Uprising, but Western news outlets would soon refer to it as the Tet Offensive.

The Battle for Hue City featured some of the most brutal house-to-house combat faced by the US Marine Corps since... well, ever. The Marines drove the NVA and Vietcong from the city. The result:

more than six hundred Marines killed, somewhere between four and ten times that number of enemy dead, half the city reduced to rubble and, despite the ultimate victory, a public relations disaster in the US.

In the days leading up to Tet, the North Vietnamese struck bases south of Hue in coordinated attacks on the Marines stationed around Phu Bai and Phu Loc and all along Route 1. Those strikes might have been meant to weaken support for Hue from the south prior to assaulting the city, or they might have been the random mayhem of war throughout the province.

It didn't matter to Danny Osterchuk. He missed it all, lying in a hospital bed.

On December 24th, 1968, Ngo Pham, a buddy of Osterchuk's and fellow member of Combined Action Platoon Hotel 6, had invited Osterchuk to dinner at the home of one of his cousins. Combined Action Platoons were an amalgamation of a Marine rifle squad and local militia known as Popular Forces, or PFs. They worked together to deny the VC operational support at the village level and ran interdiction and combat patrols throughout their assigned area. Ngo wasn't a Christian, but he saw how glum the big-eared kid from Minnesota was at being away from home on the holiday. In Ngo's tin-roof shanty on stilts by the Troui Lagoon, Osterchuk ate exotic fish coated in pure fire and washed his burning tongue with warm beer. Seated on a wood plank floor, he and all of Ngo's extended family held a three-legged conversation with Ngo translating and Osterchuk sweating an ocean. Osterchuk sang Christmas carols, and the family clapped along, chiming in at *fa-la-la*, which left Osterchuk rolling on the floor, laughing so hard he pulled a muscle.

Late that night, he and Ngo left the shack and headed for their racks. It was dark as a coal mine at midnight. A narrow country lane connected the village to Route 1, which would take them west, back to their base six klicks east of Phu Loc. They carried only sidearms, and both wore civvies. In retrospect, those were stupid choices—given the tension and enemy activity—as well as a violation of regulations, but it was Christmas Eve, and Osterchuk wanted to set the war aside for a time.

He was more than a little drunk, and his reactions might not have been at their fastest as he walked next to the tiny—by comparison—Ngo Pham. He blundered into Ngo and knocked the smaller man to the ground when Ngo stopped in the middle of the dirt road without warning.

Three figures detached from the darkness beside the road. Osterchuk gaped, boggle-eyed and woozy. Blades glinted in the moonlight. Were they Communist infiltrators, VC, or street thugs?

Ngo and the three men jabbered back and forth. The words made no sense, but Osterchuk recognized the tone: *Give us your money, or else.* They were street thugs, then.

Lance Corporal Danny Osterchuk had a bit of a temper in those days. This was his second time as a Lance Corporal, since he'd been busted for breaking the jaw of a stupid shit stain from Brooklyn in a bar fight over a hooker. A rage demon lived deep inside Danny Osterchuk. When it possessed him, Osterchuk transformed from a human being to a wrecking ball. He felt no pain. He lost all reason and all memory. He lived to hit people and break things. He'd fought the red demon inside him all through high school and basic training and the first six months of his deployment and, with rare and notable exceptions, had won that battle.

When one of the scrawny thugs waved his knife under Ngo's chin, Osterchuk felt the demon take him. His face burned hot, and the pressure inside him expanded the way a steam boiler overheated. One second he was sane. The next, he was not.

With one mighty fist, he launched the nearest mugger like an Atlas rocket. Bones crunched at the impact, and Osterchuk knew in his gut that he'd broken the man's neck. And his demon rejoiced.

Secret fact and the reason he kept his demon under control: Osterchuk liked hitting people. He could hit people harder than a falling telephone pole. Yes, he could.

The rest of the fight blurred to a series of snapshot images. He remembered glimpses of it later, but he couldn't put together a coherent narrative. Later, Ngo told him he'd ignored the jabbing and slashing knives and thrashed the remaining two thieves as though possessed by a mighty dragon—a thing known as a *long*—and wreaked such destruction that the earth trembled. Osterchuk doubted that last part and told Ngo he was full of shit.

But secretly, he liked it. Yes, he did.

Ngo had sprinted the three miles to the village of Ngoc Ngot and raced back with a corpsmen, who patched Osterchuk's leaking holes. By the time help arrived, the red demon had faded, and Osterchuk lay in the dirt, cold and shivering, his blood soaking the clay soil. He was only vaguely aware of the corpsman yelling at him to stay awake.

Osterchuk had killed three men, and not with the pistol at his waist but with his fists. His knuckles resembled raw meat. He had sixteen stitches in his colon, and sixty-eight more decorated his body in a railroad-track map.

His knife wounds earned him a trip to the Naval Support Activity Station Hospital in Da Nang, where he stayed long enough to miss the destruction of his unit. Ngo Pham died on 7 January, when a swarm of one hundred fifty VC overran the hamlet of Ngoc Ngot and decimated CAP Hotel 6.

He ate ice cream and sucked soup while the 1st Battalion, 1st Marines counterattacked the NVA in Hue City and beat them back into the jungle.

Osterchuk had kept his demon under control ever since.

SINCE HE AND PETTIGREW had approached the camp from the south, Yeager arbitrarily assigned their starting point as the six o'clock position. He numbered the structures clockwise—his recon had circled behind building four and building three. His stalk around the perimeter of the camp had ranged to the twelve o'clock position and uncovered a number of new facts.

Pettigrew, moving clockwise, would have rounded behind building one and two.

Yeager's reconnaissance had located a fifth cabin, smaller and more compact than the others and set farther back, tucked between buildings two and three. It had its own generator, which kicked on less frequently than the larger one attached to building three. Dim lights glowed from inside. Their random flickering indicated the presence of someone moving around the interior. The rumble of a deep voice reached Yeager as he passed the place, too far away and too low to make out.

Yeager found a good observation point near the skeletal remains of a dead tree and settled in to wait. His muscles complained form the strain of hours of belly crawling and constant vigilance. There was no sign of Pettigrew.

He tried to relax and let his body recover. From his vantage point, Yeager had a good view of the back of the small cabin, which he designated as building five.

Another discovery: all along the northern side of the camp, a steep cliff fell away into a big, deep, empty bunch of nothingness. Yeager had found the drop by almost crawling directly into space. It was too dark to see the bottom, but a few experimental stone drops gave him a best guess of around a forty-yard fall.

Particularly stupid to situate a camp with no back-door escape route.

Then he found the back-door escape route. At some point in history, a chunk of the cliff wall had fallen away, leaving a wedge cut in the rock face. A natural trail led down from the ridge like a chute filled with gravel and overgrown, in places, with Hawaii's tenacious and ever-present ferns. Yeager had hiked a good ways down the cut, far enough that he was relatively sure the route would provide a second egress from the campsite. The fissure started at approximately the one o'clock position and pointed almost due north.

A quick peek at his phone under the cover of his shirt revealed the time as 2:20 a.m. The guards had changed over at midnight and not since. Four-hour rotations? If so, that was a long stretch to remain on sentry duty. Longer shifts typically meant fewer personnel, so maybe there weren't as many terrorists as Yeager had at first feared.

There was no sign of the hostages, though Yeager had convinced himself that one of the two central barracks housed the prisoners. Based on the guard positions, he would put his money on building two. There were no back doors on the buildings he had reconnoitered.

Yeager spotted Pettigrew only because he was looking for movement and knew about where to look. The old vet was slithering along, visible by his tan jacket and not much else. Yeager rattled some brush to get the man's attention.

Pettigrew shifted direction, and when he approached, Yeager gestured and led them both to the back-door cut he had found in the ridge. Going down, they were at least able to stand and work their way toward the bottom in a more human fashion. Both maintained their silence until they reached the end of the rockslide, a solid quarter-mile from the lip of the ridge.

When Yeager turned right and kept going, Pettigrew whispered, "You know where you're going?"

"Think so."

After nothing else came for a time, Pettigrew grunted. "Huh. Well, okay, then."

Yeager hiked along the base of the cliff for a solid ten minutes. The effort was rewarded when his ears picked up the hiss of falling water.

"Is that—" Pettigrew said.

"Waterfall."

Another five minutes brought them to a pool fed by a thin stream of water from the bluff above. Yeager had to restrain himself from diving headfirst into the hot-tub-sized pond. He dropped to his belly and cupped water out with his hands, drinking in deep, sloppy gulps. Pettigrew was quick to copy him.

"Probably get the shits," Yeager said after he'd slurped enough water to wash a buffalo. "But that's the least of our problems."

"Roger that." Pettigrew splashed water on his face, scrubbing with both hands. He blinked, and droplets fell from his eyebrows. "Did you find anything helpful? Besides this here water, I mean. I didn't see much on my side..."

Pettigrew's report mirrored Yeager's observations. Five buildings—one short and four long—fanned out in an irregular spread that surrounded the central clearing. Overhead was camo netting with sod piled on top.

"These boys are ready for overhead surveillance," Yeager noted.

"Agreed."

Two guards were visible, one rover and one posted and within sight of each other except when the rover went around building two on his patrol route. They were armed with AKs and sidearms, with radios clipped to their belts.

Yeager and Pettigrew settled on a flat rock near the pool, and the older man fired up one of his diminishing pack of Marlboros. "We can get the rover when he goes around the building," Pettigrew said, though he didn't sound thrilled by the idea. He sucked a deep drag and exhaled smoke through his nostrils.

"Then we have to get the other guy right away." Yeager lay on his back with his hands behind his head. He stared at the vast blanket of stars. "So, one for you, one for me. With what? Rocks?"

"Better than spitting on them."

"Mm. Say that happens. Then what? Will they have keys on 'em? If not, we have to bust the lock off the door." Yeager sighed. "That's a lot of noise."

"Uh-huh. Every injun in the teepee be on us."

Yeager's eyelids grated, heavy as steel doors. He was tired to the core. Short night, long day, no food, and lots of exercise had taken a toll he couldn't afford to pay. He allowed his eyes to slide closed, took a deep breath... and drifted off to sleep.

CHAPTER TWELVE

Charlie huddled with Betty and four other hostages in a rear corner of the barracks. The group constituted an ad hoc leadership council, elected more through their willingness to lead than any democratic process. She and Betty sat side by side on the rear-most camp bed while the others either used the next bed over or squatted in the gap between the two. Many people rested on their cots, leaving Charlie and the others alone in the back.

Dave Draper, still shirtless, tended to be the most vocal and had been beating the same drum for the last ten minutes. "All I'm saying is, who's next? I mean, that guy, he could... take anybody. Anybody."

"We know that, but what are we going to do about it?" Dominick Migliozzi repeated for the third time in his thick Jersey accent. *But whadda we gonna duabowddit?* With olive skin, jet-black hair, and a tough-guy face, Migliozzi gave off the vibe of a full-on tommy-gun-toting, East Coast mobster. As it turned out, the guy owned a small chain of bakeries and designed wedding cakes for a living.

Charlie smiled, imagining Abel and Migliozzi attempting a conversation. It would be like a mule trying to understand a monkey. *Abel.* She turned her attention to the high, narrow window slit. He was out there somewhere. Charlie felt it in her bones. He might be unpolished—really, he was as rough as raw granite—but when it came to protecting his people, he wouldn't bend, he wouldn't break, and he wouldn't back up. It warmed Charlie on the inside to know she topped the list of his people.

She studied the floor between her toes, having long since given up listening to the circular arguments among her fellow "leaders" of the captives. The floor consisted of two-by-six boards, she guessed, and based on the lack of give, they were nailed to joists. Below that? Dirt. Their group would have to somehow pull up a couple of boards then tunnel their way out. *The Great Escape, Hawaiian Style.*

The walls, now… The cot creaked when Charlie stood and stepped close to the wall. She felt Betty's eyes on her as she examined the construction, which was like an unfinished house with exposed studs of two-by-four lumber framing the building. Horizontal cross pieces ran the length of the walls every two feet from top to bottom, creating a grid pattern of raw lumber. To that framework, twelve-foot-long one-by-six boards had been nailed vertically. Windows had probably been added afterward, cut out with a reciprocating saw and framed with more two-bys.

I've been watching Abel do home renovation more than is healthy. Two years ago, I wouldn't have known a reciprocating saw from a banjo.

The builders had used nail guns to attach the one-by-six slats. She noted that at least two nails sticking through the boards had missed the frame, and they were tacky with the gluey substance she'd seen when Abel used a nail gun. He had also used colorful language to describe his thoughts about not hitting what he intended.

Hmm. A nail was not a box cutter, but it was better than harsh words and wishful thinking. Charlie pinched a nail between her fingers and gave it an experimental wiggle. *Snug, but not immobile.* Could she work it loose enough to pull through the board? It would require wallowing out the hole by working the shaft without bending it, widening it enough to pull the head through. She picked at the wood surrounding the protruding nail, earning a splinter in her finger for her trouble.

A presence appeared at her shoulder. Montelle.

"Would this help?" The soft-spoken singer held up a shiny object on a silver chain around his neck—a tiny spoon no more than three inches long.

A coke spoon? It has to be. Why else would you wear a spoon around your neck?

The singer offered a wicked grin. "They missed this when they searched me."

YEAGER SNAPPED AWAKE in a full-body jerk. It was dark. The crushing sensation of having forgotten to do something very important squeezed his chest. His memory and situational awareness clicked into place like a mosaic of still images. Hawaii. Charlie held hostage. Pettigrew. Waterfall. Lying on a rock by a pond.

His jaw clenched. How could he fall asleep knowing Charlie was—once again—being held by people with bad intentions? She was undergoing a hellish experience, and here he was, having a nice nap by a tropical pool. *Stupid, lazy...*

The clock on his phone revealed he had slept about an hour. Dawn was not far off. Pettigrew snoozed cross-legged with his arms across his knees and his head down.

Yeager sat up, and every muscle from scalp to heel sang a ballad of pain—a whole choir of *Oh, hell no—that hurts. Please don't!* He ignored the aches and shoved himself upright. His legs vibrated like tuning forks until he shook off the weakness and paced in a circle to get the blood moving again. Yeager stretched his calves by leaning against a tree. The aches receded as he warmed up the muscles. Quad stretches came next, followed by hamstrings and thighs.

Pettigrew looked up with bleary eyes. "We moving again, Staff Sergeant?"

"I am." Yeager glared at the ridge top as though he could see the encampment with its guards and hostages. "Charlie's waiting for me. First thing I'm gonna do is get me a firearm or two, then I'll see what happens next."

"Mm. Great plan, Sergeant. Why didn't they make you an officer, tactical genius like that?"

Yeager twitched a smile at the old man. "I got a friend you need to meet. You and Por Que would be the best of buddies in no time. Yeah, the plan sucks. Sitting on my ass sucks worse. I want to start thinning out the herd up there. You need to slip around, get back to the trail so you can guide in the cavalry."

"Jus' in time to save the Lone Ranger from the injuns, huh?"

"Something like that."

"You gonna get killed."

"Look." Yeager collected his thoughts. "Charlie's been in a situation like this before. She still wakes up from nightmares after being kidnapped by a pair of lunatics." Yeager's hands closed to fists, and he spoke through gritted teeth. "She won't tell me everything that happened that night, but I'm pretty sure one of them tried to... assault her. She's tough," he admitted with more than a little pride. "She killed both those fuckers. I hear the deputy that responded to the scene puked his guts out when he got a look at what she'd done. But... damn. I didn't... couldn't do anything to protect her that time."

"Not again, huh?"

"Not again."

"You sure this is your brain talking and not your balls?" Pettigrew asked.

"I'm a Marine, remember? Pretty sure they didn't issue me a brain."

KIMO EKEWAKA THREW his trash over the side of the ravine and listened to it bash and thump along the side of the cliff, ending with a muffled *whump* somewhere far below. He scratched his bare chest, yawned, and returned to what he called the commander's cabin. The smaller hut was set back from the four longer barracks and contained amenities like a refrigerator, a microwave, a desktop fan, and a real bed with a mattress. The hut had its own personal generator-supplied power, so he had lights and a small television connected to an HD antenna.

He stripped the messy sheets off the bed and tossed them in a wadded ball into a corner. Some of the fluids had soaked through to stain the mattress. Kimo unrolled his sleeping bag over the gunk and lay down on top of it, wearing only his white boxers, letting the breeze from the small fan cool the sweat on his body.

It was too warm to get inside the bag—and too warm to sleep as well, but resting would be good. The next day would be quiet as the strike teams returned from their missions and everyone packed up their shit and left. In the evening, the Niho Niuhi would issue their manifesto via the internet, spiced up with videos of executing haole pigs, then they would burn the evidence, hop on a boat, and prepare for the coup de grace.

And after that?

"Fuck it," Kimo growled to himself. He stretched out on the bed and covered his eyes with the crook of an elbow. He was too tired to worry about the future. The little Korean bitch had given him a good workout. He yawned. *A real good workout.* And maybe in the morning, he would be ready to get in some more exercise.

Heh-heh. College Boy would go all green when he pulled another woman out of the pack and dragged her off for some vigorous PT. He had his eye on the skinny blond woman, though the redhead who'd stood up to him looked like a great workout partner. That bitch had some fight to her. *Be fun to find out if the carpet matches the drapes.* Kimo relaxed, visions of red pubic hair bringing a sleepy smile to his face.

AS YEAGER NAVIGATED the base of the cliff toward the cut, something heavy bounced down the escarpment and nearly landed on his head. A flash of a light-toned object crossed in front of him and thudded to brush-choked rocks a few yards away. His brain tried to make sense of what he'd seen. A deer had fallen off the cliff? A sandbag had tumbled loose? Neither of those fit.

Behind him, Pettigrew hissed, "What was that?"

Yeager held up a hand and crept forward to get a better look. When he reached the bushes—

Aw, no. Hell, no.

The naked, torn body of the activity director from the *Fair Breezes*, Lu Kim, draped the rocks and brush like a discarded towel. Yeager forced himself to examine her body, and what he saw turned his stomach. The tiny woman had suffered before dying. She'd suffered more than any human ever should. Acid welled up from his stomach, and Yeager gritted his teeth, clenching his eyes tightly to keep the scream of anger buried inside.

Pettigrew appeared beside him. "Jesus, Mary, and Joseph."

"They're not here."

Yeager welcomed the anger into his system. It was metered out in a steady drip, like an IV. Anger triggered his old friend, the warrior. The warrior killed without remorse. Hard. Fast. Merciless.

The beast inside had grown sleepy, complacent. Marriage, fatherhood, and the soft life of a modern man—fixing the plumbing, grocery shopping, beers, and barbecues—had dulled his edge. The warrior had gone to sleep, locked in its cage, buried deep in his psyche. He had thought, after Mexico, he'd put the warrior to rest forever.

When he spoke to Pettigrew, his voice came out frigid as icicles snapping. "We need to take care of her. Can't leave her like this."

"I'll do it." The old vet straightened and met Yeager's eyes. "You need to go kill some people that need it bad."

Yeager nodded once. *Roger that.*

CHAPTER THIRTEEN

Yeager climbed the slope to the top of the ravine without pausing to rest. He ignored the burning in his calves. At the lip, he gave in to the oxygen-deprived muscles and paused for a breather. He located a rock the size of an orange cut in half. It had a jagged edge and fit his hand like a wedge. *Good for head-bashing.*

He felt the press of time working against him. Already, the deep black of night had begun to diminish. The stars dimmed. He could make out individual leaves and branches from feet away instead of inches. The sun was, at most, an hour from rising, and he still had no plan aside from a series of objectives: kill people, break things, find Charlie, go home.

The objectives were tactically unsound, as Pettigrew had pointed out. Rambo might accomplish them, but then, Rambo had contracted for sequels, and bullets tattooed all around him, magically missing his overly developed physique every time. Yeager couldn't count on these guys shooting like storm troopers.

Fight smart, dummy. Hurry carefully.

When he had his breathing under control, Yeager oozed over the ground in stealth mode. He reached the edge of the clearing near the small cabin and paused to listen. Morning birds were waking, tuning up for the day ahead. The temperature had dropped overnight to the point where Yeager wished for a jacket. He shut out the cold and dampness soaking his belly and controlled the urge to shiver.

Something shuffled in the brush to his left. Yeager isolated the sound, identifying it as a pig or other animal rooting around for breakfast. An armadillo maybe, if Hawaii had such a thing. They damn sure had mosquitoes. Several spots on his neck burned to be scratched.

He snaked over the open ground to the back of the small cabin, also known as building five. When he put his ear against the boards, he picked up the faint buzz of snoring from a single individual. Yeager crept to the corner of the building and peeked around it. The roving guard was just disappearing to the front of building two, facing away from Yeager on his clockwise rounding of the long barracks. The man appeared wary and alert.

The only ambush available was the near side of building two, close to the back corner. When the guard's circuit took him around the building, he would be blind to that side until he cleared the corner. The man kept wide of the building but not wide enough. With a lightning-strike attack, he could disable the guard without raising the alarm. He had once chance only to get it right.

Yeager was tempted to cross the distance to the second building immediately. The guard would take thirty seconds to a minute to make it around the building and reappear. In that time, Yeager could slip into position and be ready when the guard turned the corner. The posted soldier was on the opposite side of the building, and the takedown of the rover would happen as far away from that man's position as possible. If Yeager was quick and quiet enough, the other guard would not be aware of any trouble until it was too late.

Problem: there was no cover near the long building. Yeager would be exposed during the crossing and while waiting for the man's patrol to bring him into range. The sentry would be facing Yeager when he rounded the corner. Yeager would need to flatten himself against the side of the barracks then slam the guard in the head with his rock the instant he appeared. No finesse, no hand-to-hand bullshit. Bang once in the head. Repeat as necessary. Pray he could keep it quiet.

Caution made him hesitate. Hesitation led to a decision to wait for the next rotation. Waiting caused him to reconsider his options.

Option one: kill the rover and take his weapons then retreat. Strike and move in true guerrilla fashion with no concerns about making noise. Run like a scalded cat and go over the rim and out of sight in seconds. He could sneak back later, hit again, and run again, whittling away at the enemy and sending them all to Buddha hell or to whatever afterlife they believed in.

Option two: drop the first guy then press his luck to eliminate guard number two. Option two would be risky—of that there was no doubt. The second man's post was virtually unassailable without a long stalk across open ground from his rear, followed by a kill from an awkward position, striking around the base of a large tree.

But if he could succeed at option two, it opened a narrow window of time to free the hostages and get them out of harm's way. With two silent kills, maybe he could get the barracks door open without a fuss. He'd have to keep the hostages quiet. Charlie was tough and capable. She would put a choke hold on the vegans from California if they started bleating.

He liked option two a lot. Maybe too much. Every second his wife remained a captive was another drip of acid on his conscience. Impatience drove him hard, and he wanted to end this quickly, but even he recognized that the house-of-cards plan he'd built wouldn't stand a strong look, let alone a gust of wind.

Option three: the nuclear option. Kill both guards, take their weapons, and shoot every terrorist asshole brave enough to come out their door.

Kamikaze this, motherfuckers. He sighed. *No. Not smart. Use your brain, Yeager.*

The guard walked around the corner. He carried a matte-black AK with a folding stock—a commando's weapon—at port arms, not strapped over his shoulder—a sidearm in a holster, and additional magazines in a harness around his torso. The guard's eyes scanned left to right and back again.

If the guy standing post was equally alert, Yeager might have mere seconds before the alarm was raised and the camp swarmed with soldiers.

Lord grant me sloppy enemies.

The guard disappeared around the front, and Yeager moved. He soft-footed across the open ground, his skin prickling at the exposure. He flattened his back against the side of barracks near the back corner and drew deep, steadying breaths. Somewhere behind him, separated by inches of wood, was his wife. He could feel it in his chest. Yeager tamped down the urge to rip the board siding loose.

He gripped the rock, mentally rehearsing the series of moves. *An overhand blow.* The soldiers wore berets instead of helmets, leaving the skull unprotected. If he cracked the guy's noggin with one shot, the guard would drop like a sack of dirty socks.

Seconds ticked by. A faint shuffle of footsteps placed the sentry on the far side of the building, coming closer. The cover of darkness was retreating by the second.

Yeager realized he could see outlines of the camp buildings, and beyond them, the trees had gained definition. If everything went to hell, he would be exposed to enemy fire for longer than would be good for him.

Gravel crunched. The guard was at the back of the building. Yeager cocked his arm, like a big-league pitcher.

The sentry turned the corner. He stepped well wide of the structure—a full two steps away. His gaze was focused outward, away from the building. *Lucky break.*

Yeager struck, whipping the rock overhead. Whether through a sixth sense or unnaturally fast reactions, the guard twisted away an instant before Yeager hit the top of his head. The rock slashed across the man's face—a glancing blow. The soldier reeled back, grunting, dazed but not down.

The man screeched in surprise and pain. Loudly.

Option two, gone at first contact.

Yeager rushed in and slammed the rock down overhand. The man threw up a blocking arm. The rock thunked atop the guard's head, slowed by his block.

Hard, but not nearly hard enough. Drop him! Drop him fast!

Yeager's nerves screamed at him to *move*. He felt trapped in honey. He was too slow, too slow. The noise hadn't been great so far. There was a chance to keep this contained to the two guards, *if* he could knock this guy out before—

"Jio ming! Jio ming!"

Yeager spun and snapped a left elbow into the man's throat. His right arm followed, slamming the sharp leading edge of his stone into the side of the man's skull. A dull crack reverberated up his arm, and the guard dropped.

Running footsteps pounded the dirt. The other guard was coming.

The sentry had dropped his weapon in the dirt at Yeager's feet. Yeager dropped to a knee, grabbed the AK, and targeted the place where he expected the man to appear. His thumb struggled to find the selector switch for a gut-twisting second that stretched forever. He found it and moved it to a middle position without looking, hoping he was off Safe and the weapon would fire when he pulled the trigger. AKs were all pretty much alike, but it had been a long time since he'd handled one.

Yeager registered the scuffing sound when a second guard skidded to a halt before rounding the corner. *Smart play. Lord, please. I asked for sloppy enemies, not pros.* It seemed wrong somehow to pray for the guy making a mistake that would get him killed, but...

"Jianguo?" the man called out.

Yeager didn't know whether that was a name or *What the fuck?* in Korean. What he did know was that every second was a second too long to sit around and wait. He groaned, hoping his decoy of pain sounded enough like his buddy to fool the guard.

Guard two lost his patience. He appeared, having circled wide out from the corner.

Thank you, God. Blasphemy or not, Yeager shifted aim and fired. The AK bucked in his hands, rattling out a satisfying torrent of full auto. The remaining guard flew back, slammed in the chest by at least four solid hits.

Shouts echoed from the other barracks. Options one and two were gone, and Charlie would yell at him for trying the kill-them-all option, even if she had to chase him to hell to do it. It was time to go. *Di di mao,* as Pettigrew would say.

Yeager paused long enough to tear the harness off the dead guard at his feet. The door to the small cabin slammed back, and the ugly giant Yeager had seen on the trail appeared. He wore no clothes but carried an AK of his own. He shouted at Yeager and ripped loose a burst, firing from the hip. The rounds zinged past Yeager's nose. Yeager triggered off a shot one-handed, pointing his weapon blindly while running away. He didn't look to see if he'd hit the big bastard but just kept running.

He ducked into the trees and cut left then zigged back right. Bullets chipped leaves from the surrounding vegetation. Yeager pounded through the jungle, a halfback dodging and weaving through the defensive line of low branches, exposed roots, and entangling vines. After twenty seconds of all-out, panting effort, he crossed a clearing and pivoted around the base of a solid tree trunk. Gun up, he aimed back the way he had come.

Brush crackled, and the naked monster with the AK appeared at the far edge of the clearing. Yeager targeted the ugly bastard, centering his weapon's iron sights between the man's brown nipples. Motion must have given him away, for the big man's eyes widened, and he dove away. Yeager held his fire.

When the man didn't reappear, Yeager sprinted away again. He made the top of the slope leading to the valley below and hit it at full-tilt boogie. Scrambling at a reckless pace, Yeager jumped from boulder to boulder, scrape-slid on his butt in the loose gravel, and wind-milled his arms down the chute. It was a miracle he avoided tumbling ass over elbows all the way to the bottom.

Yeager found Pettigrew placing stones on a mound of banana-tree leaves, below which, he assumed, lay the body of Lu Kim. The gnarled man looked up from his task when Yeager appeared.

"I heard the shooting," Pettigrew said. "What happened?"

Yeager held up his hand with the AK and the wadded ammo harness, too winded to speak.

"Hostages?"

Sweat spattered the ground when Yeager shook his head. He gasped for breath. "Killed... two guards."

"Now what?"

Yeager waved his free hand. "Come with me."

They slipped along the faint trail to the base of the chute Yeager had narrowly avoided falling down. Bushes grew in the gaps between tumbled boulders. Tangles of rambling vines choked the brush, making it a natural hiding place. Yeager hunkered down tight between two coffin-sized stones, hidden by the brush from any observer following the path he had taken off the ridge.

"What are we doing?" Pettigrew asked.

"Shhh."

"What are we doing?" Pettigrew repeated in a whisper.

Equally quiet, Yeager said, "Ambush." He added, "I want to nail me a couple more if possible. Back 'em off for sure."

"Good." Pettigrew nodded. "I need a gun too."

HONOLULU, OAHU

Sunday, 9 May

0640 Local

At first light, Victor tried Yeager's cell. Voicemail. He called Charlie's cell. Voicemail. He tried the main line of the tour company that operated the *Fair Breezes*. "Your call is very important to us. Please stay on the line."

The Coast Guard said, "No, sir, we don't have any distress calls from the *Fair Breezes*."

The local news stations: "Your call is very blah-blah-blah."

"Out to sea," Alex said. "They're probably out of range of a cell tower."

"The ship has Wi-Fi. It says so on their website. Right here."

"Wi-Fi is not a cell signal—"

"I know, but damn. Got Wi-Fi, you should have a cell tower, right?"

"Try emailing them. They emailed us from the ship the other day, true?"

Victor sent an email.

No response. He drank a bottle of water. Hit refresh. Refresh. Refresh.

"*Mi hermano*," Alex said with a touch to his shoulder. "They're on their honeymoon. They're probably still in bed. Why don't you go work out or something? Lift some pianos. Speaking as your doctor, this would help you relax."

"Speaking of relaxing..." Victor turned in his seat and slipped his hands over her hips. "You wanna play doct—"

"No!" Alex laughed and spun away. "Stop that. I told you I need to go to the hospital. They probably need some help for all the injuries."

"Wait. I know who to call." Victor scrolled through his contacts—and scrolled again when he reached the end. "Damn. I just have to find his number."

CHAPTER FOURTEEN

Molokai Forest Reserve
Sunday, 9 May
0642 Local Time

Danny Osterchuk considered himself a generally happy person. The list of things he loved far outstripped the list of things he hated. The guys at the auto-parts store he managed were always amazed by how he could deal with cranky customers and turn them into puppy dogs wagging their tails. His grandkids called him a foolio, which they defined as a big, goofy, lummox from Minnesota. He was okay with that. The grass where Osterchuk stood was always greener than anything over the fence, and his glass wasn't just half-full—it was waiting to be topped off. Preferably with beer. Osterchuk liked beer.

Sleeping out in the open with no tent, no sleeping bag, and no cooler full of beer made the short list of things he did not enjoy. Fortunately, his wife had forced him to carry a backpack with water and granola bars... not enough granola bars, but—hell, *granola bars*? Ugh.

"Shoulda packed some Vienna sausages, you bet," he muttered while digging into his pack for any granola crumbs that might have escaped into the crevices. Osterchuk liked Vienna sausages.

Gomer gave him that look—the one that said *I didn't hear you, but I'm gonna pretend I did.* Osterchuk shook his head. It wasn't important enough for him to repeat himself with the exaggerated, slow-lip movements that Ted could read. Gomer reclined against the bole of their sheltering tree, looking semi-awake and morose, having gotten up during the night six times to pee. Osterchuk had made five similar trips. Heavy dew had left both of them damp and chilled, Gomer more than him because he didn't have nearly the padding. Osterchuk shivered a bit despite his bulk.

Early dawn had arrived, and none too damn soon. His ass hurt, his back hurt, and he needed to take a dump something fierce. Add toilet paper to the list of things not present, along with a porcelain throne like the one he had at home with the magazine rack and the super-strength exhaust fan. As a kid in Vietnam, he had never thought twice about relieving his bowels in the bushes. He and his buddies called it "leaving behind a memento of American digestion." When you were deep in the boonies, it was just something you did... though come to think on it, back then he'd remembered to squeeze a roll of Charmin into his ruck.

Have to talk to Jan about that. No more hikes without some two-ply Charmin in the pack. And some real damn food, you bet.

It was time to move. Osterchuk stifled a groan as he climbed upright and waved for Gomer to get moving. Gomer stood and dusted off the seat of his shorts, which, given his spindly old-man legs, made him look like a chicken dressed in a man's clothes. Osterchuk wore loose pants—Jan claimed no one should be subjected to the sight of his bare thighs. He didn't object. He liked long pants as much as shorts, and more now that they kept his legs warm.

Osterchuk took point. There was no trail. For most of the previous day, they had paralleled the hiking trail, weaving back and forth as nature demanded. Staying off the tourist path had seemed conducive to not dying in a fiery hail of lead. But the options narrowed as they approached the overlook where the tour jeeps had dropped everyone off the previous day. The overlook was an overlook because—guess what?—it overlooked a damn big gorge. At some point, they would need to skirt the gorge and navigate their way to the trailhead. *Where a smart man would have positioned troops to cut off retreat.*

A shallow rain-cut gully went the right direction, and Osterchuk led the way into it. His instinct told him to keep low relative to the horizon and this wash—arroyo, whatever—fit the bill perfectly. His feet sank into the spongy soil, adding the benefit of keeping their progress quiet.

The chance of reaching the overlook and finding a pair of jeeps and drivers waiting with open smiles and open beers was a bit god-damn small. *As much chance as a finding a creme-filled donut at church after services.*

Osterchuk liked donuts, you betcha. His stomach growled.

The first indication their luck had run out came with the clack-ety-clack of an AK bolt being thrown. The sound was imprinted on Osterchuk's subconscious, hardwired into his hindbrain. Reactions coded into his nervous system put him in motion before his mind could form a single *Oh shit.*

"Down!" he screamed, throwing himself backward and knocking Gomer flying.

A short burst ripped leaves where he had been standing. Oster-chuk speed-crawled through the undergrowth, as graceful and agile as a walrus on a beach. Dirt and twigs scraped his belly, and he did not care one damn bit. He slithered with the same vigor and mud-eating drive he'd shown in boot camp, crawling under the barbed-wire obstacle with live fire overhead.

Osterchuk stayed on Gomer's churning heels, the deaf bastard scrambling through dirt and debris as fast as his chicken legs could push him along. *I guess you heard that, huh? Seven-dot-six-two crack-ing overhead. You didn't need hearing aids for that sound.*

They wiggled through the gully. Shouts in a foreign language sounded too damn close behind them. Osterchuk tasted dirt. He gasped for air. His heart rate was off the fucking charts. At least—so far—he had managed not to shit himself. That was a plus. *Silver lin-ing, meet black cloud.*

The gully would peter out not far from the tree where they'd spent the night. After that, nothing but deep forest stretched for miles and miles in any direction. Assuming they could break contact long enough between here and there, they might be able to juke sideways and lose their pursuit. For the moment, though, the depression in the earth was keeping one damn big foolio from getting his king-sized butt filled with a lead enema.

Gomer reached the point where the depression leveled out and twisted around. His face reflected the same barely contained terror that bloomed through Osterchuk's bloodstream with the bongo drumbeat of his overtaxed heart.

Osterchuk risked a look behind them. Men called back and forth. Two of them. Eighty to a hundred yards away. The foliage lining the gully and the surrounding forest blocked them from view. In a mental replay, he guessed that the incoming fire had come from a copse of trees at least fifty yards from the point where Osterchuk first heard the racking of the bolt.

Huh. The team blocking the overlook had not charged directly after them as Osterchuk had assumed they would. Had they done so, they would have run straight up his backside and shot both him and Gomer without breaking a sweat. But they were coming on—silently now, but coming. He could feel it in his bones.

Now or never, amen and pass the ammo. Osterchuk hauled himself upright, grabbed Gomer by the shirt collar, and dragged the smaller man to his feet. Holding Gomer's arm, he ran for the deeper forest as fast as his big, fat foolio legs would carry him.

HONOLULU, OAHU
    Sunday, 9 May
    0750 Local

Victor waited at a hospital near downtown Honolulu while Alex talked the administrator into letting her help. The hospital admin, an older Hawaiian man with an explosion of white hair around his crown and deep circles under his eyes, raised an eyebrow at her Mexican license before deciding to ignore where it came from and press her into desperately needed service.

Alex bussed Victor on the cheek after pulling on a loaner lab coat and rolling up its too-long sleeves. "Go. I'll call you when I'm ready to go."

Victor surveyed the madhouse of an ER and said, "Sure," but she was already gone, wrapping a stethoscope around her neck and conferring with a fast-walking nurse. He sighed. "Some vacation."

Victor fired up the rental sedan and followed the signs to Interstate Highway H1. That struck him as funny—an interstate highway in Hawaii. "Need one goddamn long bridge to be an interstate," he said to himself.

He navigated a snarl of interchanges and headed eastward on IH 3, across the narrow end of Oahu. He tuned into talk radio to pass the time and agreed with the callers who wanted some balls nailed to the barn door over the downed plane, the *Oceanus Delphinius*, and all the other terrorist attacks. The most heated comments came from people who were raving mad about the destruction of the Arizona Memorial. It was December 7, 1941, all over again.

After reaching Kaneohe Bay, on the far side of the island from Honolulu, he pulled off the highway and hunted the side streets with the help of his navigation app. He found the place Cassidy had specified after Victor had found his number and called him. He was within two miles of Marine Corps Base Hawaii.

The restaurant was fashioned on a Denny's model. Victor took the offered booth and ordered a pot of coffee to go with a stack of pancakes big enough to qualify for a building permit.

"Them carbs will kill you."

Trayvone "Butch" Cassidy slid into the booth across from them. At six feet, two inches of oiled black steel, Cassidy could eat gunpowder and spit fire. Except for the man's creepy and unnatural preference for fixed-wing aircraft, Victor considered him the second-best pilot the Marines had ever produced. More importantly, as S-2 for Marine Aircraft Group 24, 1st Marine Air Wing, Butch Cassidy would have his finger on the pulse of activity surrounding the situation in Hawaii.

"Hawaiian pancakes." Victor wiped his hands on a napkin and reached out for his coffee cup. "I thought they'd taste like pineapple."

"Well"—Cassidy glanced back at Victor and consulted his multidial watch—"you have exactly eight minutes to ask whatever favors you think a to-go order of breakfast burritos will buy, then I have to depart the pattern."

"Busy, huh?"

"It is Charlie Foxtrot out there. Only my great pity for you as a rotorhead buys you the eight minutes. CO expects a report on available assets by yesterday. I'm damn near AWOL just by coming here."

"What's the situation?"

"Fucking bunch of home-grown terrorists ripped us a new asshole, is the situation. All commercial flights are grounded as of eighteen thirty last night. The ports are closed. Cruise ships are embargoed until the crews are vetted and the ships inspected. You see the news on the *Delphinius*? Jesus, what a nightmare those people are going through. The islands are a raging nuthouse. The stores are stripped bare, and the local warehouses are damn near sucked dry. The food reserves on Hawaii were never deep—they rely on almost daily shipments to keep the shelves stocked."

"What about the tourists?"

"The brass has decided to start moving tourists off the island by military transport. We're pushing a bunch of tin out there—C-17s and C-130s, along with some F-18s to fly CAP and some Apaches to rain down extra-strength hurt on any SAM that pops its head up. We're off-loading relief supplies from incoming birds as I speak." Cassidy glanced at his watch. "Four minutes."

"Can you get me some intel?"

Cassidy paused. His eyebrows asked the question.

"I'm looking for a boat." Victor asked. "How many burritos would it take for you to check on it?"

THE BLACK-CLAD ASIANS came down the slope like professionals—darting from cover to cover and maintaining overwatch positions and doing it... quietly. No talking, no radio comms. Hand signals only. Yeager's opinion of their professional demeanor cranked another notch higher. The oncoming operatives were either Spec Ops or the equivalent of Army Rangers. Not, of course, as good as Force Recon Marines, but still pretty decent.

Yeager shifted aim, chasing the point man as he flashed in and out of view. He'd have a split second to locate the man, center the sights, take up trigger slack, *annddd...* no. The man would vanish behind cover. It was like a game of whack-a-mole using live ammo. Yeager wanted a one-shot hit. Killing him would be best, though a wounded man might pull in other heroes to try to save him. In any event, the instant Yeager pulled the trigger, return fire would obliterate his position. And letting the entire squad of six troops reach the valley floor unscathed would be unacceptable. He had to even the odds before they spread out and flanked him.

Pettigrew watched from the safety of the rock to his right. The old man's nasal passages whistled faintly from sinus congestion, although his breathing stayed slow, or only slightly faster than normal. Yeager could feel the old veteran's glittering eyes fixed on him.

Patience, Yeager cautioned himself. The last twenty yards of the trail were bare. Anyone wanting to reach the tumbled field of boulders would need to cross a kill zone of gravel-covered slope. Yeager placed the AK's sights on a point midway down, selector on single shot. No doubt, the commando would hit the last patch at a dead run, depending on speed to keep him alive.

Can't outrun a bullet, son.

The commando burst from cover right where Yeager expected him.

Bam! Bam! Bam! Three shots banged his shoulder. Three hits. The enemy soldier rag-doll tumbled down the slope. Yeager rolled left before the body came to rest, not a second too soon. Leaves and twigs at his previous position blew apart in a hurricane of bullets. Had he remained, Yeager would have been ripped to shreds.

"Fuck," yelled Pettigrew. He lay curled in a ball, ears covered with cupped palms. "These guys are good!"

Yeager scrambled to another crevice that afforded a view of the slope. Two men approached the open ground. Yeager cranked off a couple of snap shots at the nearest one, who disappeared under cover, probably untouched. Incoming fire cracked the stone next to Yeager, peppering his face with hot shards of rock. He flinched and dove away.

The terrorists used suppressive fire to cover their movement. At least two would maintain a base of fire, spattering the rocks in random bursts, while the others would move. Whenever Yeager found a firing lane, rounds would impact nearby. He was forced to duck back and seek different vantage points. The soldiers coordinated their actions with hand gestures. *Silent, disciplined, and deadly. Hell yes, they're good.* They were better than any opponents Yeager had ever faced, by a wide margin.

"Plan B!" Yeager yelled to Pettigrew. He got a thumbs-up in return.

Yeager backed away from the tumble of boulders, eeling through cover as fast as he dared. Between the forest and the field of boulder lay a strip of open ground, about two seconds' worth at a sprint. Two seconds was a long time to be exposed to well-aimed fire from professional soldiers. Yeager's only advantage was that the enemy would need to compensate for his appearance at a different location than they expected. There would be a delay while they acquired the target—him—and sent rounds downrange.

Would it be long enough to keep him alive?

"Let's find out," he growled softly and bolted for the trees.

A shout came from the hillside. Yeager hit the gap between a pair of old-growth eucalyptus trees as instant chips of bark exploded near his shoulder. He juked right, putting the largest tree at his back. Zips and zings of probing bullets followed him into the vegetation, while still more rounds *thocked* into the spongy bark.

He didn't pause to check on Pettigrew. Their hastily improvised plan was for Yeager to lead the surviving enemy soldiers into the forest, where he would find ambush points, whittle down their numbers, and eventually break contact. Pettigrew would go into hiding until the squad passed. When all was clear, he was to scavenge any dead bodies—hopefully not Yeager's—and slip away, unseen. They had planned to rendezvous back at the waterfall ASAP after dark.

Yeager ducked through slapping fronds at a run, one hand up to shield his face. He breathed savagely, already winded. Sweat slicked his face, which felt overheated. Dehydration was a serious complication. He had no canteen and would be forced to rely on streams found along the way to keep from stroking out.

Yeager had the confidence of a born warrior. He was a weapon, shaped and honed by a cadre of the proudest, toughest sons of bitches on the planet: a United States Marine. Tested in battle. Hammered in the hottest flame. A protector of the flock. A knight tempered with honor, blessed with skill, and trained by the best. America's enemies feared him. Their widows hated him.

And for the first time since he was a kid in Afghanistan, a tight knot of self-doubt settled in his belly and took root there. His opponents had him outgunned and outnumbered and were highly trained. Disciplined. Skilled. Head-to-head, he would put himself up against any single one of them. But there were five of them firing at him. And how many more waited above in the barracks where his wife was being held captive?

Just how in the hell was he supposed to do this?

The First Law: Come home at the end of the day.

But home had never looked so far away.

CHAPTER FIFTEEN

The sounds of Yeager crashing through the forest, leading the enemy away from his position, faded with distance. Pettigrew grinned. Yeager was a good man in the woods when he could move slowly and quietly. When he was in a hurry, Yeager sounded like a bull loose in a cymbal factory.

A few yards back from Yeager's initial ambush point, Pettigrew had found a spot under a rotted, fallen tree. The gap beneath it was thick with vines and heavy with shadow. Bugs and slugs were everywhere, and it smelled of wet wood and green moss. Winston Pettigrew squirmed into a hole that a gopher would find constricting.

It was like coming home. His thing—the talent he'd learned in that Southeast Asian vacation courtesy of Uncle Sam—was to find a place any man would overlook as too tight, too narrow, too confining, or too intimidating to search then ferret himself into it and hide every molecule of his presence from the outside world. Many a canny, sneaky Victor Charles had stepped over Pettigrew and walked on, unaware of the skinny black man under his feet.

Once burrowed in tight, Pettigrew concentrated on a spot in front of his nose and... folded in on himself. He didn't know any other way to describe it. To him, it was like pulling the drapes at night. He felt himself... diminish... in relation to the rest of the world. When he pulled it off just right, he could damn near fade into the wallpaper in a crowded room, change color like a chameleon, and be as forgotten as yesterday's news. Guys standing right next to him would forget he was there then turn around and bump into him.

The enemy soldiers following Yeager zipped past Pettigrew's hiding place without a second glance. Some rounded his fallen tree in front of him, others behind, splitting and bypassing him without slowing. Had he a weapon, Pettigrew could have nailed three of them easily.

He counted them off as they passed. *One... two... three... four.* All moved in disciplined silence. Pettigrew pinpointed them by the sounds of their passage as they spread through the jungle—a scratch of cloth on a branch, a crunch of grit underfoot... one so close that the stench of garlicky sweat infiltrated Pettigrew's nose and threatened to break his concentration.

They came and they went, one after another. After a long pause, number five appeared, slipping from tree to tree and sweeping right, left, up, and rear, his eyes glued to his weapon's sights. Pettigrew could see individual beads of sweat trickling down the man's face as he passed. Asian features, black uniform, carrying an AK... now, didn't that bring back some memories?

Oh, how I wish I had my Betty Ann. His preferred weapon in the 'Nam: six inches of icy-sharp double-edged blade—a single piece of Sheffield steel from needle tip to rubber-coated grip, completely nonreg. As if killing was only okay with gear supplied by the lowest bidder. The Marine Corp had issued him a K-Bar, which was a handy knife for camp chores and whatnot—sturdy, capable, and good for opening C-rations and cutting branches for shelter.

For killing, though, nothing equaled Betty Ann. Named after a wicked little bitch from Mobile who had blown him, rolled him, and stolen his car, Betty Ann had sliced more throats than Sweeney Todd on free-shave Saturday. Man, he missed that blade.

Minutes ticked off the clock. Pettigrew had no idea how long he stayed immobile. In his folded-in state, time had no meaning for Winston Pettigrew. The critters crawling over and under his body did not register in his conscious mind. The damp ground chilling his belly and balls was as comfortable as his king-sized four-poster at home. Well, okay, that was a lie, but the point was, he could ignore the discomfort.

After an unmeasured space of time later, something clicked in Pettigrew's subconscious. Sounds of the jungle returned to undisturbed harmony. His sixth sense detected no enemies within a noticeable distance. Pettigrew decided he was as alone as he was going to get. He unfolded, and a deep breath filled his lungs for what felt like the first time in hours. Wriggling from under the tree trunk, he stood on shaky legs and brushed off the debris clinging to his clothes. The chill of damp clothes made him shiver in the brisk morning air. Returning to the world brought with it a reminder of his aching bladder, his swollen, arthritic joints, and his tobacco-deprived lungs. *Getting old sucks.*

Pettigrew navigated around the tumble of rocks at the base of the cliff and scrambled to the earthen ramp leading up into the cut in the steep wall. "Aha!" he whispered.

The enemy soldiers had moved on too quickly to stop and secure the body of their fallen comrade. The commando lay in an awkward heap halfway up the gravel path, caught on a stewpot-sized bush. Pettigrew hiked up the slope and recovered the man's rifle first—he'd need to check it for grit and obstructions later—then slung it over one shoulder and climbed up to inspect the body.

The ammo harness came off first. Six magazines and—*oho, look!*—two smooth baseball-sized grenades. Next came the flak jacket, which Pettigrew slipped over his shoulders. Rolling the body around had dislodged it, and the heavy weight of the corpse slid into Pettigrew's legs, threatening to unbalance him but also revealing—

"Oh yeah, baby. Come to Daddy."

A sheathed knife was secured at the man's back. Double-edged. Four inches of blade instead of six. Plain wooden grip. Not a patch on Betty Ann, but...

"You'll do, my sweet thang," Pettigrew cooed, holding the blade low to keep from catching and reflecting sunlight. He repressed a chuckle and settled for a satisfied smirk. "Let's go do some hunting, little sister."

MOLOKAI FOREST RESERVE
Sunday, 9 May
0815 Local

Kimo Ekewaka stalked the camp, pacing like a caged lion. The two dead "advisers"—soldiers supplied by the nation that had agreed to fund and support the Niho Niuhi—lay under blankets in the center of the clearing. He couldn't give a shit about their dead carcasses. The attack, on the other hand, made his blood boil. *Who was it? What was his objective?* Clearly, the guy was not a cop or a soldier. He wore plain clothes and had brought a rock as his only weapon. Plus, he had taken first blood. Those were not the actions of any type of authority.

Kimo had ordered a squad out after the lone-wolf attacker. The man had escaped down the ravine and disappeared before Kimo, running bare-assed and pricking his feet on a thousand fucking thorns, could catch him.

Hunter? Off-duty military? Kimo guessed the guy was in his midthirties and six feet tall with a wrestler's body. Killing both guards had required skills beyond those of a casual hunter or passing tourist trying to play hero. These advisers were not conscript soldiers—they were commandos, supposedly Special Forces. It should not have been so easy to take them by surprise. Kanoa said they were North Korea's best, though Kimo had been to Korea several times, and these men struck him as less Korean than pizza. That awareness was based more on gut feeling than any fact Kimo could point to.

The mystery attacker, however—now, *that* asshole was pure haole, a white cockroach who badly needed to get stomped on. Before Kimo needed to report the attack to Kanoa, he wanted that white hide tacked up on his wall. Kimo did not do failure. Failure sucked.

Six men had left the camp more than two hours back. *Closer to three.* The chatter of shots had crackled in the distant gorge for a while early on. Since then... nothing.

One of the new sentries called a challenge from the south perimeter. The response came back friendly. The team leader, Manu Ho—the one who had carried out the resort hotel shootings—led his team and the Pearl Harbor mortar crew into the clearing. More advisers. The only native Hawaiian in the group was Mal, who came in dragging the tail end.

Kimo greeted his fellow native first. "Aloha, Mal. You win?"

Mal's answering grin was tired but happy. "The monuments are toast, my bruddah. Pearl Harbor burns again."

Kimo had argued for the Pearl strike to happen during the day, when the tourist attractions would be flooded with haole pricks. The slaughter of haole always warmed Kimo's heart. Kanoa and his mysterious companion, Mr. L, had vetoed the idea. Too many people were around the launching area during the day. The mortar teams would be seen setting up the weapons and not achieve the objective. Still, the gutting of the Arizona Memorial would strike directly at the heart of the pigs infesting his nation.

Manu Ho approached, reporting to him since Kimo was senior member of the Niho Niuhi in camp. With a respectful nod, the strike-team leader said in his stilted broken English, "Strike team leader, reporting all objectives achieved." The man slurred his Ls and Rs, so his words came out *lepohting arr objectives achieved.* Ho's gaze fell on the two shrouded corpses. "Who killed?" *Who kirred?*

"Your sentries got sloppy, *brah*." Kimo laced the last word with contempt. He stepped in closer, using his height and strength to intimidate the smaller man. The commando was forced to look up to meet his eyes. "A fucking tourist killed them and ran away. Six more of your men are on his trail. Assuming they don't fuck up, too, I expect they'll have his nuts in a sack pretty damn quick."

Ho must have understood the gist of his comments because his brow lowered and his jaw clamped tighter than a vise. He stalked over, stiff legged, and flipped back the blanket covering first one soldier, then the other. Soft curses in a foreign tongue flowed from his mouth. The language did not sound Korean. Ho glared at Kimo.

"You... ah," Ho growled, "re-responsible... this?"

"No, brah. Done told you—your guys fucked it up. Let a haole come in, and *skrickkk*!" Kimo made a throat-slashing gesture.

Ho's eyes narrowed to slits. He nodded curtly and spoke to his men, this time in Korean. The foreigner troops collected their dead and carried them off into the woods. Kimo knew just enough Korean to order a beer and a whore, so he could only assume the leader had instructed his men to bury their dead in the forest. Ho followed after them.

Mal trailed him. "What's this about a haole killing sentries?"

"Nothing big." Kimo shrugged. "Some asshole playing soldier. The Koreans will get him." Kimo smiled and punched Mal on the shoulder hard enough to jolt the smaller man. "Hey, but get this: I caught me some bitches hiking yesterday, dude, and College Boy brought some lookers with his haul. We are plussed up on pussy, brah. Come and see what we got, man. I got eyes on the skinny blond gal, but you can have your pick of the rest."

HONOLULU, OAHU

Sunday, 9 May
1218 Local

Traffic in Honolulu had become a total bitch migraine, crotch-rotting horror show. Everybody in the city had decided to go for a drive at the same time—some leaving, some ransacking grocery stores, and some just wandering to no purpose. Checkpoints further solidified the traffic as the police looked for gun-wielding nutsos.

The spot between Victor's shoulder blades had twisted into a Christmas-light tangle of nerves, muscles, and pain by the time he made it back to the city after seeing Butch. He inched through traffic to his hotel. Miraculously, he made it without pulling from vehicles and beating to death anybody in a minivan or a BMW. After arriving, he was so tense that he worked the hell out of the hotel's inadequate gym for a solid forty-five minutes.

After that, showered and dressed and with totally no idea of what to do next, Victor wandered out to the bench seat under the motel's portico and picked through the sparse articles of a pathetic newspaper to find some new piece of information about the attacks. Hunger nibbled at the edges of his stomach, though not enough to make him get up and do something about it.

His cell rang.

"Yo."

"Victor, it's Butch."

"You find my ship?"

"Nada, amigo." Cassidy's voice conveyed a verbal shrug. "The vessel has not checked in with its parent company and is unreachable by radio, and the Coasties have nothing on her. She has, for real, dropped off the radar. Last known position: headed for anchorage off the south coast of Molokai."

"Well..." Victor leaned back into the bench. Sirens wailed, making it hard to hear. An ambulance cut across his field of vision, light bar flashing as it weaved through traffic. "That sucks."

"Yeah, it do," Cassidy said. "Look, buddy, I got to run. Shit has blown up into a class-A clusterfuck of giant proportions out here. But hey, did you hear? We got one."

"Huh?"

"Yeah, a sport fisher was intercepted by the Coast Guard leaving the vicinity of the *Delphinius*. They fired missiles at the cutter, who blew the ship out of the water. No survivors, unfortunately."

"Yeah, I'm so sad," Victor said. "My heart, she is breaking."

"Intel, buddy. We needed the intel."

Victor grunted an assent. A fire truck followed the ambulance, blowing its horn and howling through traffic. "Kind of approaching a clusterfuck out here too. Thanks anyway, dude. I owe you." Victor ended the call.

Now what was he supposed to do—snatch up a helicopter and fly around, buzzing ships, to see if he could find Yeager's? Volunteer as a CareFlight pilot and do some good like Alex? Or go back to the hotel and drink beer and eat peanuts while watching movies at fourteen dollars a pop? Logic suggested no one would be turning him loose in a borrowed helicopter, and staying in a sterile hotel room all day sounded like a torture made for the hell bound.

An idea crept up from a dark corner of his mind and begged for attention. *Maybe...?* With the use of his phone's browser, Victor checked his way out-of-date social-media pages for news of a certain someone who...

"Oh, hell," he said after a time staring at the screen. "Alex is gonna be so pissed."

Victor smacked the fist holding his phone into his other hand a few times, jaw tight. He spat between his teeth, got up from the bench, and headed for his rental car. There was one trick left up his sleeve, and it would mean getting out into the craziness seizing Honolulu and driving *back* across the island to a spot near where he'd met Cassidy, but it beat doing nothing.

CHAPTER SIXTEEN

Molokai Forest Reserve
Sunday, 9 May
1235 Local Time

When the barracks door opened, Charlie tensed and broke out in a cold sweat. She relaxed a tiny bit when two guards entered carrying boxes, a third man maintaining watch with his rifle held across his chest. In the seconds between the sound of the lock and the entrance of the three terrorists, Charlie had been convinced the gargantuan monster who took Lu Kim was returning for another victim. She clamped her thighs at the sudden need to pee.

The guards brought in two boxes the size of totes she used to store quilts and winter blankets, each requiring two hands to carry. They set the boxes on the floor by the first cot and barked orders for the captives to clear the central aisle. One man exited and returned with an empty five-gallon bucket. The previous night, some of the men had stood two cots upright and leaned them together to form a rickety wall around the waste bucket that afforded users a tiny amount of privacy. The bucket carrier kicked over the cots and exchanged his empty container for the one full of waste.

Seventeen people had made a tremendous number of contributions to it. The guard's features twisted into a mask of disgust as he walked the waste bucket to the door, holding it by the handle away from his body. The contents sloshed over the rim, and some spattered the floor. The other guards laughed when gunk landed on the unlucky man's boot and he hissed in displeasure.

The trio exited, and the door banged shut and was locked.

Ed Collins, a fellow Texan, was the first to reach the boxes. "Hey, y'all. Food. And water!"

People scrambled to claim meals and bottled water. There had been no breakfast that morning or dinner the night before and nothing to drink either. One tote contained field rations similar to the MREs the US military used except with Asian markings. The water was the type Charlie bought from a warehouse club, still shrink-wrapped. The tote contained forty-eight bottles, or about two and three-quarters bottles for each person.

"Oh, yum." Betty Pyle's lips twisted in a sour way when she got her meal open.

Charlie had to agree. Inside her MRE, she found a sealed packet of sticky rice mixed with pungent bits of an unnamed fish. Another packet contained desiccated fruit—pear, maybe—that was almost tasteless. She ate everything and drank a full bottle of water.

Someone had rebuilt the makeshift privy, and already, there was a line for the "toilet." The sound of urination into the plastic bucket triggered the urge to go for Charlie as well, but she could hold it until the rush passed. She was amazed that people who had not had much to drink in the last eighteen hours could find so much fluid to dispose of

Migliozzi, the baker from New Jersey, belched and returned to the topic of conversation he had been drumming all day. "So who was it, ya think, who killed the guards?"

The loose confederation of leaders had hung together throughout the night, hashing and rehashing everything from how to escape to what the terrorists wanted with them. Would they demand ransom? Would the prisoners be executed on the internet, like those poor folks caught by the Taliban or ISIS? Would the ape-man who'd taken Lu Kim come back to claim more victims?

"Like Charlie said," Betty responded to the baker's question, "it was probably her husband, who was a Marine—*is* a Marine, because once you're a Marine, you're always a Marine. So is Ted, though I don't see him taking out two armed men... not anymore, at least."

"What is he *thinking*?" Melissa said. The pretty, slender blond from California was standing close by, in line for the potty.

Charlie and Abel had tried getting to know the California couple early in the cruise, since they were all around the same age. She soon gave it up. Every time either of the vegans made a political or social observation, Charlie felt Abel's eyes roll so hard they clicked in their sockets. At one point, when Austin was carrying on about gun control with unsupportable assertions, dubious facts, and numerous clichés, she sensed her husband would spontaneously explode. His restraint was admirable, but Charlie was sure it wouldn't last, so she had steered them to other social contacts—the Leatherneck Legends, for instance.

"I mean, for real?" Melissa continued. "He's going to get us *killed*!"

"Pretty sure we're slated to die anyway," Dave Draper said. Charlie had learned that not only was Dave the king of car sales in Southern California, but he was also a currently sitting congressman in the US House of Representatives. The pudgy man had a no-bullshit approach she really liked. "I mean, where's the ransom demand? If they wanted money, they would have already demanded something, right?"

"I believe I agree." This from the lean Ed Collins, who turned out to be a no-kidding Texas oil baron from Houston, though he wore running shoes, athletic shorts, and a T-shirt with a Just Do It logo rather than boots and a Stetson. He was CEO of a well-supply company that outfitted oceangoing rigs with everything from drill pipe to light bulbs. "These folk ain't acting like they're in it for the money."

Migliozzi threw in, "Maybe we're supposed to be exchanged for some political prisoners, huh?" That was another idea he'd introduced a couple of times already.

"Who understands their cause?" Montelle wondered in his soft voice.

"It's oppression, of course," Melissa said. "Their land was annexed against their will. You, of all people, should understand how greedy white Europeans have built the United States on the backs of oppressed people."

Montelle laughed softly. "Oh, honey, I own a villa in Italy and a nine-thousand-square-foot house in Beverly Hills. I ain't in no way oppressed."

"We should talk to them," Melissa insisted. She ignored her turn at the bucket to stay and speak her mind. "Let them know we understand their cause and that we sympathize with how they've been treated. If we can establish common ground—"

"Fuck common ground." Charlie had spoken with more force than she'd intended, but once committed, the heat rose in her voice and colored her language, and she let it loose. "And fuck them too. They kidnapped us, killed Tom, and raped Lu Kim. My husband, assuming he's not dead, is a goddamn US Marine and a veteran of Afghanistan and twice beat the shit out of Mexican drug cartels. Killed a fuckton of them. The three men with him are US Marines, too, and they fought for each other in a faraway jungle to stay alive and to keep your lily-white ass safe from communism—which, by the way, has killed and enslaved more than all the white European settlers of the American continent ever have." She sucked in a lungful of air as if pausing to reload. "I hope the four of them are out there right now. I hope Abel killed those guards and stole their guns. I hope that because I hope Abel and his fellow Marines take this camp and stomp the everlasting shit out of every goddamn, mother-*fucking* one of them."

The entire hut fell silent. Charlie hadn't realized that she had that much profanity in her. Getting all that out of her system felt like lancing a boil. She regretted none of it.

Melissa's face, pinched and pale, looked as though she'd bitten a bug in two and swallowed half of it. The woman's husband appeared at her elbow, as slender and almost as pretty as she. He looked as though he wanted to say something but didn't know quite what.

Montelle laughed aloud, a bright, brittle sound. "Right on, sister!" he crowed. "Preach it!"

MOLOKAI FOREST RESERVE
Sunday, 9 May
1402 Local

By 2:00 p.m., all the strike teams had returned to base camp... except for team three with Makani and the *Delphinius* gang. The head count came to six Niho Niuhi, seventeen hostages, and thirty-four "advisers"—including the six-man squad chasing the asshole in the jungle, and the three men dispatched to the overlook to intercept anyone trying to enter or exit the remote areas of the forest via the main trail. That made twenty-five in total, including Manu Ho, the leader of the advisers.

Kimo erupted with several choice curses in Hawaiian. Makani and his men could be lost, captured, or dead. For security purposes, only Kimo and Ho knew the position and name of the extraction ship, *Kekepi*. If Makani was captured, he might give up the location of their Molokai camp under torture, which would make having hostages as human shields a prudent form of insurance.

There was a limit on how long they could wait for Makani and the others. Throwing off the timing was not crucial for a successful conclusion, but logistics being what they were, it would not be good if they missed their exit timing by a wide margin.

Before extraction, they had to destroy all nonportable equipment, burn their papers, scrag the computers, and video the execution of the hostages. At that point, they would march to the rocky eastern shore of the island for the rubber boat ride to the waiting *Kekepi*.

Kanoa and the creepy little Mr. L—who was a spook of some kind, and no doubt about it—had remained aboard the stolen yacht, from which they would launch the last operation before separating from their advisers and going to ground—assuming Mr. L didn't double-cross them and throw the Niho Niuhi to the sharks after which they were named.

Kimo stomped to the command hut and slammed the door open. Kenny Po lifted himself up from his bunk in the back of the room, bleary-eyed and sloppy-haired. Hambone, in the bunk next to him, didn't stir a muscle, but then, a rocket attack up his butt would fail to wake Hambone. The nerd, Alapai, sat in front of a laptop, a mouse under one palm.

"Hey, College Boy!" Kimo snapped his fingers as though suddenly recalling something. "I forgot to save you some poon, bruddah. Oh, well, never mind. I pretty much bored it out, so I doubt your little dick would touch the sides. Maybe next time."

Alapai kept his gaze fixed on the screen, though he seemed more aware of Kimo than he was letting on.

"Gimme the sat-phone thing," Kimo demanded. "The fancy spy one."

With a tilt of his head, the skinny kid indicated the device lying at the end of the table. Kimo snatched it up and stabbed the buttons to establish a secure communication link with Kanoa. When the leader of the Niho Niuhi answered, Kimo wasted no time relaying the bad news.

"Some dumb fuck hit us this morning, killed two guys. Not our guys. The other guys."

"What? Who?" Kanoa's voice came through strong, although clicks and pops marred the transmission.

"I don't know who," Kimo admitted. "I sent a patrol out after him, but they haven't come back yet."

Kanoa cursed then went quiet for a long moment. "Okay, it doesn't matter. Does it? Maybe we should advance the timetable. Hold on. No, I'll call you back. I need to discuss this with Mr. L. Stand by the phone."

Without warning, the line went dead. Kimo squeezed the plastic case until it crackled with stress. *Discuss this with Mr. L. Fuck.* Who was in charge of this operation, exactly?

The civilian guy running free was a nuisance. A fly. A mosquito. This end of the island was practically deserted, with only a few homes and a couple of tiny towns. If he reached somebody's house and called the cops, they would respond with a patrol car. Next might come a detective, who would have to investigate. Maybe by late, late afternoon, they would send a four-wheeler up the trail or dispatch a helicopter to take a look. The first would be handled by the men at the overlook. As for the second, good luck trying to spot the camp from the air. Either way, it would take Five-O a minimum of twelve hours to mount an effective operation—probably longer. But what if...?

Kimo dropped the phone and paced the room. He ignored the glances from the domino players and pretended not to notice the tense silence. If the Molokai police called the US military, they might send in a combat team. Would they take the word of a lone hunter, or tourist, that a bunch of insurgents were hiding in the middle of the Molokai Forest? And if they did, how long would it take them to plan and execute a mission? Probably hours longer than Kimo expected to be around, given that the military liked to plan, then plan, then plan some more before committing troops. His short time in the corps had taught him that.

Kimo grunted under his breath. Realizing he was slapping one fist into an open palm over and over, he stuffed his hands in his pockets. "Haole motherfucker," he muttered. Not for the first time, he wished he had a do-over for the missed shots when he had the guy under his gun. There were reasons, of course. *Too sleepy, too tired. Caught by surprise, dick waving in the breeze. Hard to shoot straight in those conditions.*

Before his bad-conduct discharge from the US Marine Corps, Kimo had qualified as sharpshooter. That he'd missed a shot when it counted chapped his ass. He wanted another shot. Just one. Better yet, he wanted a few minutes of hand-to-hand combat so he could snap the guy's neck and piss on his corpse.

He jumped when the sat phone jangled.

Kimo reached to answer it before the second ring had started.

CHAPTER SEVENTEEN

Molokai Forest Reserve
Sunday, 9 May
1530 Local Time

Eight hours of heavy jungle hiking without sighting an identifiable landmark led Osterchuk to conclude they were lost as shit. He planted his butt against a tree, braced both hands on his knees, leaned over, and retched up a little bile then spat the taste out of his mouth. Dizziness swished through him, and blackness tickled the edges of his vision. He shook his head to clear it.

Gomer took a knee not far away, sucking down great gulps of air and drizzling a rainfall of sweat. The smaller man looked as worn-out and red-faced as Osterchuk felt. They had paused near a clearing filled with head-high grass, the stalks sharp as razors. Osterchuk already knew they were sharp because he and Gomer had flayed their way through a similar field earlier in the day, and he still carried the red stripes on his hands and face as evidence. This time, they would go around, by damn.

Osterchuk swiveled his head to get his bearings. The shooters at the overlook were somewhere way, way, way back *there*, he decided, and the main trail into the forest was somewhere way, way, way over *that* way, to their right. Maybe. Probably.

Ever since avoiding pursuit—or to put it more accurately, running away from the terrorists in a blind panic—he and Gomer had maintained the goal of returning to the rendezvous point where Yeager had said to meet back up. At some point, they'd made a wrong turn at Albuquerque and ended up into big goddamn middle of jack all. You bet.

The gunmen had not followed them. Maybe they had orders to hold their positions and turn back anyone trying to reach civilization. Osterchuk forced a weak chuckle. More likely, they'd seen two Mutt and Jeff geezers hightailing it for the woods and laughed themselves into convulsions. Anyroad, he and Gomer were as alone as two guys in the middle of a jillion acres of forest could be—Hansel and Gretel without a bread trail to follow.

Aw, by damn. Why'd I have to think of food?

Tok-tok-tok. At the sound, Osterchuk's head snapped up. Gunfire. Close. He checked Gomer, nearly asking him if he'd heard that, but the deaf man stared into space, oblivious.

Tok-tok-tok-tok-tok-tok. The tempo of firing increased. There were at least two weapons, maybe more.

"Somebody's havin' themselves a little do-si-do, you betcha."

Pinpointing distance and direction was tough, the way sounds bounced around the jungle. If he had to guess, he'd say the shooters were less than a mile away and somewhere ahead and to the right, at or near the ridgeline—about their ten o'clock position.

Osterchuk waved to get Gomer's attention and motioned him closer. "At least two shooters," he said into the man's ear. He pointed with a bladed hand. "Over there. Automatic weapons. Sounds like AKs. Should we head that way, see what's up?"

Pyle frowned and shook his head like a dog worrying a stick.

"Any idea which way to go?"

Pyle shrugged.

"What, you stop talking as well as hearing?" Osterchuk asked.

"Too tired to talk."

"Roger that." Osterchuk listened as gunfire sporadically rattled through the jungle. "Okay, then. Here's my thinking. This is a goddamn island, right? We stay on any single bearing, we bound to hit water, hey?"

Gomer nodded.

Osterchuk undertook another survey of the surrounding mountains. There was the tall ridge to the right, which was probably—maybe—the ridge they'd paralleled when they'd been with Adventure Tours. To the left was nothing but goddamn jungle. Behind them was eight hours of uphill travel that he had no desire to retrace, ending with more gunmen lying in wait at the overlook.

"So I say we go due east. Path of least resistance. Take a bearing on the mountaintop over that way. See it?"

Another nod.

"Okay, then." Osterchuk grunted and pushed off the tree. "Let's go."

Pyle shot him a thumbs-up and led off, walking point as he'd done most of the day. He skirted the razor-grass field and picked an easterly bearing on the far side, sliding through hip-deep ferns and ducking under floppy-leafed trees. Osterchuk was content to follow along as Gomer blazed the trail. The man was good at finding the easiest path and avoiding dead-end pockets of heavy, impassable brush.

The firing had died off, leaving behind sounds of a pristine forest. Twice since their run from death, Osterchuk had spotted deer, prime specimens he would have been proud to bring down on a hunt. He'd also caught a flash of a brown pig scuttling away into the forest. Squawky birds and buzzing insects infested the place, providing a natural soundtrack of background music.

He was marveling at a brilliantly colored butterfly when Gomer threw up a fist and froze. Osterchuk had to tap dance to keep from plowing into the smaller man's back.

"What?" he hissed when he regained his balance.

Gomer pointed. A pair of boots, solid black, protruded from under the canopy of a low bush. Osterchuk touched Gomer on the shoulder and eased past him. Crouching low, he lifted the fronds.

Sprawled in a dead heap lay an Asian soldier dressed in black trousers, black uniform blouse, and black beret, exactly like the terrorists-slash-soldiers they had seen on the trail the day before. His automatic rifle lay near his hand. A lake of scarlet soaked the ground, watering the bush with the dead man's blood. The toe of one boot had dug into the ground, carving a trough in the soil as if he'd spasmed in death. His throat had been cut from ear to ear.

Osterchuk touched the back of his hand to the dead man's calf. "Still warm."

Gomer lifted his chin in acknowledgment and pointed to a bare patch of red soil between the low bushes. Osterchuk duckwalked around the corpse to get a closer look. Footprints were impressed in the soil. They pointed almost due north, the same direction as the gunfire, and were small and rounded, with a zigzag pattern of the kind that he associated with cheap tennis shoes. Keds, maybe, or PF Flyers—though come to think on it, neither of those brands was cheap anymore. The only guy he knew who wore shoes like that was...

Osterchuk squinted at Gomer, who was haloed by the sun. "Winston. Does that look like Winston's footprint?"

"Yup," Gomer said in his overloud voice. "I'd say that's Winston."

Osterchuk groaned and rubbed the gritty overnight growth of beard on his cheeks.

He retrieved the AK-74, which, on closer inspection, he decided was some knockoff variant like the North Korean Type 88-1. Except for the sand sticking to it from having been dropped, the rifle showed the signs of meticulous care. The bolt slipped back in glassy-smooth perfection, and every moving part visible to the naked eye carried a faint glimmer of oil. Oiling a weapon required Goldilocks precision—not too much, not too little. Whoever the dead guy had been, he knew how to care for his weapon.

Osterchuk liked a well-tended weapon. He dropped the magazine and cleared the breech then checked the bore for obstructions and found none. He reloaded and chambered a fresh round. Meanwhile, Gomer stripped the corpse of its spare ammo harness, which he handed to Osterchuk. He had also found a pistol in a hip holster when he rolled the man over. At first glance, it looked like a Czech CZ 75, but a closer inspection revealed it to be a North Korean copy called the Baek-Du San.

Osterchuk handed the sidearm back to Gomer after the man had buckled the holster and ammo pouches around his waist. Gomer checked the chamber, thumbed the decocker, and holstered the pistol. The expression on his face mirrored Osterchuk's own feelings.

"We going after Winston?" Osterchuk asked.

Gomer nodded once, a quick jerk of his head.

"Well, let's go, then."

MOLOKAI FOREST RESERVE
>**Sunday, 9 May**
>**1540 Local**

And then there were three.

Yeager studied the man he'd just shot at a distance of over one hundred yards. The body remained motionless. Considering he'd used iron sights on a rifle he didn't know—shooting on a downhill slope while panting like a marathoner carrying a bus—Yeager allowed as how that was a hell of a shot.

He hunkered behind a natural breastwork of stubby palms and jutting stones halfway up a damn steep hill. Aside from his hiding spot, the hill sported almost no cover. Sometime around noon, while

Yeager had led the pursuit farther north, the terrain changed from deep tropics to tall hills covered in a carpet of knee-high brush and dotted with the rare outcropping of trees.

And the hills were a stone bitch to climb. Yeager had given up seconds ahead of what felt like his heart exploding, and he'd tumbled into the one spot of cover he could find. And it was a close thing, too, because the point man had appeared at the bottom of the hill and peppered the surrounding palms with controlled bursts of automatic-rifle fire. The guy had charged up the hill without waiting for his buddies to provide covering fire. He must have either been tired of the chase and trying to end it or gotten too excited.

"Now look at you, son," Yeager told the distant body with sadness, though not regret. "There ain't no do-over for stupid out here."

Where were the other three? That was the question. Of the six, Yeager had dropped one at the ravine, and another had fallen to his second ambush—which had nearly been his last, as the others had flanked him and damn near pinned him with covering fire before he vacated the kill zone. And this one made number three. He was no math major, but he figured there were three left.

"Come on, boys," he muttered. "I'm tired of running. Now's the time."

Yeager settled into a prone position and struggled to get his breathing under control. The elevation challenged his Texas-acclimatized lungs, and a headache threatened to clamp down on his forehead from lack of oxygen. His heart pounded as well, sending miniature tremors through his hands. These transmitted to the rifle, affecting his aim. It was a wonder he'd hit the man coming up the hill.

The day had turned into everything a visitor to paradise could wish for. High sixties, low seventies. Cloudless, crisp blue sky. A mild breeze flitted with through the greenery and carried a scent of tropical flowers along with a faint tinge of salty sea.

A great day to die. Yeager banished the thought with a grunt. Aloud, he said, "A great day for *them* to die."

At the base of the hill, shadows moved just past the edge of the jungle growth. Ferns stirred in ways not moved by the wind. Company had finally arrived. Yeager sighted on the moving brush but held his fire. No reason to give away his position unless he had a decent shot. Plus, throwing bullets into an unseen target went against the grain. Winston Pettigrew was out there somewhere, and Yeager would never forgive himself if he shot the old man by mistake.

Poor guy. The man was seventy-something years old and having to endure sleeping rough, no food, limited water, and being chased by armed terrorists. That would be tough on anybody, but for an old man, it would be pure hell.

A black-clad commando stepped into view at the edge of the jungle. He stood motionless, looking up the hill. *Trying to draw fire to pinpoint my location?*

"You're either very stupid or very brave." Yeager settled his sight picture, adjusted down for the slope, and squeezed off a shot. Dirt exploded three feet in front of the man, and he dived back into cover. Yeager winced. He should have waited and let them come closer.

"Dumbass," Yeager berated himself. "Hurry carefully."

And now it was time to play Alamo. They had Yeager pinned. There was no escape uphill until nightfall. One guy could keep him ducking with covering fire while the other two flanked him and came at him from different directions.

Movement flickered, first left, then right. Too fast to react to. The commandos blurred from the forest and dived into the tall foliage coating the hillside. Yeager had no shot, and the enemy had disappeared. Instead of alternating between fire and movement, it appeared that they planned to advance under cover of the tall grass.

Where is the third guy?

Yeager risked a pair of single shots into the moving brush where he *thought* the left-hand flanker was located, firing out of frustration, hoping for a lucky hit. It would be nice if he could draw some return fire from the third man and spot his position. Nothing happened other than him chopping down some leafy greenery. Fronds stirred in the breeze, making it difficult to follow the movement of the commandos, who remained belly down and under cover. They advanced sporadically, keeping their movements random, leaving no straight line for Yeager to track.

He squirmed into a new position, sliding around a shaggy palm-like tree and using its bulk to protect his right flank. The ground cooled his stomach. Yeager braced his legs against the earth, solidifying his shooting stance, molding himself into the ground. Misalignment would lead to discomfort, which would lead to awkwardness, which would translate to missed shots.

With no bipod, Yeager supported the rifle's foregrip with his left hand, his elbow in the dirt, anchored bone to ground the way a Marine sniper had once showed him. When he achieved that state of zen with the earth, as the sniper had described it, he breathed in... and out... slowing his heart rate, controlling his twitches, and shutting down his doubts and fears and worries.

Then he waited. Sooner or later, the enemy soldiers would have to pop up. Sooner or later, he would get a shot. Sooner or later, someone would die.

CHAPTER EIGHTEEN

Honolulu, Oahu
Sunday, 9 May
1540 Local Time

Victor stopped his rental car at the entrance to the crowded parking lot of Heeia-Kea Harbor, where it looked as though a mass exodus of Oahu was underway. Apparently, those people who could tow trailers had brought their boats to the harbor. A line of six deep waited for a turn to launch off the small boat ramp, and empty trailers attached to vehicles occupied every extra-long slot or were jimmied in wherever they had room, regardless of the marked spaces. Along both docks, cars without trailers filled most of the available spots, and people hustled aboard their craft, dragging coolers and suitcases and grocery tote bags. Watercraft from a forty-foot sport fisher to a green-hulled johnboat motored toward the harbor mouth.

Victor blinked at the two guys puttering along in the johnboat. *You dudes gonna drown.*

A pair of Super Stallions thundered overhead, crossing Kaneohe Bay from the Marine Corps Base Hawaii at wave-top level. Victor spared a quick thought for Butch Cassidy, less than two miles away on the other side of the bay, probably mainlining coffee and machine-gunning his keyboard in an effort to keep his people up-to-date on current intelligence. *Here's some intelligence, Butch: everybody on the island is bugging out.* Victor parked his car beside the road, got out, and thumbed the remote to lock it.

Heeia-Kea Small Boat Harbor featured two concrete docks that stuck out into the shallows of Kaneohe Bay like thin fingers. The Kaneohe Sandbar protected the harbor from the heavy rollers of the Pacific Ocean, making it a great spot to berth and launch the smaller craft its name referred to. Victor hiked onto the left-most dock, to the side of which was moored the larger craft—primarily sport fishers with flying bridges riding high over the waterline and festooned with poles and long whip-like appendages that Victor suspected had something to do with catching fish. Despite being a Marine, the most Victor knew about the ocean was that it was wet.

"Aloha, jarhead," called a broad-shouldered woman from a lounge chair on the rear deck of a low-riding sailboat. She held a steaming mug in one hand, which she raised in salute. "Want some coffee?"

"Did you make it, squid?" Victor stood at the edge of the dock, hands on hips, and cocked his head at Monalisa Montgomery, former petty officer, USN. He stepped onto the deck of the boat, uneasy at the sway under his feet. "If so, I'll pass. I filled up on 10W-40 this morning."

"Wimp."

"Hag."

"C'mere, you." Monalisa stood to accept Victor's backslapping hug. A head taller than Victor, Monalisa was not a small woman, and her hugs tended to be of the crushing, full-contact variety. The feel of her body, along with the smell of the apple-scented shampoo she favored, activated Victor's guilty conscience. He stepped back so fast the woman nearly spilled her coffee.

"Hah!" Monalisa barked a laugh, eyes dancing. "You're seeing someone, aren't you?"

"Uh..." Victor looked everywhere but at Monalisa. "Beautiful day here, huh? This your boat?"

"No, I stole it." She squinted one eye. "I'm a pirate, arrr."

The boat ran a good thirty-plus-feet long with a low, enclosed cabin that extended from near the prow to past the midpoint of the deck, lined with portholes. Dead center stood a mast tall enough to make a monkey dizzy. Lines and turnbuckles rattled in the breeze, tinking the aluminum pole with a sound like wind chimes.

"Your dream, right?" Victor asked. "Sailing around the world?"

"Aye, aye, Lieutenant." With cropped brown hair bleached by salt and sun, her eyes flecked with green and gold, Monalisa Montgomery appeared born of the sea. In a tank top and shorts, she showed off her wrestler's build—wide in the shoulders and hips, stout, and muscular.

Both gym rats, she and Victor had met at NAS Whiting Field when he offered to help spot her on the bench. She was pressing one twenty over and over and over, regular as a piston. Monalisa spared him a sidelong look. After a pause, she said, "Fuck off, jarhead. I don't date Marines."

"What gave it away, *chica*?" he asked. "My low forehead or my obvious disregard for death?"

"Your T-shirt says"—pump, relax—"Marines Do It Hard."

Master-at-Arms US Navy Petty Officer Monalisa Montgomery and Second Lieutenant US Marine Corps Victor Ruiz had come together like a pair of jumper cables—shooting sparks and lighting up the ionosphere with high-voltage discharge. Despite her contention that she didn't date Marines, Monalisa back-heeled him into bed with a judo throw and didn't let him back up until he'd pulled a groin muscle and strained his abs so badly he walked bent over the rest of the day. They went at it hot and heavy for six weeks while Victor learned how not to crash helicopters, and they parted only when he graduated and went on his first tour of the mountain wonderland known as Afghanistan.

He had not seen her since.

She asked him, "So what happened to 'I'll call you?'"

"I did call."

"Yeah, half an hour ago. Nothing for eight years, and *bing!* I get a call from Por Que Ruiz, famous dickman of the"—she made a cross-eyed face—"Ew Es Maw-reeen Corpse."

"That's stickman, not dickman."

"Whatevs." Monalisa rolled her eyes. "Never mind, dude. I'm just fucking with you. I didn't expect anything, didn't want anything, and it all turned out anyway." She waved a hand in a Vanna White impersonation. "I got my boat. I'm doing what I want."

"You make it around the world?"

With a hand on her hip, Monalisa struck a suggestive pose, her tongue poking into her cheek. "I go round the world alla time, sailor." She laughed. "No, seriously. I stopped here for an overnight two years ago. Haven't left yet. I'm in no hurry. The world will be there when I decide to kick it loose and move on... or so I hope. So what's up? On the phone, you sounded like this was more serious that a booty call."

"I need to go to Molokai."

"*¿Por que?*"

"Find a missing ship."

"I repeat: *por que*? Why?"

Victor sighed. Hands on hips, he studied the sky, following the flight of a gull dipping and curving on the breeze. The putter of small engines filled the air, along with a dead-fish-and-diesel-oil smell. After a time, he looked at her. "I don' know, chica. I got a bad feeling, is all. Can you take me there?"

"To Molokai? Sure. How fast?"

"Faster is better than slower." Victor eyed the mast. "How fast will this thing go, anyway?"

"Not fast enough for what you want. Minimum six hours to Molokai if the winds are in our favor the whole way."

"Six hours?" Victor shook his head in disgust. "*Madre de Dios.*"

"But..." Monalisa's freckled nose wrinkled in a grin. "Lucky for you, I have boyfriends with big toys."

MOLOKAI FOREST RESERVE
Sunday, 9 May
1548 Local

Yeager braced for impact when an AK opened up from the bottom of the hill. His first thought was that the third man had made an appearance. He had to reconsider when no rounds impacted his position. Instead, greenery erupted near the place where he suspected the left flanker was hiding.

The man leaped from cover, popping out of the low grass like a jack-in-the-box, twisting with a hand held against his back. He ripped off a burst downhill, firing one-handed and spraying lead into the trees—wild, un-aimed fire. Dust flew from the man's flak jacket, and red sprayed from his throat as more rounds from the shooter down below impacted him.

Pettigrew. Who else could it be?

Yeager put the top of the front sight at knee level and added his own counterpoint to the deadly barrage hammering the enemy soldier. Pummeled from above and below, the soldier pirouetted in an almost delicate fashion, blood spraying in an arc from a huge hole in his neck.

The right-hand flanker jumped up as well. He stitched a burst into the tree near Yeager's cheek, turned, and ran at an oblique across the face of the hill—away from both Yeager and Pettigrew. Yeager chased him with a pair of snap shots, but the distance, angle, and speed of the running man worked against him. Pettigrew—assuming that was who it was—sent a few rounds in that direction. Holding

hard against the tree, Yeager braced his rifle, led the target, and...
crack!

The soldier dropped like a bag of rocks.

Winston Pettigrew stepped out into the open and waved his weapon overhead in an exaggerated all-clear signal. Yeager stalked, stiff legged, down the hill. He paused by the left flanker, who was clearly dead, and stripped the man's body of extra ammo. He helped himself to the backpack as well. A quick examination revealed it contained some water and energy bars. Yeager's stomach grumbled at the sight.

Pettigrew had hiked toward the right side. He stood near the spot where the second man had gone down and scratched his head, wearing a puzzled expression, as if he'd misplaced his reading glasses. When Yeager trekked across the hill, Pettigrew looked up. "It was here, right?"

"Near enough."

Hunters often misjudged the spot where game had dropped. Birds fell into brush when shot and sometimes disappeared as if they'd fallen into the earth. Deer would go down from the first strike, then recover and run away before the hunter reached them, leaving a blood trail and nothing else. Wounded men were the same, though when one was well armed, trailing him into the brush was a stupid as poking along after a wounded tiger.

"Watch your ass," Yeager growled. "He could be sighting in on you right now."

Pettigrew grunted and dropped to one knee. Yeager joined him. The brush came to chest level, offering concealment if not cover. Nothing moved across the open hills except from the sway of a light breeze.

Sweat dripped off Yeager's nose. "Glad you came along when you did."

Pettigrew offered him a sly look. "I got one from behind. Ssskit!" He made a throat-cutting motion with a thumb.

"Humph."

"They weren't real good at watching they ass."

Motion at the tree line had Yeager snapping the rifle to his cheek.

"Wait, wait, wait." Pettigrew laid a hand on Yeager's shoulder. "I think that's..."

Danny Osterchuk and Ted Pyle stepped into the clearing. Both wore huge shit-eating grins and carried scavenged weapons.

"Hey, hey," Pettigrew said. "The gang's all here."

Jesus Christ, Yeager thought. *Geriatric guerillas in Hawaiian shirts.*

MOLOKAI FOREST RESERVE
Sunday, 9 May
1630 Local

"Some friend." Victor braced one hand on a stainless-steel rail next to the dashboard of a forty-foot yacht. Monalisa stood behind the wheel and flashed a grin at him. She had the beast throttled down to navigate the heavy boat traffic zipping around the peninsula of Marine Corps Base Hawaii. Using a joystick near her right hip, Victor's former girlfriend dinked and dodged the wedge-shaped sport cruiser—a boat she'd called a Cobalt A40—through a gaggle of fishers and sailboats. The inevitable comparison of a shark among a school of fat groupers came to his mind.

"Thad's a good guy," she told him. "A little spoiled maybe."

Victor cocked an eyebrow.

"Okay, a lot spoiled," Monalisa admitted. "But he lets me borrow the *Guppy* whenever I want. Yeah, I know. Don't give me that look.

Stupid name for a boat, right? But you gotta admit, she's a fricking racehorse."

"Roger that."

With gleaming fixtures, elegant electronics, soft seating, and an enclosed cockpit, the *Guppy* was a forty-foot-long wet dream. All it lacked was Dr. Alex in a string bikini, lounging on the forward deck.

A six-foot-long duffel bag lay across the plush leather seats just aft of the bridge. It contained a big chunk of Monalisa's personal arsenal—a 9mm Beretta, a souped-up Wilson .45, a Mossberg 12-gauge, and a wicked-looking Ruger M14 in .308 caliber—all nestled inside foam-filled cases. Another case held ammo for each.

As Victor had watched her pack the duffel bag prior to leaving her sailboat, he made a comment about being prepared for Armageddon.

Monalisa had grinned and told him, "Some girls like face powder." She'd shrugged. "I like gunpowder."

At the helm of the *Guppy*, Monalisa glanced at him. "Once we pass Moku Manu, we can hit the afterburners on this thing and really fly."

"What's Moku Manu?"

"See that big rock sticking up out of the water over there?" Monalisa pointed off the port bow at a wedge of weathered rock jutting from the Pacific, about the size of a block of condos, with a smaller cousin next to it. "Moku Manu is Hawaiian for Wreck Boat Here. My butt tightens up every time I run the gap with in the *White Wing Dove*. No worries with the *Guppy*. This thing will slip through a bedroom door without scratching the paint."

Off to port, flight operations continued at Marine Corps Base Hawaii. Victor worked his way around the pitching deck to get a close-up view as a pair of Hornets roared down the strip in tandem, their needle noses pointed almost directly at him. When their wheels were inches off the deck, the jets sat on their asses and burned aloft, howling into the sky. Victor watched them until they vanished in the distance. He felt like cheering.

"There's some dry food in the galley," Monalisa said. "Power's been off, so nothing in the fridge and no ice. There's warm beer and a gajillion kinds of booze in the bar, or you can make coffee."

"No, I'm good."

She fixed him with a look. "Or you can make coffee."

"*Dios,* chica. You're a caffeine junkie, *entiende*?"

"No way. I can quit anytime I want."

Victor went below and found the modern-aesthetic galley filled with neat little fixtures and equipment, all ingeniously stowed in nooks to maximize space. He found a space-age coffeemaker in a cabinet, pulled it out, and puzzled out how to brew a cup of high-voltage dark roast. He carried it back up the swaying ladder and handed it off.

Not long after, they cleared the gap between the Mokapu Peninsula and Moku Manu, and she eased the throttles forward. The *Guppy* responded by nearly throwing Victor on his butt. The Cobalt A40 planed up atop the waves and did some howling of its own. The sleek yacht shed all respectability and gave every indication she intended to achieve escape velocity.

Monalisa whooped and pumped her fist. She stood with easy grace, muscular legs flexing in time with the boat's movement. The wind through the cockpit window whipped her hair across her face and plastered her T-shirt across her breasts—which, he noted, had come to pointed attention.

Oh man. I'm on a million-dollar yacht. My ex-girlfriend's nipples are standing out. Alex would rip my balls off if she saw me here and now.

He chanted a Hail Mary under his breath, praying for forgiveness and mercy from a woman who knew how to use a scalpel. *It's for a good cause.*

"C'mon, buddy!" Monalisa's teeth flashed in a wide grin. "Let's go find your friend!"

CHAPTER NINETEEN

Molokai Forest Reserve
Sunday, 9 May
1610 Local Time

Yeager gathered the older Marines into a circle at the edge of the forest. He passed out all the trail bars and shared the bottled water from the soldier's backpack. The blood smeared on the bottles didn't seem to bother anyone. Yeager inspected his firearm while he chewed, confirming that the action wasn't fouled—he had a full mag seated, a round chambered, and the safety on.

He took stock of the other men. Osterchuk seemed worst off. Overweight, red-faced, and sweating buckets, the big Minnesotan sat with his head down, hands hanging loosely over his knees. Gomer Pyle wasn't in much better shape—he leaned back against a tree with his eyes closed, breathing with his mouth open as if he couldn't get enough oxygen.

Pettigrew knelt, using his captured AK as a prop. He had found a strangely marked pack of foreign cigarettes on one of the bodies. He tapped out a butt, lit it up, and winced at the first drag. "Harsh."

They all carried scavenged rifles. Pyle and Osterchuk had pistols tucked in their waistbands, whereas Pettigrew had a double-edged dagger in a belt sheathe. Everyone had extra ammo in shoulder harnesses, and the two smaller men wore flak vests taken from the enemy dead. None of the vests they'd found so far would fit Yeager or Osterchuk.

"Well," Yeager said. "Ain't we a bunch of badasses."

"What now?" Osterchuk asked without looking up. "We going back or what?"

Yeager sucked his teeth and spat out a bit of trail bar. "I aim to do just that. You boys..." He sighed. "I don't think that's wise."

Gomer, who had opened his eyes when Yeager spoke, said in his overloud voice, "My wife is still up there. I'm going."

"Yeah," Pettigrew added, "we da four musketeers, baby. One for y'all, y'all for one."

"Look here," Yeager said. "I reckon it's an hour hike back to the ridge. We gotta figure they'll have that back door locked down, so any assault up the chute will be opposed."

"Talk about Heartbreak Ridge," Osterchuk said.

"Exactly." Yeager nodded. "So I have to scout another way up, which will take... well, I don't know how long that'll take. You boys—no offense, but y'all look about done in."

"Au contrary," Pettigrew said. "I'm ready to go." He tapped the butt of his knife with a thumbnail and grinned with yellowed teeth. "Me and Little Bessie will slip up dat chute and slit us some throats. In the dark, they won't never see me coming."

"I..." Yeager drew a breath, searching for the right words.

"You know what I hate the most?" Pettigrew directed the question toward Osterchuk and Pyle, both of whom looked up in expectation. "The pity. People today, they ashamed—some of them are—of the way they treated us when we came back from overseas. They look at us now, and they shake they heads, thinking about how they acted like babies and smoked dope and ran off to Canada. They ashamed of being class-A pussies. Liberal white guilt." Pettigrew ground the last of his unfiltered cigarette into dust under his heel. "Or they say... they say, 'Aw, them poor dumb fucks. They didn't know what they was getting into. Gub'mint sent 'em off to war and'—how's that song go?—'sent them off to kill the yellow man.' Like we was fighting some race war even back then. They make documentaries and write books, make us look stupid that we went to Vi-et-fucking-Nam. Shee-it."

"Amen, brother," Osterchuk said.

Pyle, who had probably heard one word in three, nodded.

Yeager's face scrunched up. "How's that help this situation—"

Pettigrew held up a pink palm. "Excuse me a sec here, Staff Sergeant, and listen up. Hear me true. The three of us here are not *victims* of the military-industrial complex, sent to war so General Motors could sell more tanks. We are not baby killers. We fought with honor and dignity and a goddamn *ferocity* not seen since the Spartans held the Hot Gates against that fascist bastard Xerxes. We are not each and every one fucked up by post-traumatic *bull*shit. We serve our country every day, every week, every god*damn* minute. We are ready to step the fuck *up* and lay down our *lives* for our people. Our fellow Americans. We do the hard thing so overpaid asswipes can kneel during the national anthem and whine about how tough they gots it. We are not *ex*-Marines, as they ain't no expiration date on Marines, Staff Sergeant Yeager. No, we goin' up that hill, and we gonna kill enemy *combatants* until they ain't no more left to kill. You hear me *clear*, Staff Sergeant Yeager? You best not expend one ounce of pity in my direction, cause I had it up to fucking *here* with pity." Pettigrew accompanied the last statement with a hand at eye level.

Yeager surveyed the determination in the faces confronting him. One corner of his mouth lifted in a grin. "Well, okay, then. Best strap your shit down tight, Marines. We have a long walk in the jungle, followed by a gunfight against heavily armed opponents."

"Been there, done that!" Pettigrew crowed. "Let's go get some more."

MOLOKAI FOREST RESERVE

Sunday, 9 May
1730 Local

Charlie sat on the floor and studied the nail in her palm. *Pathetic. A weapon of minimal destruction.*

Her—ahem—*weapon* was two inches long, max. She pushed it between her ring and middle finger, making a fist so the nail stuck out like a unicorn horn. Maybe she could punch somebody in the eye or throat. Would it be enough to incapacitate a giant like the one who'd taken Lu Kim? That guy would laugh off anything except a nuclear strike to the forehead.

Better than nothing, though, right?

It had been quiet in the camp for several hours. Parties of soldiers had arrived and disappeared into barracks. Some moved the bodies out of camp and came back an hour later without them. A burial party, evidently. Aside from a doubling of the guards, nothing much had changed since Abel—and she knew in her gut it was Abel—had raided the camp.

The prisoners had maintained watch through the high windows, one at a time volunteering to balance on a cot and keep tabs on their captors. Everyone took a turn except, of course, Austin and Melissa and their small group of followers, who nattered on and on about reasoning with the terrorists, finding common ground, and using persuasive words to avoid rape, torture, and certain death. When it came to that triumvirate, Charlie preferred a more direct response: shoot the bad guys until they didn't breathe anymore, then shoot them some more. It was a mystery to her why some people thought terrorists were reasonable but misguided people who only needed enlightenment to be productive members of society. As far as she was concerned, terrorists could provide the most benefit to the world by becoming fertilizer.

Charlie rubbed the pads of her fingers, which ached from hours of patient effort to recover the nail she now held. Across from her sat Dave Draper, his wife using his thigh as a pillow as she slept. Betty Pyle curled up on the cot next to Charlie, sweat plastering her blouse, outlining her thin ribs. Whether or not she was asleep, Charlie couldn't tell.

The other so-called leaders of Camp Molokai—as Betty had nicknamed their place of incarceration—had drifted off to their own cots, their own thoughts. Montelle stood watch, his calves flexing to remain upright on the rickety cot. It creaked with his movements. Ed Collins had fallen asleep, his eyes buried in the crook of an elbow. Migliozzi, the baker from New Jersey, picked through the remains of his boxed meal, digging out single grains of rice and popping them into his mouth. He looked up and gave her a wink when her gaze fell on him.

Trapezoidal blocks of light from the late-afternoon sun tracked up the eastern wall of their barracks. Nightfall was only a few hours away. What would happen at nightfall—business as usual at Camp Molokai, or Kong returning for another toy to help him pass the night? Who was next on his playlist? Sarah Rae Draper? Melissa? Or Charlotte Buchanan Yeager?

Or would Abel storm the camp single-handedly and get himself killed trying to save her? Lord knew he was hardheaded enough to try such a stunt. Charlie's gut clenched, and her body chilled at the thought of her husband tangling with Kong one-on-one. Abel was a warrior, surely—a killer even, given the right circumstances. She had no doubt he was tough, resilient, and a badass to the core. All that was a given.

But... the man who had slapped her and taken Lu Kim was a different order of magnitude—a bigger monster than Charlie had ever imagined. Skeeter Davis, the man she'd killed with a box cutter and her bare hands, was a pussy compared to the Samoan. It gave her chills to think of Yeager taking him on without a platoon of Marines at his back.

"Something's happening," Montelle hissed. He leaned forward on tiptoes, fingertips gripping the open window frame.

"What?" Charlie demanded when Montelle refrained from saying more.

"Uhh, a soldier just came running in from the north. He was bleeding all down the side of his face. He went to the soldier's dorm and went inside."

A minute passed, then another. Charlie was on the point of relaxing again when Montelle reported, "No, wait—now he's coming out with an older guy. Uhhh... they're going to the boss's hut."

"The guy came from the north?" Charlie looked at Betty Pyle, who had sat up and pushed damp gray hair back off her forehead.

"Was it the one of the soldiers who chased after our guys?" Betty asked. Like Charlie, she was convinced the morning raiders had been Abel and the Leatherneck Legends.

"I can't tell," Montelle said. "But he came from that direction."

"Six went out." Betty shared a significant glance with Charlie. "One came back."

Charlie smiled for the first time in ages. "That's our boys."

MOLOKAI FOREST RESERVE
Sunday, May 9
1737 Local

Kimo Ekewaka had both hands wrapped around a ham sandwich when the command hut door banged open. Manu Ho, the senior commander of the Special Forces troops stormed in, followed by a bleeding commando in black BDUs and a muddy flak jacket.

If Kimo's guess was right, the man called Ho was either a captain or a senior lieutenant in the Special Forces of the DPRK army, and his men where part of an elite unit acting undercover. Mr. L was undoubtedly their spook controller, and part of the North Korean State Security Department. How Kanoa had managed to connect with Mr. L was a mystery, but Kimo grudgingly admitted to himself that without their advisers, they would have never pulled off the depth, breadth, and devastating results they had achieved in the past few days.

Ho stomped to a halt in front of Kimo. "The men? Who are they?"

Kimo ground the bite of ham sandwich in his mouth, leaving the Korean to fume and glare at him. He swallowed and chased the bite with a slug of coffee from a tin cup. "What men?" he finally said.

"The soldiers who attack camp!"

Kimo frowned. "I only saw one man. Civilian, not military. Your guys should have wrapped him up by now." His eyes flicked to the injured commando. "If they were any good, that is."

Ho's English became even more fractured as his temper heated. Kimo made out about one word in three as the troop commander blew up and ranted, but he managed to piece together an account of his patrol being chopped to shreds by at least two attackers and maybe more. They came under repeated ambushes from the one they chased, losing three men to direct assault. Another soldier had been taken from behind, killed with a knife. The wounded man had broken off contact when he and another came under fire from the rear as they assaulted a hill.

"These men soldiers! Soldiers!" Spit flew from Ho's lips.

Kimo leaned back in the rickety folding chair. It creaked under his weight. "Could be," he said. "Could be some off-duty military from Pearl or MCBH. Maybe they were out hiking or camping and found us sitting out here in the boondocks. Molokai don't have many people, but that doesn't mean it's deserted either. Hunters and hikers are all over the place." He checked the time on his watch. "Look, Ho. It's nearly eighteen hundred. We were going to pull out under the cover of darkness, which is about... uh, three hours, give or take. We'll move up the timetable a little. My guys will start packing up camp, burning what needs to be burned, then we'll start doing the hostages. On video, like we planned, right?"

Ho nodded once sharply.

"You sprinkle your guys around the perimeter, right? You know..." Kimo twiddled his fingers like a man playing a keyboard. "Around the camp? That way, if these heroes come back, they'll get their dicks caught by thirty guns. You know, brah? Like an ambush."

Ho nodded again. He muttered a grudging, "Yes. Yes, good."

Kimo took up his sandwich and bit into it to hide his smile. *Elite unit* might have been too strong a description. *Dumbass Koreans.* If the commander of the advisers needed Kimo, a guy who'd been kicked out of the Marines, to teach him basic tactics, then Kim Jong-un's boys were harder up for military talent than he'd imagined.

Ho cuffed his wounded soldier and rattled off a string of orders. The captain was pissed, no doubt. Kimo got that. The man had lost seven troops in one day, which was probably a hanging offense back in the People's Republic of Love and Forgiveness. He was probably scared his whole family would disappear one night over this fuckup.

Still, he had twenty-nine other men to go up against... what, two or three off-duty military types? The firefight, if the heroes came back, would be one-sided and short.

Kimo shifted in his seat. He dismissed Ho from his mind, instead thinking about what he could do with the three hours he had left before they wasted all the haoles and headed for the boat. Three hours meant he had time for only one bitch to play with, so he had to decide.

Blond or redhead? Maybe he'd flip a coin...

CHAPTER TWENTY

A board the *Kekepi*
Sunday, 9 May
1740 Local Time

Kanoa leaned against the rail of the *Kekepi* and allowed the sun to drive the chill from his bones and the nausea from his stomach. Neither the coldness in his body nor the queasiness in his gut had anything to do with the gentle rolling of the *Kekepi's* deck. They had everything to do with the hours of news coverage he'd watched on the ship's big-screen television.

The sun dropped toward the sea. Sunset was due at 2020—in less than three hours. Not long after that, Kimo would begin executing hostages with a *hoe leiomano*, a handheld, paddle-like club lined with shark's teeth along both edges. Alapai would videotape the executions for posting on the internet.

The thought of the tourists dying gave Kanoa no heartache at all. However...

A lot of Hawaiians had died in the past few days—many more than he ever imagined in his wildest estimates. He had never doubted some of his own people would be sacrificed in the struggle to bring attention to their cause. *Collateral damage*, Mr. L called it. In the sterile environment of a planning session, the deaths could easily be justified. Rationalized.

Seeing limp bodies carried from rubble, hearing the interviews of stricken family members... that was not so easy to brush off.

So many. So very many.

"You have struck a great blow for freedom," a voice behind him said.

Kanoa jerked, startled. He spun to find Mr. L. Somehow, the man had approached him across a steel deck in hard-soled shoes without Kanoa hearing a thing.

"I have killed many of my countrymen today," Kanoa replied, then he added words that spilled from his heart without warning. "I wonder if it was worth it."

"That is the freedom fighter's conundrum, is it not?" Mr. L stepped up to the rail and clasped his hands over it as though praying to the sea. Small in stature, wearing a conservative black suit, the man always reminded Kanoa of a slimmer version of the North Korean leader, Kim Jong-un. He spoke like a college professor, pushing his round glasses up the bridge of his nose. "We must somehow burn the overseers without harming the workers he enslaves. Consider this: your people will never be free until the United States government revokes its claim on your territories. Without provocation, the establishment will not act. Without pecuniary damage, the capitalists will not cede ownership."

Kanoa hung his head. "I know this—"

"Then you know you had no choice but to strike at the heart of their greed—drive away the tourists, make the corporations beg for mercy, and make the cost of holding Hawaii to dear for them to accept. The Americans will fold. They always do. They have no stomach for sacrifice. Their progressives will demand reparations to the victims of the robber-baron ancestors in order to assuage their guilty consciences. Their people will weep on TV, and others will scream for fairness, as if such can be granted in a capitalist state."

"*My* people weep on TV at the moment," Kanoa said with a burst of fire behind his eyes. "And it tears my heart."

"Of course it does." Mr. L patted Kanoa on the shoulder. He had to reach high to do so. "But you must harden your heart."

The wind off the ocean carried to Kanoa's lips the taste of salt. His skin felt stiff, brittle. He swallowed with a dry throat and nodded without speaking. A sleek yacht zipped across the sea, throwing a sparkling bow wave. A short, muscular man observed them through binoculars as the smaller craft zipped past. Kanoa ducked his head.

"Listen to me." Mr. L had turned his back to the rail and spoke away from him. "Our last strike will be devastating to the American military. Your casualties will be justified."

Kanoa frowned. "When we blow the charges..."

"True," Mr. L conceded. "A horrible event. But necessary."

"I don't know..."

"But I do." Mr. L straightened and walked toward the nearest hatch. Kanoa noted that his footsteps were almost silent. Had he not been paying attention, he would never have heard them. The Asian man glanced back. "Now is not the time for cold feet, my friend. Come. We need to get a status report from our shore team. It will not be long before they return."

Kanoa hesitated only a second before following the tiny man in the dark suit.

MOLOKAI FOREST RESERVE
Sunday, 9 May
1756 Local

"Soldiers are pouring out of their barracks," Montelle reported from his place at the window. He teetered, and the cot creaked and wobbled under him. "They're spreading out into the woods."

Charlie jumped up and tapped the singer on the leg. "Let me see."

When she chinned up to the high window, Charlie saw the last of the contingent of Asian troops scattering into the forest. They were dressed for combat in full "battle-rattle," as Abel called it, and carrying military rifles—Abel got annoyed when she used the erroneous term *assault rifle*—and each hefted a small rucksack on his back. The impression she gained was that the soldiers were not coming back to their barracks.

The soldiers vanished into the foliage, and the camp went quiet.

It was a very oblique angle, but she could just make out the front door of the command hut. When it banged open, Charlie put her cheek against the boards and craned for a look. Her bladder twitched when Kong stepped out. The man had grown larger since she'd last seen him—at least, that was her gut reaction.

"I've ridden in smaller SUVs," she said under her breath.

When he stomped toward their barracks, Charlie scrambled off her perch and hissed a warning. The tension in the sweltering cabin hit like a wave of fresh sweat as people shifted and exchanged worried looks. Melissa and Austin held hands, Dave Draper and Ed Collins stood up to face the door, and Betty Pyle crossed to the adjacent cot and pulled a visibly trembling Sarah Rae Draper to her bosom.

The lock rattled, then their tormentor filled the doorway.

If all of us rush him at once, right now...

The thought died the moment it was born. Not only was it problematic that all the able-bodied people in the hut could make a dent in the block of granite in the doorway, but they also had a forest full of armed men to contend with. They would all be shot to ribbons before they made it a hundred yards.

The warm sweat on her body turned to ice as the giant stepped in and surveyed the group. His narrow, puffy eyes lingered on the women.

"What do you want?" Dave Draper marched forward. His short, pudgy body contrasted with the monster at the door like a mouse approaching a tiger. "You're not touching another—"

Smack!

Charlie jumped. The man's hand had moved faster than her eye could follow. The backstroke caught Draper alongside his head and sent him reeling into a cot occupied by the German tourist, Schweighofer. Both crashed to the floor as the German tried to catch the congressman.

Kong pointed. "You. Come with me."

"No!" Melissa shrieked.

An ugly sense of relief flowed through Charlie when that sausage-sized finger pointed at Melissa. A pang of shame at her own cowardice followed. She pushed the nail in her hand to poke out between her fingers. Maybe, if she could hit him in the eye...?

Austin stood as Kong approached. "Wait, wait, wait. We can talk about this." He held up a hand like a traffic cop, and the giant caught his wrist and twisted. The bones in Austin's arms shattered with a sound like gristle crackling. He screamed and went to one knee.

The monster kicked him aside and reached for Melissa, who squealed and shrank into a ball at the end of her cot. She jerked and kicked when he reached for her, looking like a small child afraid of a shot. Ed Collins and the baker, Migliozzi, ran over and jumped on Kong's back. Even skinny little Montelle raced in and swatted at the giant, slapping ineffective punches into any open space he could find.

Charlie stalked forward, her fist tight and slick with sweat. The nailhead dug into her palm. She sidestepped a rolling Migliozzi as he was pitched off the terrorist's back and flung across the floor. Cots banged and crashed together in the melee, further tangling the approach with obstacles. Charlie picked her way through the debris. She dodged a pair of captives who were escaping the area. Screams and shouts from the others faded into the background of her perception.

Kong shrugged off Ed Collins and swatted down him as easily as knocking over a toddler. The big man ignored Montelle, who rained feathery blows on the monster's back. Like King Kong after

Fay Wray, the Samoan zeroed in on Melissa and caught her by the ankle. He dragged her across the floor.

"Not me! Not me!" the blond woman screamed. Wet eyes rolled in her beet-red face. They landed on Charlie, who was sliding up from the giant's left rear. "Her! She's the one," Melissa wailed. "She has a weapon! Take her!"

Kong glanced around. Saw her raised fist.

Damn you, Melissa. Charlie rushed in and punched at the man's piggy left eye. Her fist smacked Kong's palm. It felt like hitting a side of beef. The protruding nail stabbed deep. The man took no notice. His meaty hand snapped closed on her bunched fist like a Venus fly-trap. Warm blood—his, she hoped—seeped around her knuckles.

Kong's lips curled up on one side. "I like you," he rumbled. "You've got spirit."

He squeezed. The bones in her hand cracked like small twigs. The pain registered as cold white heat firing through her fist, followed by a blast of agony that ripped a scream from her guts. Charlie's eyes blurred, and her legs gave out. When the giant released her, she fell at his feet, all the fight crushed out of her. Her hand burned with pain. She cradled it against her body.

Kong's voice came from a distant shore. "Now, you, little bitch—I don't like a tattletale. C'mon, honey. We're gonna go play."

Charlie was vaguely aware of Melissa howling as she was dragged past. The woman clawed at the floor, digging grooves in the soft wood with her fingertips. A wet, bloody bit of metal fell by Charlie's knee. Her nail. Tossed back to her in a show of contempt.

The door slammed shut, and the lock clattered home.

Charlie rocked her broken hand and blocked out the gabbling of the other hostages. Salty wet tears splattered the floor. Hers, as it turned out.

MOLOKAI FOREST RESERVE
Sunday, 9 May
1800 Local

Yeager returned from his reconnaissance, following the sound of the waterfall back to the pool where he had left the others. It was the same pond where he and Pettigrew had spent a very short night. He had left the older men to rest and rehydrate while he scouted a way up the ridge that didn't involve a suicidal assault on a defended position. The three men were resting in the shade of a massive tree. Osterchuk sat up as he approached, and Pettigrew toed Pyle awake.

"Okay, Marines. I found a way up." He settled on a rock next to the pool, dropping like a sandbag. He stuck his face in the water and drank his fill. He shook off the water and used the front of his shirt as a towel. "Let me draw y'all a picture."

With a stick as a pencil and a patch of wet sand as his drawing board, Yeager diagrammed the camp layout. He drew five rectangles like the spread fingers of a hand. "Here are the four barracks and a smaller hut. They all face a central clearing. From here"—Yeager poked a hole in the middle of the clearing, where the palm of the spread hand would be—"starting left and reading clockwise, barracks A is at the nine o'clock. B is at straight-up twelve. The hostages are in this one. A guard post is in between those two, next to a big tree. Next up, we have this little building—call it C—here at the one o'clock, but it's set back from the others. At the two o'clock position is barracks D, and E is at the three o'clock position. Clear so far?"

"Sounds like an IKEA project," Osterchuk said.

"Wait until we start inserting tabs into slots," Pettigrew said with a chuckle.

"On the south side of the camp is a creek." Yeager drew a wiggly line. If the buildings were a spread hand, the line would slash the wrist. Well above the fingertips, he drew a second line. "On the north side is the ridge. I suspect the creek is the source of the waterfall here—it must bend north at some point. Off to the east of the waterfall, away from the camp, there's a game trail that goes up to the top. We'll climb that and make our approach by following the stream from the top of the waterfall back toward the camp." Yeager looked at each man in turn, making eye contact. Weighing. Assessing. If there were any doubts, the older men hid them well. "Okay, then," he said. "Here is where it gets tricky."

CHAPTER TWENTY-ONE

The *Guppy*, Off the Coast of Molokai
Sunday, 9 May
1822 Local Time

Victor, scanning the ocean with binoculars, saw it first. He pointed. "There."

Monalisa nodded and canted the wheel to port, aiming for a small cruise ship riding the ocean swells about five hundred yards away. It looked like the picture of the *Fair Breezes* she had pulled up on her phone from the company website—emerald-green hull and white superstructure with green accents. She gripped the wheel with one hand and toggled the radio mic with the other.

"*Guppy* calling *Fair Breezes*. *Guppy* calling *Fair Breezes*. Coming up on your stern, *Breezes*. How copy?" She repeated the call as they approached. No one answered from the cruise ship.

"This don' feel good, *mi hermosa*." Victor trained binoculars on the ship. Even with them braced against the dashboard, the image juddered around with the *Guppy's* motion. "No one on deck. No passengers, no crew, no nobody."

Monalisa cut off the forward throttle at a hundred yards and let inertia carry them closer. She used the joystick-driven motors to jockey them in close to the well deck on the cruise ship. The well deck was a drawbridge-like ramp at water level that allowed the cruise ship to launch and recover kayaks and inflatables. It could be raised or lowered as needed, though at the moment, it was lowered. And unattended.

Monalisa brought the *Guppy* in close and turned it side-on to the bigger ship.

"We'll never fit in the boat well. Hold it here," Monalisa told Victor. "I'm going to throw out the fenders so I don't scratch Thad's paint."

"Aye, aye, Skipper."

Monalisa ran out of the cockpit, opened lockers on the yacht's starboard side, and draped thick bumper pads over the rail. When the fenders were out, she yelled to him to bring them in closer. Victor joggled the controls, and the yacht bumped into the *Breezes*'s stern. When the sides touched—well, slammed together—Monalisa picked up a coiled rope, one end of which was tied to a davit on the *Guppy*'s side rail. Nimble as a goat, she jumped the gap of blue water and tied off the line to a similar davit on the bigger ship.

Victor monkeyed with the joystick, trying to keep the *Guppy* from bashing into the cruise ship while keeping it close enough for Monalisa to jump back. It was harder than it looked.

His guts refused to settle, and not all of that was from seasickness. There was no response from the cruise ship to their radio calls. No response to the yacht pulling up to their back door. No activity on the decks.

"Hey, what was that famous ghost ship?" he said when Monalisa returned to the bridge. "The *Frying Dishpan*?"

"*Flying Dutchman*." She shoved him off the controls. "And yeah, the same thought crossed my mind. Can you jump it?"

"You kidding? They don't call me the Mexican Superman for nothing."

"Ow. I rolled my eyes so hard they broke. You want a gun?"

"Always. You should stay here. Be ready."

"Always," Monalisa said.

Victor claimed the .45 and tucked it in the back waistband of his jeans. He climbed onto the gunwale, eyed the gap, and jumped before he could think about it. He splashed into ankle-deep seawater on the rubberized surface of the ramp and clambered up the sloping incline, past the pivot point, and onto the deck proper, which was more like a wide back porch than a deck.

Overhead, a sundeck jutted out partway over the launching ramp, like an awning over the porch. Racks of kayaks hung from brackets on the port side, and bundles of paddles were tied to the railings. Empty brackets on the starboard side looked big enough to hold an inflatable boat.

Flotation rings and gaffing hooks hung from the back bulkhead, and a closed door was located closer to the starboard side than the port. A stairway—or *ladder*, as the squids called it—slanted from port to starboard and connected the well deck to the deck above.

A crew member's jacket with a *Fair Breezes* logo sewn on the breast pocket sloshed in the water surging across the well deck. A sleeve button was caught in the joint between the ramp and the deck. Seeing it there, lifeless and empty, gave Victor the major willies from his gonadal region all the way to his chest.

Chingade tu madre, he thought. *Fucking ghost ship.*

He hesitated, a hand on the lever that opened the door. *Loud and stupid—or sneaky and dangerous?* If he went in loud and stupid, and everybody was playing Yahtzee and drinking mai tais, no harm done. If there were nefarious characters involved—he liked the word *nefarious*—then going in loud and stupid would get him killed.

Sneaky it is. Victor checked Monalisa, who remained on the *Guppy*'s bridge, one hand shading her eyes as she followed his progress. Sweat trickled down his back. He pulled the gun from his waistband, thumbed off the safety, and held it low against his thigh. His left hand eased down the lever until he felt the latch give way. Victor raised the weapon and oozed through the smallest gap possible.

A narrow passageway led to a dining area with tables covered in white cloth and place settings arranged with precise care. Doors opened on either side, leading to what appeared to be cabins for paying passengers. The passageway was painted a soft ivory and splattered with crimson.

On the deck at his feet lay an older man in white T-shirt, khaki shorts, and white socks. He wore one sandal—the other appeared to be missing. So did a large chunk of the man's head.

MOLOKAI FOREST RESERVE
Sunday, 9 May
1900 Local

When someone banged on the door to his cabin, Kimo left the woman and stomped to answer it, not bothering to put anything on. He flung open the door to find Alapai and Manu Ho. Kimo grinned when College Boy's eyes flicked down to check out his swinging dick.

"Uhh..." Alapai's cheeks flushed, and he locked gazes with Kimo.

"What is it? I'm in the middle of something."

Manu Ho said, "News report say boat killed. Strike team three. Everyone dead."

"Makani?" Kimo asked.

Alapai shrugged. "We have to assume he's gone."

"Then there's no reason to wait, hey, brah?" Kimo said. "Start burning shit—"

"Already started," Alapai said.

As if conjured by his words, Kenny Po and Hambone exited the command hut with arms full of paper, which they piled into a fifty-five-gallon drum they had placed there previously for just that purpose. Flames flickered up from the barrel, and Kimo smelled the faint tang of smoke.

Manu Ho spoke up. "Half men go to beach. Security for boats."

"And the three at the overlook?"

"At beach."

Kimo scratched his bare ass. "That's it then, huh? Gimme a minute."

He closed the door and started dragging on his clothes. When dressed, he looked around. Patted his pockets like a man ensuring he had his wallet and keys. Kimo considered the skinny blond on the bed. Her blue eyes were watery and dull as though her soul had already departed. Nobody home.

"Sorry, babe. I can't stay." He shot her in the head, once. Then Kimo walked out to join his crew in clearing the camp.

THE *Guppy* **and** *Fair Breezes*, **Off the Coast of Molokai**
Sunday, 9 May
1900 Local

Victor hopped back aboard the Cobalt yacht. "Call the Coast Guard."

"What the actual *fuck*," Monalisa barked. "You've been gone forever. I had no idea—"

"They're all dead."

"Who? Who's all dead?"

"The passengers, the crew." Victor drooped his head like a sad hound dog. "Everybody."

"Oh no." Monalisa touched his arm. "Your friends?" she whispered.

Victor perked up, a rekindled spark. "No. For true, that's what took so long—checking the bodies. No Yeager, no Charlie. I found this, though." He held up a sheet of paper. The back was stamped with a bloody boot print.

"What's it say?"

"Today's activity: A hike into the Molokai Forest Reserve."

"So they might be...?"

Victor shrugged. "I have to hope so, chica. I need you to drop me off at this..." He squinted at the pamphlet "Cow-and-caca? No, Kaunakakai Harbor. Then call the Coasties. I need to go up in this Molokai Forest thingy."

"What? And leave me to deal with *this* mess?"

Victor cupped Monalisa's broad, open face in his palms. "Ah, *mi que linda pirata*, you have done your job, yes? You have delivered the marine to fight. This is what the navy does. You must stay and watch over the dead, *mi hermosa*."

"Aw, hell. I know when you start using Spanish on me, I'm getting a snow job. Your act is not as charming as you think it is."

"Call the Coast Guard," Victor said. "Call the Molokai police or—what is it? The forest rangers? Yeager and Charlie, they're probably sitting around with a bunch of tourists, waiting for a boat ride back to the ship, going 'What the fuck?' Or they came back, saw the situation, and left already."

Monalisa narrowed her eyes. "You're doing that macho shit again, trying to protect the little lady. Need I remind you, Lieutenant, I was a master-at-arms in the navy."

"Then you know your duty," Victor said with a wink. "Never leave a crime scene."

Her mouth opened... and closed. No words came out.

"Hah!" Victor laughed. "Gotcha."

Monalisa's shoulders slumped. "Asshole."

"Sea hag."

"Cast off the line. I'll give you a head start, then I'm calling the Coast Guard from Kaunakakai Harbor."

MOLOKAI FOREST RESERVE
Sunday, 9 May
1910 Local

Yeager advanced through the trees. Pyle flanked him on the right. The older man moved well enough, though he was breathing hard and his face glowed red from exertion. Pyle appeared "switched on"—eyes sweeping, weapon ready, alert to danger. Even though he couldn't hear a plate drop on a tile floor, he seemed totally engaged in movement to contact.

The sun had fallen below the hills to the west, though it hadn't truly set. Darkness seeped into the spaces under the vegetation. Before long, Yeager would be traveling by feel more than sight.

They had swung wide south to approach the camp along the same trail he and Pettigrew had used the night before. It had the advantage of both familiarity and decent cover, at least until they reached the stream bordering the south side of the camp. Having scouted the camp, Yeager had a fair guess as to the likely position of any observation posts or ambush sites. He very much intended not to blunder into either.

Yeager heard the trickle of water before he saw the stream. The scent of water carried through the foliage moments later. He held up a fist to halt the advance. Pyle took a knee by his side. The acrid tang of sweat wafted from him, and Yeager knew his own body smelled like a dead goat. At least the breeze quartered in from the east, carrying their scent away from the camp. One of the things he learned early in Afghanistan: sweat stink gave away a stalking enemy as often as sight or sound.

Yeager leaned over his watch—a cool-looking G-Shock with dials and buttons and a rubberized case that Charlie had bought him for Christmas. A teeny button that Yeager's thumb always fumbled over activated a dial light.

"Nineteen ten," he whispered then remembered to hold the watch where Pyle could see it. He motioned Gomer to a prone position. "We'll hold here. Take a breather."

Go time was set for 1930 hours. Yeager stayed on one knee as his companion rested. He was too keyed up, and too close to the enemy, to take his own advice and relax for the next twenty minutes. His head was filled with thoughts of his wife, kidnapped and under duress. The last time she had been taken, he'd been useless to her. She'd faced down her captors and escaped on her own. The next time she faced a killer, he was in Mexico getting some good men killed—again, unable to protect her. In fact, the dog had been more useful than Yeager.

This time... this time he had the deep-rooted conviction he was failing her once again. The clock was ticking, and Charlie needed him more than ever. And yet, here he was, stuck in a forest less than three hundred yards away. Close, but not close enough.

Hold on, Charlie. I'm coming.

MOLOKAI FOREST RESERVE
   Sunday, 9 May
   1915 Local
   Winston Pettigrew snaked along at a crouch, as low as he could get and still be on his feet. *I am a shadow*, he chanted in his mind. Habits learned in a different jungle, in another age, snapped into place as if they'd only been waiting for the switch to be flipped. Moving in the forest was never truly silent. The trick that Pettigrew learned was to avoid sounding like a human animal—avoid the

crackle, the scuff, the shuffle of human footsteps. Break the regularity of movement so his sounds blended in with the surroundings.

He approached the camp from the west, edging northward toward the ridgeline. His objective: the rear of barracks B. Somewhere farther back, Osterchuk waited, allowing Pettigrew to clear the way.

A huff of wind stirred the palm trees. Their brittle fronds clattered. Along with the breeze came the sharp reek of smoke. Individual trees took shape, backlit with an orange glow—fire in the camp.

That ain't good. He picked up his pace. Terrorists lighting fires meant all kinds of bad news. He'd seen on the internet some video of people in a cage burned alive by ISIS, and the barracks were made of extremely flammable material. He wouldn't put it past these assholes to try the same thing.

Someone coughed.

Pettigrew froze.

Directly ahead, covered in shadow, a terrorist must have gotten a whiff of smoke that irritated his lungs. Rushing forward had nearly gotten Mama Pettigrew's little boy killed. He might as well have stomped right up the sentry and stuck the man's gun in his mouth.

The glow from the fire brightened as though more tinder had been added. With the enhanced light, Pettigrew could just make out the regular outline of the target building forty—maybe thirty—yards ahead. Not on fire, thank God. Not yet, anyway.

Between him and his objective was a hidden sentry—based on that one cough, about halfway to the barracks. *And don't forget the guard post between the buildings, by the tree. And there could be a rover.*

Yeager was due to kick off the party in mere minutes, and Pettigrew needed to be in position within seconds of the first bang. The distraction would pull the sentry's attention to the south and give Pettigrew an edge. The question was, could he wait that long? There was a lot on his plate, and after the balloon went up, time would be shorter than a Kardashian marriage.

Pettigrew eased to his belly and crept forward. *I am a snake. I am a shadowy snake.*

CHAPTER TWENTY-TWO

Molokai Forest Reserve
Sunday, 9 May
1925 Local Time

Kimo met Alapai in the clearing, the *hoe leiomano* dangling from his left hand. Its shark-tooth edge gleamed orange in the firelight. Two burning barrels of material—maps, supply lists, timetables—provided a bright-yellow glow to the open space. *Like a campfire*, Kimo thought. Kenny and Hambone ferried stuff out of the command hut, adding to the blazing contents. Sparks and swirls of red-tinged confetti spiraled up whenever they dropped another load.

"Damn, bruddah," Kimo observed. "That's a lot of paper for one little rebellion. Gonna hafta get us another barrel."

"Yeah, who knew?" Alapai grumped.

"Just set the damn building on fire, da kine? Be faster."

"And light a beacon for everyone to see? Yeah, great plan."

Kimo tapped the younger man on the neck with the *hoe leiomano*. Alapai yelped and clapped a hand to the bright points of blood welling from fresh holes.

"Don't be a smartass," Kimo warned.

Near the center of the clearing, a full-sized tripod held a mini-camcorder. Kimo walked over and examined the video device. "We good to go? Got batteries and shit? Don't want to be like that movie, the one with Arnie and the terrorists."

"It's ready," Alapai said, smearing blood along his neck and examining his red palm afterward. "Soon as the guys are finished with the docs, we can start on the hostages."

Kimo swished the ceremonial knife like a musketeer with a rapier. His palm ached from the hole put in it by the redheaded bitch. A fucking nail. He wondered when he'd had his last tetanus shot.

The last of the daylight seeped from the sky, and the first stars were winking on, showing clear and bright in a cloudless sky. Fitful puffs of wind whipped the flames rising from the barrels. The night birds, usually vocal at this time of day, were holding their peace. In fact, it seemed to Kimo that every native creature had gone quiet, leaving behind nothing but the rattle of palms and the gurgle of fire.

"Why wait?" Kimo flexed his sore hand. "You and I can handle these pansies, da kine? At least the bitch I want to start with."

KUANAKAKAI HARBOR, South Coast of Molokai
Sunday, 9 May
1925 Local

Monalisa maneuvered the *Guppy* alongside the Kuanakakai Harbor pier with the gentlest of bumps. Victor hopped out and tied the boat off with a half hitch, which Monalisa retied as a bowline as soon as she cut the motors and joined him. She returned to the yacht to finish locking up while Victor recovered his legs.

Many people described the shape of Molokai as resembling a shark, with the south coast forming the underbelly. Made up of alluvial and volcanic runoff from the mountains to the north, the southern and western side of the island resembled West Texas more than Hawaii, which was to say, *flat and brown*. From his spot on the concrete pier, Victor had a good three-sixty view for several miles in any direction. Pinpoints of lights from houses and businesses dotted the coast, concentrated on the town of Kuanakakai, while the orange ball of the sun dropped into the western sea. To the south and east, twinkling yellow lights of container ships edged across the darkening sea.

And less than a mile away, hidden by nightfall, a ghost ship lay at anchor, its crew and passengers ripped apart by gunfire. Victor shivered.

Closer in, all along the dock, gulls stood in scattered packs, feathers ruffling with the breeze as they roosted in place. Voices carried from other boats. The tinny sound of a sitcom laugh track drifted faintly from the other side of pier, and Victor caught a whiff of smoke from a hibachi.

Monalisa joined him, pocketing a set of keys. She'd thrown on a light jacket as nightfall brought a lower temperature. Victor was both relieved and disappointed at the concealment of her twin peaks.

"Let's go find someone in charge," Monalisa said.

"Uh... okay." Victor had a long-standing dislike of involvement with any law-enforcement types, but he could see no way around it. He didn't have the resources to run all over the island looking for Yeager by himself, and the cops might already know what happened to the tour group from the *Fair Breezes*. It would save him a lot of trouble if that were the case. "Let's go find the po-po."

The harbormaster's office was closed. Victor cupped his hands around the door's window glass to check inside. The office was dark and deserted. To the right of the door was a box full of envelopes, a pencil hanging on a string, and a mail slot labeled Slip Rental. A sign with rates advised people to drop their money through the slot when the office was closed.

"The honor system, huh? Now what?"

"Now I use some of Thad's petty cash to take care of the boat." Monalisa squinted toward the narrow two-lane blacktop leading into town. "Then I guess we hike to the police station."

"Dial 9-1-1. See who shows up."

"Or that."

Victor wandered into the parking lot while Monalisa scribbled on the back of an envelope and stuffed some bills into it. Several of the docked craft were occupied, either by live-ins or weekend sailors. Overriding the smell of the grill, the tang of pot smoke drifted on the breeze.

A scarecrow materialized under the light from an overhead fixture and approached an antique Willis Jeep that might have been abandoned by Douglas MacArthur. He was carrying a five-gallon bucket, a seven-foot-long fishing rod, and a stringer of silvery fish in one hand. The other hand pinched a joint tight between finger and thumb. Older than Methuselah's babysitter, the guy stood a hair under five foot six and wore a floppy straw hat and janitor's overalls. Flip-flops scuffed the tarmac as he approached his rust-and-primer truck.

The scarecrow sucked a final hit on his joint, stubbed out the coal on the Jeep's fender, and tucked the roach in a shirt pocket. He regarded Victor for a long second and spoke on the exhale. "You looking for Dave?" A gray cloud billowed up from under his hat brim.

"Depends on who Dave is."

"He da harbor man. Run da office dere, brah."

"What we need is the cops," Monalisa said, coming up to stand next to Victor. "You know where the station is?"

"Sure." The scarecrow took the time to heft his tackle and string of fish into the Jeep's rear bed. With a vague wave toward the town, he said, "Dey off up dere. Not far."

"Wanna give us a ride, señor?" Victor asked, though he wasn't sure if the guy could drive in a straight line.

The old man scratched his chin, the rasp audible from six feet away. "Ten bucks."

Monalisa flicked a sideways glance at Victor, who shrugged and dragged the folded itinerary from the *Breezes* out of his seat pocket.

He angled it to catch the overhead sodium-vapor light so the old man could see where he was pointing. He was careful to keep the bloodstains hidden. "How much to take me here?"

The fisherman shook his head. "Too dark up there. You won't see nothing."

"He's right," Monalisa said. "It's pitch-black up in the reserve. You might as well come with me to the cops. Maybe they know something."

Victor tapped the folded sheet of paper into his palm, a sour feeling in his guts. Getting tied up with answering a bunch of official questions was not his idea of a vacation. "Me and cops don't always get along." He cocked his head at the fisherman. "Another twenty do it?"

The man's grin looked like a broken picket fence with peeling paint. "*Da kine.*"

"That means yes," Monalisa said.

"*Bueno.* Let's roll."

MOLOKAI FOREST RESERVE
Sunday, 9 May
1930 Local

Yeager found the enemy's observation post where he expected it—in a thick stand of trees to the right of the main trail, directly across the stream from his position. The bright flickering from the camp provided enough backlight that he could make out one outlined figure kneeling between two leaning palms. Once he'd spotted the first man, careful study gave him the positions of two more concealed under the fronds of low-growing bushes. No doubt, more lay in wait, better hidden in the thick, shadowed vegetation.

They were twenty yards away, maybe a shade more. They had been lucky to approach so close without being seen or heard. The stream chuckling between them must have served to mask Yeager's sound, and the fire at the enemy rear was probably more hindrance to them than help. Light would reflect back at them from the fronds, leaving everything beyond in total blackness.

He tapped Pyle and pointed out the enemy position. With Pyle's nod of acknowledgment, Yeager counted down with three fingers. Three... two... one! They simultaneously pulled the pins on a fragmentation grenade, popped upright, and tossed together. He and Pyle dropped back to the ground and covered their heads.

The grenades crashed into the brush like thrown rocks. Yeager knew in his bones his throw had been on target, damn near hitting the enemy's head. He had time to draw a single breath before two heavy cracks split the jungle. The concussion thumped him through the ground.

Someone screamed. Yeager pushed his AK forward and rained fire on the enemy position. The muzzle flare blinded him—he aimed more by memory than design. With two solid bursts, Yeager was moving. Pyle fired as well, though Yeager didn't stop to check how he was doing. The man knew the plan and the fallback point.

Slithering to his right, Yeager pushed through bracken on his belly. He caught the flicker of muzzle blast from the opposite side of the river. None of the return fire had come close—so far. He didn't expect that to last. This was the worst kind of fight, in his opinion—in the dark, with no solid intel on enemy strength or position, no fire support, and absolutely no margin of error. Each side blazed away into the jungle. Random chance decided who'd die and who would live.

He tasted dirt. Sweat burned his eyes. Yeager targeted the strobing light of an enemy's weapon and squeezed off a burst. The firing ceased. Injured, killed, or repositioning? Yeager couldn't know. He moved again. More weapons opened up from the far bank. Bullets zipped and zinged overhead, chopping leaves and smacking bark, distinctive sounds despite the ringing in his ears.

At least he and Pyle had the easy job. After reluctantly concluding that Pettigrew was a better woodsman, Yeager had detailed him and Osterchuk for the hostage rescue while he and Gomer provided the diversion. It was a risky play, but the decision was made, the die cast. Now it was up to him and the deaf Vietnam vet to draw as many attackers as possible and leave the back door open for Pettigrew and the big Minnesotan to get their people out of harm's way.

Muzzle flashes lit up the far bank from multiple locations. Yeager shifted and fired, fired and shifted. One mag ran dry, and he popped in a second.

How long before the enemy crossed the river and dislodged them? As soon as the terrorists advanced, he and Pyle would be forced to retreat. Their only advantage lay in keeping ahead of the enemy, drawing them out, and making them pay for ground with casualties. If the terrorists reached this side of the stream, they could easily flank and pin them down. Outgunned, he and Pyle would be destroyed in minutes. They had to keep pulling back.

The tenor of firing changed. The pace slacked off. Then elements on his left began laying down suppressive fire, lighting up the jungle with steady pulses in three-round bursts. Rounds peppered the branches close to where he estimated Pyle had withdrawn. Yeager saw no response from Gomer's position. *Is he down? Injured? Or already moving to a backup position?*

The terrorists would be crossing the river soon. Yeager readied his weapon, resting it against the shaggy bole of a palm tree. He had a good position, overlooking the river crossing. All he had to do was wait, then he could drop at least one, maybe two. Yeager steadied his breathing and waited.

CHAPTER TWENTY-THREE

Molokai Forest Reserve
Sunday, 9 May
1930 Local Time

He had fifteen minutes to cover six feet of jungle, moving slower than growing grass. Pettigrew had traveled less than half the distance to his target. Stumpy trees protected the sentry's sides as he hunkered between them, all but invisible in the foliage draping the gap. Only the man's single cough, and a rare crackle of brush, betrayed his position.

Pettigrew gritted his teeth. *A direct assault or a long, slow crawl around to the man's backside?* Of the two, he preferred to be in Philadelphia. Circling around from behind would take time he didn't have, and a bull-rush attack would mean a good chance of getting shot.

The sharp *bang* of two grenades exploding made his decision for him. He sensed more than saw the sentry twist in surprise, his attention pulled toward the sound of Yeager kicking off the party. Pettigrew coiled his lean muscles and ripped through the brush like a sprinter at the starter's gun. He lunged at the form between the trees and slammed into a solid body. They fell in a tangle, Pettigrew on top and the sentry sprawled awkwardly, his left arm pinned under him.

The man grunted, and Pettigrew jabbed with his knife. His blade punched through flesh. He felt the brief moment of resistance followed by the meaty feel of a steel parting skin. The sentry reeked of garlicky sweat. Pettigrew held him as close as a lover, feeling the man's muscles move against him, surprisingly warm and intimate.

Being attacked at close range panicked the most stalwart of men. Pettigrew had seen it many times before. The shock of being stabbed added to the disorientation. Training failed, especially for combat rookies, when they were wrestling for their life at point-blank range of a sharp blade. This soldier was no different. He was younger, stronger, and would have cleaned Pettigrew's clock in a stand-up fight. But in the animal brawl of it, down in the dirt and leaves of a foreign place, hurt and shocked and scared, he forgot everything he ever knew and scrambled only to *get away*.

The soldier twisted under Pettigrew and bucked. Pettigrew punched his knife into the man's body again, striking blind, adding fear as much as seeking something vital. His left hand snaked up and located a sweat-slick throat. The soldier's hand locked onto his, and bones grated. Pettigrew's grunts of effort and strain matched those of the younger man. He twisted his hand free and clamped it back at the man's neck.

Using this left thumb as a place marker, Pettigrew shoved his blade deep into the notch at the base of the sentry's throat, and the bucking body under him turned to a frenzied, thrashing animal. The blade grated on the hard bone of the man's spine. Pettigrew shoved harder, capping the palm of his left hand over the knife's hilt and bearing down with the weight of his shoulders and upper body.

The blade grated on bone and sliced through cartilage with a crackling that Pettigrew felt through the tips of his fingers. The sentry shuddered and voided his bowels. A few brief thumps of the dead man's feet marked the end.

Pettigrew allowed himself a moment for his shivering muscles to calm. He remained atop the slack body, too tired to move even with the blood stink of death heavy in his nostrils. With the aid of the thin, uneven light from the camp, he could make out the dead man's features. Canted eyes open. Mouth slack. A pair of brown moles on the boy's chin—for in truth, he was a boy, probably in his early twenties.

War is best left to old men, Pettigrew thought, *as no one should have to bury a child so young.*

Osterchuk rumbled up as subtle as a tank. "Hsst! You okay?"

"Yeah," he whispered.

"C'mon then, hey? We got a lot to do." Osterchuk hustled away at a crouch.

Pettigrew levered himself up and wiped his knife clean on the dead boy's uniform—an action he had repeated more than a dozen times in his life when leaving behind another dead son on the field of battle. This young man would join his personal house of horrors in the back of his mind, a place he visited often and stayed in too long.

You'll be in good company. Lot of boys your age in there. Pettigrew followed Osterchuk toward the camp without a backward glance.

MOLOKAI FOREST RESERVE
Sunday, 9 May
1930 Local

Kimo was reaching for the lock on the hostage barracks when the concussive detonation of grenades thudded from the jungle behind him. The sound sent a jolt of momentary paralysis through his body, turning it to stone. Was this it? Had they been discovered? Was an FBI HRT team charging in to take them down?

He forced himself to turn. Small-arms fire chattered along the creek bank. It sounded loud, violent, and urgent... but not like a full-scale assault. No, more likely, the wannabe SEALs had come back for more easy kills and had instead run right into Manu Ho's squad of professional soldiers, ready and waiting.

Alapai, Kenny, and Hambone were frozen in place, like people playing Simon Says. Kimo read fear and doubt in their eyes... well, except for Hambone, who was too dumb to be afraid of anything. All of them looked at Kimo.

Kimo filled his lungs with air and bellowed, "Get your weapons! Drop what you're doing, and get your guns."

He spun on a heel and jogged toward his small hut, where he'd left his gear. Kimo sent repeated looks over his shoulder toward the south side of the camp. Automatic weapons rattled and spat in staccato bursts. During his few short weeks in Marine boot camp, Kimo had heard weapons fire—on the range. This was the second time he'd had live rounds flying in his direction, the first being earlier that day. He found himself running in a crouch without thinking about it. He bashed into his hut's door and fumbled with the knob. His hands were slick with sweat.

Kimo pushed inside and closed the hut's door. He tried to shrug off the sudden tightness in his chest. Ho and his people could smash a pair of bugs like these two, given a seven-to-one advantage. The two weekend heroes would find they'd grabbed a chainsaw by attempting a direct hit on the camp. Kimo could easily wait it out and not have to lift a finger.

They were probably already dead. And speaking of death, the stink of it lay heavy in the enclosed space. The blond woman had soiled the bed when he'd shot her. Kimo's nose wrinkled. *Damn woman, you ain't pretty anymore.* He grinned, feeling his tension dissipate. Killing hostages was his priority now, anyway. Ho didn't need his help, and they were on a schedule.

Kimo shrugged into his ammo harness and clipped a pistol in a clamshell holster to his belt. He felt much calmer knowing what he had to do. Murder had never been a problem for him.

MOLOKAI FOREST RESERVE
Sunday, 9 May
1930 Local

The pain in Charlie's hand had settled to a low-level scream when explosions thumped the wooden building and a hurricane of shooting kicked off. Nearly every hostage in the barracks had crammed onto cots to try to peer through the high windows. Migliozzi's cot toppled, and he fell with a clatter and curses.

"Them walls are too thin to stop a bullet," Ed Collins advised. He, Charlie, and the Drapers had stayed down, along with Betty Pyle and Austin. All of them huddled in a small group near the rear of the barracks. Betty held Austin and rocked him as a mother would an injured child, crooning into his ear. Since his wife's abduction, Austin had not spoken a word. He wore the look of a man whose soul had been blasted away.

Charlie cradled her right arm at the elbow, trying to keep pressure off her broken hand. Whenever her swollen fingers brushed against anything, however slight, electric-blue pain knifed up her arm. She'd considered several suggestions from her fellow hostages, including using a bra as a sling or wrapping the hand with a spare T-shirt. She'd turned them all down, and not because their ideas didn't have merit. She just didn't see the point.

Kong would be back. She'd seen the promise in his eyes. And when he came, no wrap or sling would save her from the same fate suffered by Lu Kim and Melissa. An incredible lethargy had settled over her. All she wanted to do was sleep.

Then came the bangs and the rat-a-tat of gunfire. Charlie cocked her head as though tuning in to hear a radio station. "It's from the south. The gunfire."

"Do you think it's the army?" Montelle asked.

Dave Draper shook his head. "Probably the FBI."

"But it means we're saved, right?" The hopeful expression on Montelle's face was reflected by several others in their small group. Clearly, the other hostages believed rescue was imminent. Several were bouncing on their toes, chattering back and forth. The two Japanese, Haru and Goru, hugged each other and beamed.

Draper and Collins exchanged looks. Draper finally said, "The FBI would have hit this place with helicopters and lights and about a hundred guys. This doesn't sound like that."

"Abel," Charlie said into the quiet that followed. "It's Abel and the guys."

Betty looked up and met her eyes. She nodded. "I think you're right."

Dominic Migliozzi had given up trying to chin himself up to the window. "Everything's happening out front. Can't see a thing."

"What are you saying?" A female hostage from the Lanai resorts, a woman in her fifties wearing garish designer clothes twenty years too young for her, had approached the group. Charlie thought her name was Kristen. "Your husband is attacking these people by himself?"

"Along with some Marines from our cruise ship. Her husband, for one." Charlie nodded to Betty.

"What are they thinking?" Kristen demanded. "They're going to get us killed!"

Charlie's jaw dropped. "You think we're getting out of this alive any other way?"

"The police—"

"On Molokai?" Draper laughed. "They can muster a couple dozen guys at best. They don't have any Steve McGarritts out here, for real."

"Then, like you said, the FBI." Kristen's cheeks and neck had turned turkey-wattle red. "Someone who knows what they're doing."

Charlie snorted and let her body sag against the back wall. She tuned out the conversation as Betty and the others tried to explain the facts of life to a woman who wouldn't listen and wouldn't learn. Secretly, deep in her heart, a worm of doubt had crept in. It had expanded and spread through her nervous system and metastasized to a cancerous malaise. Abel was no doubt a capable warrior—he had survived countless battles and overcome some stiff odds in the past to prove it. But he was one man, teamed up with a trio of geriatrics who should be breathing oxygen from tanks instead of breathing hot gun smoke. The guards would overwhelm the Marines by sheer numbers. And even if by some miracle they killed all the guards, Kong remained. The brutal Samoan seemed more Terminator than human.

Not too long back, she and Abel had sat together, watching an action flick on DVD. Abel laughed himself silly when the hero of the movie chose to face the evil leader of the opposition by tossing away his weapons and fighting him bare-knuckled. "If I saw this guy coming," he'd said, "I'd shoot him with everything I had then go find a bazooka and shoot him some more. A grease spot would have more life after I got done."

I hope you brought a bazooka, Abel Yeager.

When the wall at her back jolted as though struck by a heavy object, Charlie yipped and jerked upright then regretted it when her hand screamed in pain.

Draper cocked an eyebrow. "What was that?"

A voice, muffled, came from the other side. "Hey, this is the US Marines. We're here to get you out."

MOLOKAI FOREST RESERVE
   Sunday, 9 May
   1936 Local

Gomer had thrown his grenade and frozen.

Yeager had said *Hit hard and then retreat*, but Gomer Pyle could no more skedaddle than he could flap his arms and fly to Pluto. Gomer Pyle was frozen up. Ice cubes were less frozen than Gomer. He knew he was catatonic. He perceived everything—sight, sounds, smells—and his brain screamed at his muscles to aim the rifle, squeeze the trigger, jump up, and run away.

Nothing happened. He could feel the air whistling through his nostrils, the thud-thud-thud of his pounding heart, and the cool moisture of the ground under his belly. The iron bar of the rifle's collapsible stock pressed his cheek, the hard metal imprinting a groove there.

A faint scent of gun oil reached his nostrils. Automatic weapons blistered the night from the other side of the creek. Bright yellow flickering tongues of fire sparkled against the black backdrop of jungle foliage. It was almost... pretty.

He had a great view of the creek. His position was upstream of the ford where the trail to the camp crossed the water—low down, near the water's edge, with a view through a gap in the brush. The position reminded him of a duck blind. He guessed the buildings of the camp were on his ten o'clock, a good hundred or more yards away.

And he still couldn't move.

Yeager was somewhere far to the right, judging by the concentration of enemy muzzle flashes. Gomer should have gone with him. Fire and maneuver. Fire and maneuver. Staying in one place was a death sentence.

The firing slacked off. Yeager must have pulled back, hoping to draw the defenders away from the camp. If it worked, the enemy would soon begin crossing the creek. When they did, the odds were good they would move right past the marble Gomer statue in his duck blind. Movement attracted the eye. Firing would bring return fire. If he did neither, they would probably overlook him.

How aggressive was the enemy commander? Would he commit troops to the pursuit of the attackers? Yeager had said he thought the guy would be pretty pissed at losing his men and also would want to neutralize the continuing threat. He would send guys across the stream in a counterassault, which was why Gomer wanted to stick and move, just like the VC of the olden days.

Gomer concurred. Great idea. Too bad he couldn't move.

He knew they were coming when suppressive fire broke out all along the bank. The enemy commander had reacted to the assault by shifting resources to the point of attack, which was just what Yeager wanted—to relieve some of the pressure on the rescue effort and focus everybody's attention in the other direction. Gomer estimated four to six firing positions, all laying down heavy streams of copper-jacketed *oh shit* designed to keep the opposition from standing up and firing back. Under this hail of lead, a gaggle of three, then four, then a total of six black forms broke out of cover and entered the stream. Some crossed at the ford. Others flanked out and splashed into deeper water, disappearing up to their waists. Given the night, the jungle, and their black uniforms, the men could have easily been VC crossing any unnamed river in Vietnam.

Gomer could nail two, easy as breathing. That would concentrate all the enemy fire on his position, but at that point, he didn't give a shit. He would be doing his part. Yeager and the rest were counting on him. Betty was counting on him. All he had to do was pull the trigger.

He closed his eyes and concentrated all his willpower on a one-eighth-inch strip of skin pressing against the curved metal trigger. Sweat broke out, wriggled across his eyebrow, and circled down past his eye. Through the cocoon of silence that normally wrapped him, Gomer could hear the slosh of water the VC made as they crossed the river. They were coming. He had seconds to act. Half seconds, maybe.

Just pull... the damn... TRIGGER!

CHAPTER TWENTY-FOUR

Molokai Forest Reserve
Sunday, May 9
1937 Local Time

Charlie stood back while Draper, Collins, and Migliozzi helped Danny Osterchuk pry loose boards from the back wall. The effort seemed to require a lot of muffled swearing. Winston used the blade of a knife as a lever on the first board, enough that Danny could get his fingers under the edge and start pulling. He flexed it loose a little at a time to keep the squealing, groaning nails from setting off alarms. Once the first board popped free, the next came quicker.

They were working on a stud in the middle of the opening. The two-by-four studs were spaced sixteen inches apart, and some of the larger people would find it a tight fit. Draper sat on his butt and kicked at the base of the stud with his heel, trying to break it loose, while Danny pulled from the outside. The barracks shivered at each kick, and Charlie winced at the noise.

The hostages crowded in a tight-packed bunch. The group shifted and twitched like herd animals surrounded by a pride of lions. Charlie sensed that at any minute, they would stampede the widening gap and clog the opening. Sand in an hourglass.

She put her back to the work in progress and addressed the crowd in a low, but urgent, voice. "Listen up! Listen up, people. Some Marine veterans are here to help us get out. This is not a rescue by the authorities. We're going to have to make our own way through the forest to find help. We'll be in the dark with only a two-man armed escort." She paused to survey the reactions, which included everything from Betty Pyle's determination to Austin's blank stare. "We'll have to hike out of here on foot. The stronger people need to stick by the weaker ones. Keep one hand on the person in front of you. If you get lost or separated, find a place to hide and stay there. We'll have to be *quiet* on the move. No calling for help or jabbering about the weather. Do you hear me? Quiet."

A squawk from the stud giving way sounded behind her, followed by quiet exultation from the men working on it. When she looked, Danny pulled the board aside. Though still attached at the top, the stud could be pushed aside easily.

Danny caught her eye. "That's good enough. We're ready," he hissed. "Let's get 'em moving, hey?"

"Okay, line up," Charlie said. "Betty, go first, followed by you, and you." She pointed to an older couple from the Lanai resort. "Everyone else, form a line."

The crackle of gunfire died off. Charlie tilted her head and listened. Was it over? Winston had told her Abel was providing the distraction, along with Ted. Did the lack of gunfire mean he was dead? Her heart said no, but her brain conjured a dozen images—all bad—of how a firefight could go wrong.

Danny must have seen her expression as he stood next to the gap and helped people through it. "He's okay. Abel's a salty fu—uh, a salty character, you betcha."

Even salty fuckers can die. Charlie shook off the thought and concentrated on getting people through the hole in the wall. One by one, in a surprisingly orderly and near-silent manner, the hostages crouched and slipped through the gap while Danny held the stud out of the way and used his free hand to assist them.

Except for one: Austin. The younger man sat and refused to move. "Please," he said, eyes wet and glittering in the dim light. "I can't leave without Melissa. How can I leave without her? She's being... she's being hurt. By that man." Austin grabbed Charlie by the biceps when she bent close to him. It jarred her bad hand, and bolts of pain shot up her arm. "Can somebody go get her? One of the men with guns? Can they go get her?"

A thousand reasons to say *No, we can't risk it* flashed through her mind. None came to her lips. Charlie's throat seized. She didn't know what to say.

"What's going on?" Danny hissed. "We don't have all night here."

Charlie turned to him. "A... a man, the leader I think, has taken two women and... this man's wife was one. Is one."

Danny's eyes widened at her expression. "Oh hell. Oh, hell no. Was Lu Kim one?"

"Yes, why? How did you know?"

The big Minnesotan clamped his jaw and refused to say. "Where'd they go?" he asked instead. "Where'd he take the woman?"

"Over there," Charlie pointed with her good hand, indicating the northeast side of the camp. "The small hut next to this one. You can barely see it through the trees on this side."

"Okay." Danny glanced over his shoulder. "Pettigrew's already leading the others away. You take this fellow out and follow them. I'll go get the man's woman."

The lock at the front rattled, and a shooting star of panic blew up in Charlie's heart. She sucked a hard breath when the door banged open and the giant himself slammed through. Dressed in black fatigues and full battle harness, he carried an automatic rifle that looked like a toy in his Hulk-sized fists. His eyes tightened into slits, and a cruel grin twisted his lips.

"What da fuck is this?" Kong crowed. "You trying t'leave me, Red?"

MOLOKAI FOREST RESERVE

Sunday, 9 May
1940 Local

Squeeze the trigger. Squeeze the trigger. Squeeze the goddamn trigger!

The freeze broke, and Ted "Gomer" Pyle was back on Hill 881. The AK banged his shoulder. Orange fire blasted out. A VC in black clothing spun and fell in the water. Muscle memory did the rest. Gomer shifted aim and fired, aimed, fired, aimed, fired. Lather, rinse, repeat.

When the AK's bolt locked back, four men were down and two more had vanished. One of the downed men, in the shallows of the ford, lifted himself into a crouch and staggered back the way he'd come. Another lay half-submerged, facedown in the water. The two closest to Gomer had disappeared under the water. His instinct said they were gone for good.

Magazine change. *Click-click.* Release bolt. *Kih-chink.*

Gomer was back in business. Bits of debris dribbled down his back. Incoming fire chewed through the foliage overhead. Rounds laced the stream in a line of geysers. More slapped the mud and splattered grit in his face. The sounds came to his ears as though from a great distance. Gomer ignored it all.

Aim at the muzzle flare. Fire. Shift aim right. Fire.

He triggered the AK in short, controlled bursts, exerting fire discipline to keep the muzzle from climbing and the rounds on target. He'd learned the hard way: going full-on rock and roll killed nothing but sky and drained a mag in nothing flat. Worst feeling in the world: running out of ammo in a firefight with nothing to shoot with except your swinging dick.

A ricochet sparked off a nearby stone, and a hot, burning sensation ripped across his left forearm. Gomer noted other strikes coming closer to his position. They almost had him zeroed.

I should move. I really should.

A head and shoulders reared out of the water in front of him—one of the VC he'd thought he killed already, apparently not as dead as advertised. The Asian features were close enough that Gomer could almost touch his rifle muzzle to the man's forehead. Gut reaction more than guided thought triggered the rifle in Gomer's hands. He squeezed, the rifle banged, and gore sprayed backward from the VC's skull. The man sank below the surface.

"Come back up now, you son of a bitch," Gomer muttered.

A bullet smacked the forestock of the AK in his hands. The hot, tumbling round burned his cheek and clipped an earlobe. He touched his stinging ear and winced. *Huh. Damn near shot my ear off. No loss there.*

Where was the artillery? Somebody should have called in an artillery strike by now. Was the RTO down? Were Riddeau and Dearborn dead already? Gomer rapped a palm against the side of his head, trying to bang his derailed thoughts back on track. There was something he was supposed to do...

"Oh yeah." A grenade. He had one more grenade, and it needed to be over *there* instead of hanging off his ammo vest over here. Gomer tugged the baseball-sized grenade from his vest and pulled the pin. Leaving his rifle in the dirt—no telling if it was still functional after the bullet strike—Gomer shoved himself up from the ground and pushed his aching body upright.

A concentration of two or three muzzle flashes revealed enemy positions across the stream at about fifty or sixty yards to his right, on the far side of the river ford. *Easy peasy.* Gomer cocked his arm like a big league pitcher... and was on his back, the breath knocked out of him.

It felt like a giant fist had punched him in the sternum. His mouth worked, his chest heaved, but no air filled his lungs. Above him, fronds of exotic trees framed a night sky filled with stars. He smelled blood and dirt and sweat. No sound penetrated the cotton in his ears.

His right hand was empty. This was important. It meant something. What did it mean...?

Grenade! Where's the—

Lightning flashed.

MOLOKAI FOREST RESERVE
Sunday, 9 May
1943 Local

Yeager arrived at the rendezvous point first. A refrigerator-sized boulder lay canted at a thirty-degree angle, clearly visible from the faint path connecting the camp to the trail where the tour group had been ambushed. *Yesterday? Was that only yesterday?* Yeager crouched behind the boulder and tried not to think of how little rest he'd gotten since the nightmare had started—or how long it had been since he'd seen Charlie safe and sound.

Yeager estimated the boulder to be about a quarter-mile from the stream. It was the same spot to which he and Pettigrew had retreated twenty-four hours previously, after they'd first discovered the terrorists' base.

Shots cracked from the direction of the camp. Was Pyle still engaged or were the opposition shooters probing the forest with random fire? The latter didn't make sense, given the professionalism of the soldiers he had seen up to that point. Pros didn't fire at random, wasting ammo on a hopeful hit.

"Come on, Pyle," he said to the darkness. "Get your ass in gear, Marine."

The next question mark in his mind was whether or not their distraction had provided Pettigrew and Osterchuk the time they needed to infiltrate the camp and free the hostages. They had no way to communicate, so he had no way of knowing.

The decision to let the two older men go after Charlie and the rest had been difficult. In the end, Pettigrew's ability to ghost through the forest had been the deciding factor. Yeager knew he was good in the boonies and more silent than the average woodsman, but Pettigrew was in a class by himself. At seventy years old, the man could move like poison gas. Yeager couldn't imagine what he'd been like at nineteen. With Osterchuk to follow along behind him and provide muscle, Yeager figured the two of them stood a better chance of success than he did.

Focusing the enemy attention and keeping it directed away from the camp was the hard part. Yeager and Pyle had to hit and move, remaining in contact enough to lure the enemy fighters to the south while Pettigrew got their people out and moved them northwest. With any luck, they could escape detection and be well gone by the time Yeager and Pyle broke contact and retreated.

Yeager and Pyle would meet the others at the overlook at dawn the next day, where they would have to deal with any blocking force left by the terrorists before evacuating to the nearest town.

A grenade cracked in the distance. The sounds of firing died away.

The sweep second hand of his watch rolled twice around the dial without further movement or sound. Yeager waited. A sinking feeling pulled at his guts. His instincts told him Pyle was injured or dead. He was not terribly surprised, despite the sick sensation of loss that he held at bay with an effort of will.

Yeager checked over his rifle. He dropped the magazine and worked the bolt, reloaded the ejected round and reseated the mag, cocked the weapon and clicked on the safety. Four magazines left. One hundred and twenty rounds. Unknown number of enemy combatants. A few hours left to make them all dead.

"Best get to it." Yeager levered himself upright and went to work.

CHAPTER TWENTY-FIVE

Molokai Forest Reserve
Sunday, 9 May
1947 Local Time

Austin surprised Charlie by jumping into Kong's path. He jostled Charlie when he bounced up, knocking her on her butt. Instinctively, she tried to brace her fall and banged her broken hand on the floor. Light bombs exploded in her head, and it was all she could do to keep from passing out. She curled into a ball and bit her lip, hissing like a steam kettle, while Austin bulled up to Kong, chest to chest.

"Where's my wife!"

One of Kong's blocky hands grabbed Austin's chin, and the other snagged in the back of the Californian's hair. He twisted as though jerking a wheel, and Austin's neck cracked. Kong dropped the limp body.

"C'mon, Mizz Yeager!" Danny yelled. "Get out of there!"

Charlie scrambled for the hole in the wall on elbows and knees. Electric bolts of pain jolted her right forearm. Behind her, footsteps thumped closer. Danny grabbed her shoulders, snagging a handful of blouse. He pulled, and her top rode up, though she gained a little momentum. The outside air felt cool against her feverish cheeks. Danny's sweat stink was strong as she pushed her face into his side. He was half helping, half obstructing her escape, his big body clogging the hole while he struggled for a good grip.

Hands seized her ankles.

"Nooo!" Charlie's bare stomach scraped the floor as Kong dragged her backward. Danny's fingers scrabbled for a better hold, raking her back. She slid farther away, and Danny grabbed her broken hand. She screamed. He let go like releasing a hot rock.

Kong's paws clamped around her waist, and he tossed her behind him with the ease of a man forking hay. Charlie cradled her hand to protect it as she crashed into a cot and skidded over the rough planks. Splinters stabbed her back. The cot bounced away with a clatter. She banged her head on the floor, and light bloomed behind her eyes.

Charlie heard Danny shout, "Oh, hell no!" and when her vision cleared, the big man had pushed himself inside the barracks like a walrus flopping onto a wharf. He'd left his weapon outside, and Kong had deposited his somewhere when he had come for Charlie. The two men faced each other unarmed, an equal match for size, though Danny was more pear shaped and Kong was more like a hewn block of granite.

The Hawaiian terrorist laughed. "Okay, old man. Let's see whatcha got."

Danny roared, and the two giants slammed together.

MOLOKAI FOREST RESERVE
Sunday, 9 May
1950 Local
Manu Ho, leader of the special operations force attached to the intelligence officer known as Mr. L, chewed his lip and considered his diminishing chances for a long and successful career in the armed services of his country. The corpse of the man at his feet was more than a bit mangled by a grenade blast, though not mangled enough to obscure the man's civilian clothes or advanced age.

Manu considered a number of answers to the questions his superiors would pose to him, chief of which was *How*? How had a grandfather decimated his command? Of his original forty, the only acceptable casualties on the mission had been the four on the *Delphinius* mission. Those he could have lived with as they had died in action against the US Navy during the exfil of a primary mission. But the others...

Of the remaining thirty-six, he had lost eleven while hiding in the jungle and playing nursemaid to the idiot sadist Kimo Ekewaka and his band of barbarians. Two sentries had been slain by stealth and five lost chasing their killer through the forest. In a logical world, he could not be blamed for those, as the men had been under the temporary command of the *gweilo*. However, the men were his responsibility. He would be blamed for their deaths.

Four more dead and two wounded in that night's attack by... by an old man with a stolen rifle and grenades? No. It made no sense. There had to be others—younger, more capable men. Maybe even special operations soldiers. If he had to return to his superiors and report his losses, attributing them to this fossil, this white American grandfather... he would be executed, and rightfully so. He had lost face, too much face.

Manu Ho surveyed the expressions of the two men near him, Sergeant Zhao and Private Tuan. Both men gripped their weapons tightly, their eyes wide and constantly scanning the black surroundings. Sweat ran down Tuan's cheeks, and the man swallowed frequently. Zhao twitched at every small noise. This was Tuan's first combat deployment, so it was understandable he might be nervous. Zhao, however, was a veteran with more than fifteen years of service. Apparently, high losses from unseen enemies could unnerve even the toughest soldier.

I need to get these men out of here. Mission parameters allowed for losses, but they still had to execute a difficult and stealthy assault, followed by a dangerous exfiltration. High attrition before the final phase would degrade their chances of success. Tired, anxious soldiers would also reduce their effectiveness. These were tough men, the toughest his country had to offer, but even tough men needed time to rest and recuperate after a firefight.

Something knifed through the fronds nearby, followed by a thud, as though a pinecone had fallen to the ground. An object rolled to a stop at Tuan's feet. Zhao dived away, and Ho instinctively propelled himself backward an instant before the stunning crump of the grenade slammed into him. Warm, wet rain spattered Ho's face and neck. His ears rang, and his mind blanked of conscious thought.

Images. Sight only. No sound. Sergeant Zhao. Bright streamers speared from the muzzle of his weapon. Private Tuan's body somehow seated in an upright position. A dark fountain spraying from the headless man's neck.

Ho's first coherent impression was one of relief. He had been correct. There were more attackers. Perhaps US Army personnel or one of their famed SEAL units. Assuming Zhao survived this attack, he would need to be convinced the attackers were special ops soldiers and not geriatric civilians.

"Sergeant Zhao," he snapped. His voice sounded hollow and far away. "Take five men, and run this ghost to ground." He used the form of the word *ghost* that, in his native language, was more a racial epithet for white people than a supernatural entity. "Keep the pig fucker pinned down and on the run. Meet us at the exfil point at oh four hundred hours."

Zhao nodded sharply and disappeared into the jungle.

Face can be maintained, but not if we fail the next phase. He had to focus on getting as many troops as possible to the *Kekepi* and rally for the final assault. Playing nursemaid to these Hawaiian simpletons accomplished nothing except getting his men killed. It was stupid and wasteful.

It was time to go. If the Hawaiians wanted to go with him, fine. If they wanted to stay and kill the ghosts, fine. Either way, Manu Ho and his team were headed for the beach.

MOLOKAI FOREST RESERVE
Sunday, 9 May
1950 Local

Danny Osterchuk's rage demon had been caged for fifty years. It had a lot of catching up to do. Osterchuk opened the cage and let the demon take him. Conscious thought vanished. Reason evaporated. Fear fled. Only one goal drove Danny Osterchuk, and that was to beat the ever-lovin' shit out of the brutally ugly Hawaiian thug in front of him. His first punch started in Wisconsin and brought with it a freight train of rage. His fist detonated against the granite face, pulping the man's nose into a mashed strawberry lump.

The slab-faced goon staggered back, surprise and pain written on his features. Osterchuk's demon danced with glee. Secret fact: Osterchuk liked hitting people. He cocked and fired the same fist. Same spot. Same result: blood sprayed.

The Hawaiian matched him for size, and he'd obviously been in some fights. An experienced fighter knew how to deal with pain—block it out, and stay in the fight. Slab Face ducked his chin and blocked with his forearms. He backpedaled, blinking away the watery vision brought on by a solid strike to the nose.

Osterchuk bored in, driving hooks to the body. It felt like he was punching a suitcase full of bricks. He tried to back-heel the man to the ground, but Slab Face stepped out of it and unleashed a counter-jab that rocked Osterchuk and turned his legs to jelly. He was forced to break away, step back, and shake off the cobwebs. Osterchuk had never been hit that hard in his life. It felt like having a Buick fall off a cliff and land on his face.

Slab Face crashed into him sumo-wrestler style. Osterchuk grunted and staggered from the impact. They clinched and traded body jabs—short, piston-like punches that stole a man's wind. The Hawaiian broke the clinch and stepped back. An enormous fist filled Osterchuk's vision, delivered by a looping swing from right field.

The lights flickered and dimmed. Osterchuk's knees hit the floor. A thought percolated up from the swamp, drowning his consciousness. *Oh, shit. I'm about to die.*

Nothing happened. Osterchuk's vision cleared, and he saw Slab Face stomping away, headed for Mrs. Yeager. Bless her heart, she had circled around them and gone for the AK propped in a corner, where the ugly fuck had left it.

She gripped the rifle awkwardly in her left hand and fumbled at the bolt with her right forearm. Slab Face was on her in an instant. He snatched the gun away and popped Charlie Yeager between the eyes with a short right jab. The redheaded woman's eyes rolled up, and she dropped in a heap.

The giant Hawaiian turned and came back toward Osterchuk. He tossed the rifle on a bunk in passing. Blood sheeted the lower half of his granite face, and murder danced in his eyes.

Which was fine by Osterchuk. The demon wasn't done with him yet. He spat blood and gunk on the floor and filled his lungs with oxygen. His chest banged and shuddered like a misfiring John Deere tractor. Osterchuk gathered his legs under him, fueling his muscles with will power and pure junkyard-dog meanness.

Danny Osterchuk liked hitting people, true. Hitting bad people made him very happy. Hitting this evil shit stain felt like a dozen Christmas mornings come all at once. You betcha.

The man was six feet away. Four feet. Two—

Osterchuk launched himself off the floor and tackled Slab Face with a shoulder to the gut. He wrapped his arms around the man's tree-trunk legs and *heaved*. Slab Face fell backward. The Hawaiian's back slammed the floor with a *whump* that shook the building.

And then Osterchuk was on top of the man, knees pinning his shoulders, hitting him as if Slab Face was the world's ugliest piñata. Right, left, right, left, bouncing Slab Face's head off the floor. Blood sprayed up.

Something broke in Osterchuk's left hand. He ignored the popping sound and never felt the pain. His vision had shifted to deep red, though that might have been from blood splattering his face.

If Danny Osterchuk could have asked himself if this was the happiest he'd ever been, he would have said no. The day Jan accepted his proposal, his wedding night, the birth of any of his children, or any of several milestones since... those would have won. But not by much.

His enemy was down. Danny Osterchuk would beat the life out of him. He'd heard what had happened to Lu Kim. Knew the fate of the blond man's wife. Saw what happened to Charlie Yeager. Seventy-six years old didn't matter. Fat and out of shape didn't matter. No way was this woman-raping, murdering sack of shit getting up from—

A lightning bolt of fiery purple pain seized Osterchuk's chest and lanced down his left arm. Once again, the lights flickered and dimmed. All his strength drained away. The will left his body. The rage demon vanished. Nothing existed except the pain blowing up through his body.

All he could think was, *Not now, by damn. Not now.*

Then he was facedown on the floor. The scent of wood. Roaring in his ears. A knee settled on his back, but it was nothing compared to the crushing weight squeezing his chest. A giant hand clamped his chin, and another tangled in his hair. All he felt was relief. In a second, the pain would be gone.

Danny Osterchuk felt the crack of his own neck from a far distant galaxy. And he was right. The pain went away.

CHAPTER TWENTY-SIX

Molokai Forest Reserve
        Sunday, 9 May
1953 Local Time

Yeager dodged between a pair of tree trunks, ate a spider web, and ducked into a clump of shaggy bushes. He wriggled deep enough to be concealed and concentrated on not panting like a hyperventilating teenager. He pawed the sticky strands away from his face and prayed no spiders were crawling down his collar. Yeager's favorite response to spiders involved napalm.

A spider inside his shirt would ruin his whole day.

He had one full magazine, one partial. One grenade. He was as yet unwounded—a real bonus, given that he had struck a numerically superior enemy twice in the past half hour. Thank God the enemy had no night-vision goggles, or this would have been an extremely short fight.

Gomer Pyle was MIA, and that was bad. Yeager couldn't find him in the dark, and the silence underlined his gut feeling that the man dead or wounded. Out of the fight, anyway.

A fragrant scent from the surrounding brush tickled his nose. He couldn't place the smell... something between sandalwood and juniper, maybe. Yeager had never been good with naming scents. There were pretty smells, then there was everything else. Charlotte, for example. He liked the smell of Charlotte Buchanan Yeager, raw and fresh out of the bath, warm skinned and a little randy. Everything else came second.

Snap out of it!

Yeager strained his eyes, cocking his head to catch every sound. The night held its breath, and even the bugs were quiet for a change. The rifle in his hands felt greasy with sweat, and the ground cool and damp. Yeager wiped his face against his shoulder—first one side, then the other.

After pitching his next-to-last grenade, Yeager had been forced back in the face of a blistering response. The enemy was a just a teeny bit disturbed. Who could blame them? When executed properly, guerrilla tactics drove even seasoned fighters to a frenzy. Being stung and stung and stung created an impossible situation for a team holding a static position.

Tactical options after an incursion included flooding the area of operations with overwhelming firepower, dropping a blocking force behind the guerrilla fighters to prevent exfil, or applying a heavy dose of air support and artillery to saturate the area with munitions. Also, the commander might deploy counterguerrilla elements around the most sensitive targets, which in this case meant the terrorist camp.

Yeager figured that air and artillery support were out of the question, and the limited number of enemy forces prevented either blocking or applying overwhelming response to an attack. The terrorist leader had chosen to set up OPs—observation posts—around his campsite, believing Yeager's mission involved attacking the camp itself. Since all Yeager wanted was to focus attention away from the camp, locating and attacking the OPs had accomplished his objective. He had avoided entrapment by hitting the perimeter and retreating.

The big question remained: had Pettigrew and Osterchuk taken out the OP on the back door and freed the hostages? Yeager glanced at the luminous dial of his watch. It was coming up on thirty minutes since the first bang. By that point, Pettigrew would have either succeeded or failed. There was no way for Yeager to know or find out. He could not break off, as continuing to harass the enemy from this side of the creek fixed their attention away from the escaping hostages. Pettigrew should be leading them all to safety to the northwest, veering right to intersect the National Forest trail and, from there, heading eastward to the trailhead and, presumably, safety. The longer Yeager kept the terrorists' attention fixed on him, the more distance Pettigrew could put between the hostile force and the fleeing captives. Including his wife.

With forty-five rounds and one grenade, he would not be keeping the terrorists' attention long at all. Yeager switched the AK to single fire, holding it close in the dark to read the strange markings. The familiar scent of gun oil and burnt powder overrode the gentle smell of the native plants. He had to admit: after Charlie, burned gunpowder was next on his list of favorite smells.

The whisper of cloth brushing against a hanging limb activated his warning system. *Danger close.* Yeager held his breath and waited.

MOLOKAI FOREST RESERVE
Sunday, 9 May
2000 Local

Charlie Yeager woke up with the feeling her guts were being squeezed like a tube of toothpaste. After a second of disorientation, she realized two things. One, she was being carried over the shoulder of the giant, Kong, and two, her head ached the way it did at the beginning of a two-day migraine. Her right hand had swollen to the size of an oven mitt, and it throbbed with an electric jolt of white heat at every jounce and jostle of her captor's lumbering steps.

She had no time to assimilate more information as Kong tossed her off his shoulder. Charlie hit the ground like a laundry bag, the impact slamming the air from her lungs and leaving her gasping.

Stars glittered through a shroud of camo netting overhead. The feet of several men surrounded her.

"The prisoners have escaped," Kong snarled. "We need to go after them."

"No," said an Asian man dressed in black combat utilities. "We go. Rendezvous with boat."

Charlie had the impression the man in black was a real soldier and not a homegrown terrorist like Kong and his friends. Kong swelled up at the challenge from the smaller man as though ready to come to blows. A black-clad soldier standing behind the speaker shifted, the muzzle of his AK casually swinging into position to riddle the ugly giant if he made a false move.

Kong deflated with a growl. "Fine." Hands on his hips, the Samoan turned his attention to the native Hawaiians. "Kenny, Hambone, how much more you got to do?"

"This is about it." A chunky, overweight man with deep-set, piggish eyes brandished a pair of three-ring binders and threw them into a burning barrel. "Some computer shit to do, though."

"Get your gear, and let's go." Kong pointed to a thin man with glasses who resembled a Hawaiian Harry Potter—the clipboard guy. "You the computer whiz, da kine. Stay here, and do the computer shit."

"And then what?"

"And then run like hell to the beach. We ain't waiting for you."

Clipboard's eyes shifted to Charlie and slid away. "What about... her?"

Kong laughed. "No, she ain't for you, brah. This is my reward for a job well done." The bloody half mask of Kong's face made him look like some kind of pagan god with the blood of his sacrifices smeared over his lips and chin. Coal-black eyes glittered in the firelight. "She goes with me."

MOLOKAI FOREST RESERVE
Sunday, 9 May
2002 Local

The guy was good—Yeager had to give him that. After the first crackle of brush, all movement had ceased. Eyes straining, Yeager examined the area from which the sound had come and saw nothing but blackness mixed with patches of denser blackness covered with a patchwork quilt of monochrome shadows.

With the elevation and the absence of sunlight, the temperature had fallen to downright chilly, and the longer he remained in place, the colder he felt. Yeager swiped the back of his grimy left hand under his runny nose then scrubbed it off against his pants. His fingers brushed across a smooth, round stone, and he picked it up. Would an old trick work?

Yeager tossed the stone six feet to his left. Crackling leaves marked its passage. He counted to ten and watched for movement. Nothing. Apparently, the other guy had seen the same movies. Or was there even another guy out there? Maybe the noise had been a falling tree limb or a coconut or a critter rustling around for acorns.

No. Yeager forced patience on himself. The ticking clock in his head counted off every moment his wife remained in danger. Every second felt like it had weight, as though each one was a waterdrop on his forehead. A steady torture of helplessness. *Hurry carefully. Impatience gets you killed.* He'd seen it before—a soldier dismissed a stray sound, decided it was nothing, or lost patience, then he got up to continue his patrol, and *Wham! Here's your flag, Mrs. Smith, and we regret your loss.*

In this game, first to move was first to die.

From the corner of his eye, Yeager saw a shadow detach from a bundle of blackness, splitting off like a cell dividing. It moved like a man, slinking low and sweeping a rifle in short arcs: front, right, left. Yeager tracked it with the barrel of his AK, sighting with experience and a touch of hope as darkness shrouded the foresight. He couldn't aim with any degree of precision. This would be spray and pray at its worst.

Yeager let out his breath and triggered off three rounds, single fire. Muzzle flare blinded him, and he lost sight of the target.

And a second later, he didn't care. A half dozen weapons opened up on his position. A hot-iron poker scorched across his shoulder blade. Another round shattered a nearby rock and peppered his cheek with pulverized shards. Weapons hammered the night with sound and fury.

Yeager scrabbled backward on his belly. His shirt rucked up under his chest, and the rough ground scratched his bare stomach. A grenade banged, and leaves and debris rained down over him like confetti. His eyes watered from the dirt and grit blown into them. His ears rang from concussion. He was blind and deaf.

He found a depression and wriggled into it. The tempo of incoming fire changed from suppressive to fire and maneuver. The enemy leapfrogged toward his position, covering each other's advance. Yeager had a minute, maybe less, before they would close in from both flanks. He scrubbed his eyes and blinked to clear the grit.

Dying was not out of the question. He accepted that. If it bought Charlie and the others time to get away, he would pay the price without question, but... he didn't *know* she was free. If Pettigrew failed, then Charlie was still a captive, and his sacrifice would be meaningless. And if he died while she lived, he'd never hear the end of it. She would track down his ghost and rag him until the end of time.

As Pettigrew would say, it was time to *di di mao*. Rifle fire pounded the trees as Yeager snaked across the forest floor away from the enemy pressure. The *snap-zing* of passing rounds gave him all the incentive he needed to get his ass in gear. His son, John Riley, could zip across a floor on his hands and knees faster than a squirrel after a nut. Yeager beat that speed by a hair, even with an AK cradled across his bent elbows. The smell of rich red earth and exotic plants filled his nostrils. His ears still rang, and sounds came through muted like TV heard from another room.

After eeling through a stand of trees, Yeager guesstimated he was far enough way to stand and run. He shoved himself off the ground and kicked off into a jog, ducking and dodging as tree trunks and low-hanging limbs appeared out of the night.

The incoming fire had slacked off as the enemy probed for his position. They probably guessed their target had successfully disengaged. They would be back to a crawl once they confirmed he had retreated. A crawl suited Yeager just fine.

It was time to completely break contact, flank wide right, and circle back to the camp. Had Pettigrew succeeded, or was Charlie still a captive? The answer to that question would determine his next move.

CHAPTER TWENTY-SEVEN

M olokai Forest Reserve
Sunday, 9 May
2010 Local Time

Winston Pettigrew stepped to the side of the trail and motioned the line of people behind him to keep walking. He counted heads and waited for the appearance of a big Minnesota farm boy and a good-looking redhead married to a certain sleepy-eyed Marine.

Betty Pyle was the last in line, and she stepped up to him. "Where's Ted?"

"Off with Abel Yeager, causing a distraction." He craned to see over her head. "Where's Danny and Mizzes Yeager?"

"I looked back, and Danny was climbing into the barracks, I assume to get that idiot Austin, who looked catatonic when I left." She bit her lip. "I... I didn't wait to see if they came out."

Pettigrew patted her shoulder, his attention fixed on the trail behind them. "Don't beat yourself up, Betty. The Michelin Man can take care of himself, and I 'spect Charlie Yeager can too."

"She's injured. Charlie is."

"Say what?"

"She went after the big man with a nail. He crushed her hand like... like it was nothing. An eggshell."

Pettigrew winced. "Abel not gonna like that."

"Why is Ted with him? Why isn't he with you?"

"We needed ever' body looking the other way, with enough fire-power to make 'em all go over yonder while we snuck up and got y'all

223

out." Pettigrew shrugged a shoulder. "Yeager figgered I needed somebody who could hear."

"Damn that man," Betty swore softly. "If he gets killed…"

Pettigrew checked the line and noted the last of the hostages disappearing to his right. Osterchuk and Charlie and the Austin feller had yet to appear. "Lookie here." He squared up, held Betty by the upper arms, and locked eyes with her. "Ted's safe as kittens with Abel Yeager. He'll be fine. I need you to keep all y'all headed west, okay? The high mountain is on your left, and you can see the North Star pretty clear. Keep goin' west, and you'll cut the trail to the lookout. Where we left the cars. It's all easy from there."

"You're going back, aren't you?"

Pettigrew nodded. "I need to keep that big blue ox from doing something stupid."

"If you see Ted, tell him not to get killed." Betty scrubbed away a tear and squared her shoulders. "Get back safe, y'hear?"

"Yes'm, that is my intent."

Pettigrew snaked back through the jungle and approached the prisoner's barracks from the rear. The hole they had created in the building gaped dark and ominous as a horror-movie basement inviting the unwary teens to trot down the stairs and engage in heavy petting while surreptitiously observed by a hockey-masked psychopath lurking in the shadows. Osterchuk's weapon lay propped against the side of the building.

"That ain't good," Pettigrew said to himself.

Ducking through the hole, Pettigrew smelled the open-latrine reek from the bucket used by the captives as a toilet. The interior of the space pressed in, tight and close. A hulking obstruction blocked the floor, deeper black against the gloom inside the barracks. It might have easily been mistaken for a pile of laundry heaped in the middle of the floor. Unless you happened to have seen a number of dead bodies in your lifetime, as Winston Pettigrew had.

Pettigrew approached on cat feet, stepping carefully around upturned cots and unidentified debris. He leaned in close. The knowledge of what he would find gripped his stomach in a tight knot and made his eyes water with emotion.

His big pal from Minnesota lay on his belly, eyes wide open and staring at the ceiling.

"Aw, damn," Pettigrew whispered. "What the hell am I gonna tell Jan? And where's Mrs. Yeager?"

A sound from outside drew his attention to the front door. Pettigrew crossed the room and skulked up against the front wall. He pressed his cheek against the splintery doorframe, surveying an open clearing in front of the barracks where two barrels crackled with leaping flames. A man had just finished dropping an armload of junk into the nearer barrel, and it had flared up, sending a crescendo of sparks spiraling into the sky. The man carried no weapons and appeared to be alone. He was in his midtwenties or so, as slender and physically unremarkable as a grad student on a camping trip.

Pettigrew shouldered his rifle and touched the hilt of the knife at his waist.

The grad student turned and walked back toward the command hut, the one Yeager had labeled building D, and disappeared inside. Pettigrew flowed through the door and ghosted across the clearing. The crackle of flames masked any sound he made, which was pretty minimal to begin with. He crossed first to building A, then C, verifying no one else remained in camp. He paused at the open door to the command hut. Inside, the grad student hunched in front of a glowing computer screen. He was alone.

Pettigrew figured that in a minute or two, the lone terrorist would sincerely regret not having his buddies around for company, because one way or another, Winston Pettigrew intended to get some answers PDQ. Pettigrew slipped inside and closed the door behind him.

MOLOKAI FOREST RESERVE
Sunday, 9 May
2128 Local

The old Willis jeep jounced along a narrow, rutted excuse for a road, its one working headlight waving a weak yellow beam ahead like a drunk teenager running through the forest with a flashlight. Victor rode the bucket seat the way he would a bull at the Rio Grande Valley Livestock Show and Rodeo. The scrawny old fisherman, whose name was Jumbo of all things, worked the shifter without a demonstrated ability to mesh gears, palmed the wheel as though maintaining a straight line was against Hawaiian law, and smoked enough weed to leave a normal man comatose.

After dropping Monalisa at the police station, Jumbo and Victor had roared away in a cloud of oil smoke mixed with pot smoke. They zoomed out Highway 460 at a breakneck forty miles an hour for a few short miles, then Jumbo had left the main highway for a narrow two-lane road that cut across open fields. The two lanes turned into a gravel road that turned into a nightmare of pits and ruts. Jumbo hit every bump. Some of them twice.

The road bored through a tunnel of trees. A thin strip of stars shone overhead, but everywhere else, pitch-black night pressed in close and tight. Cool, damp air blew away Jumbo's weed exhalations and chilled the sweat under Victor's arms. At one point, the single headlight had picked out the glowing eyes of a feral dog, and later, three deer bounded across the track, lit for a fraction of a second before disappearing.

"Axis deer," Jumbo said.

"If they're the Axis, who are the Allies?"

Jumbo looked at him with the sleepy expression of the heavily medicated. "Huh?"

"Never mind—watch the road!" Victor grabbed the dash and held on as a deep rut catapulted his butt off the seat.

Victor's kidneys were about done in by the time the Jeep emerged from the jungle into an open area. A Forest Service sign blipped past, illegible in the darkness. Jumbo applied the brakes, and the Jeep skidded to a halt at a fork in the road.

"You need a piss?" Jumbo gestured to the right, where a building hulked among the trees. It was visible only by the dull gleam of reflected starlight from its pale roof. An iron rail marked the road here, and sectioned off the space.

"No, I'm good for now."

The fisherman popped the clutch, and the seat slammed Victor in the back. The old Jeep lurched forward another few dozen yards and came to a single paved parking spot adjacent to another structure, smaller and narrower than the first. Jumbo pulled into the space and stopped. The headlight revealed another rail crossing the darkness, this one accessed by a concrete path, and then the yellow beam was swallowed by darkness. A swath of stars, thick and bright, sparkled in the sky, and a quarter moon rose over the eastern peaks.

"Here you go," his driver announced. "Dis de lookout. Picnic tables there." Jumbo pointed at the building then back to the right where the road continued. "That way is the reserve. You gotta have an invite, you know?" He swiveled to indicate dead ahead, where the headlight pointed. "Walk out dat way, and you fall big-time, bruddah."

"Bueno. You got a flashlight, homes? Cool, thanks. Wait here."

Victor took the greasy dime-store flashlight, flicked it on, and was rewarded by about a candle's worth of light. He climbed out of the Jeep and stretched. Then he resettled the pistol in his waistband, wincing at the bruises from where the hammer spur had dug into his spine.

Walking felt good after two hours of Jumbo's driving. Victor craned his neck from side to side, and the crackle of joints realigning sounded like Bubble Wrap popping. Instead of exploring the overlook and possibly falling big-time, he opted to explore the trail to the reserve. Behind him, Jumbo switched off the engine, and Victor caught the distinctive sound of his cheap lighter snapping on to light another doob. *How much dope can one man inhale?* The secondhand smoke alone had given Victor a mild buzz.

In minutes, he was alone with singing insects and rustling of the foliage, following a crunchy twin-track road that could have been any backwoods camp road in any state park in America. Victor kept on, sweeping the wan light ahead of him, not sure what he was looking for or even why his instinct was driving him to look in the first place. It wasn't as if Yeager couldn't handle trouble—no, in truth, trouble often couldn't handle Yeager.

But... something itched in Victor's conscience. He needed to be out here, doing something positive, rather than sitting back in a Honolulu motel, watching pay-per-view movies.

A flash of red reflected from the darkness ahead. Victor centered the light and picked out the rear of a vehicle parked at an angle beside the track. As he approached, another SUV materialized and parked next to the first. Victor slipped the .45 out of his pants and held it down by his thigh.

The SUVs were Range Rovers, mud-splattered and dingy, with a company logo on the side: Adventure Tours Unlimited. Same company as the one noted on the brochure from the *Fair Breezes*. He shined the light inside the first car, holding it against the glass to avoid reflection. Front seat, empty. Back seat, empty. Rear compartment... dead man, bullet hole in his forehead, blood all over his shirt. Victor noted that the shirt had the same logo as the vehicle. The driver must have been employed by Adventure Tours to carry tourists to the trailhead.

He checked the second Rover and found an identical situation: dead driver stowed in the back compartment, one shot to the head, multiple gunshot wounds to the torso. Both drivers had apparently been gunned down then received a *coup de gras* to the forehead. Their killers had thrown them in the back of their own cars, then departed.

Victor prowled in an ever-widening circle and found nothing else of interest. No trace of the shooters remained, at least in the immediate vicinity. He stabbed the gun back in his waistband and stood in the middle of the trail, smelling his own sweat and listening to his own heartbeat. Victor tilted his head back and consulted the heavens.

"So now what?" he asked the white blanket of the Milky Way.

The stars glittered down without answering, indifferent to his confusion.

MOLOKAI FOREST RESERVE
Sunday, 9 May
2130 Local

For over an hour, Yeager worked at the pace of a snail harnessed to a boulder, creeping under fronded vegetation, over mud and dirt and gravel, and through hip-high water. He paused often, listening a lot and waiting for the moment when he would be the guy making the first move, not wanting the slamming impact of a bullet to be his first indication of enemy presence.

He arrived at the camp's perimeter wet, muddy, and exhausted. The place appeared to be abandoned. In the middle clearing, two oil drums plumed smoke into the night sky from long-abandoned fires. The barracks hulked with silent menace, portals open to black interiors. The building that had held the hostages lay open as well, its interior as impenetrable as the others.

Yeager studied the opening, hesitating to move forward and examine the contents. The longer he delayed looking, the longer he could imagine Charlie long gone with Pettigrew and Osterchuk. The empty building would attest to the success of their strategy and reward Yeager with joy for the future reunion with his wife.

Or... checking inside the building might reveal a horror he was unwilling to allow. It was all too easy to picture a scene of butchery so profound it would crush him so that he was unable to recover, like a submarine sinking to the ocean floor. The weight of despair at the thought of life without Charlotte would squeeze him to the point that his heart would burst from the pressure.

But remaining frozen was cowardice, and cowardice was as abhorrent to him as failure. Yeager rose from his crouch near building A and entered the clearing, eyes fixed on the black doorway awaiting him.

"There you are," a voice to his right said.

Yeager pivoted on one heel, rifle swinging into alignment at his hip. His finger was taking up slack when he recognized Winston Pettigrew at the doorway of building D, the one they had identified as the command hut. The slight man was in the process of wiping a knife blade on a piece of cloth.

He studied Yeager with a sad expression. "I nearly shot you."

"What the hell? Why aren't you with the hostages?"

Pettigrew sheathed the knife, his expression as grim as a doctor describing a terminal illness raging through his patient's body. "C'mere and take a knee, big guy. I got some bad news, and I got some bad news."

CHAPTER TWENTY-EIGHT

M olokai Forest Reserve
Sunday, 9 May
2140 Local Time

Yeager sat in the dirt and leaned his back against the side of the command barracks. The rough-textured wood jabbed his scalp with splinters. The acrid smell of burning plastic drifted from the smoking barrels, and tiny licks of flame peeked over their rims. The fires were dying out, and the darkness had all but reclaimed the abandoned camp. Exhaustion soaked Yeager's muscles, and it was all he could do to force his mind to focus on Pettigrew's debriefing.

"So you're saying," Yeager said, "that Osterchuk is dead, and the leader—"

"Second in command, but leader here." Pettigrew knelt beside him, sweat gleaming on his dark complexion.

"This guy named Kimo dragged Charlie off with the rest of the quote-unquote military advisers."

"Who are trying hard to look and act like North Koreans but the computer geek says are as North Korean as a fortune cookie."

"Who, then?" Yeager's eyelids dropped. Post-battle reaction and the dissipation of adrenaline sapped his will power. Add to that the crushing disappointment of his wife remaining a captive to these maniacs, and it was all he could do to keep from curling into a ball and giving in to the sleep that wanted to take him under.

"The kid thinks maybe Chinese."

"Who's this kid, the computer geek?"

"A homegrown wannabe terrorist all hot and bothered over Hawaiian independence. Rah-rah, Hawaii for Hawaiians. Yaaahh-hh!" Pettigrew mimed a cheerleader waving pom-poms and imitated the roar of a stadium crowd.

Yeager cut a sideways look at the smaller man. "You kill him?"

Pettigrew shook his head. "Nah. Cut a few bits off at first—got him talking."

"Heh. And they say torture doesn't work."

"Only Hollywood assholes say that. Torture works just fine if you know how to do it. The kid—his name is Alapai, by the way—is zip-tied to a table in there. He ain't going anywhere. Not on foot, anyway." Pettigrew added that last with a look that would sour milk still in the cow. Yeager chose not to pursue it. "Anyway," the Vietnam vet continued, "the point being, Kimo's got an hour head start, maybe an hour and a half. No way we're catching up, trying to follow where they're going."

Yeager grunted. *An hour-and-a-half lead and no trail to follow.* It didn't matter. He was going to have to try—

"But we don't have to," Pettigrew added.

"Huh? What?"

"We don't have to run after Kimo and his boys."

"I have to." Yeager planted a hand to lever himself off the ground. "They have my wife."

"One other thing Mr. Alapai related..." Pettigrew fished a scrap of paper out of his shirt pocket and held it up. Letters were scrawled on it in blue ink. "The name of a ship."

"A ship?" Yeager frowned, trying to concentrate.

"We don't need to follow the bad guys." Pettigrew's teeth glittered in a wolfish smile. "We just need to find the ship they're headed for."

MOLOKAI FOREST RESERVE

Sunday, 9 May
2350 Local

Victor glanced at his watch. Mickey's big hand and Mickey's little hand were both pointing almost straight up. At nearly midnight, he still had no plan. So far, what he'd come up with was A, throw the stoned, sleeping Jumbo into the back of the Jeep and drive back to town to report the dead bodies in the Land Rovers, or B, hike up a pitch-black trail into the jungle with nothing but a dime-store flashlight and a handgun. His head said A, and his balls said B, which left the default of plan C: insert thumb in ass, and wait for the killers of the tour people to reappear while watching for a bright star to blossom in the sky and lead him to Jesus.

The moon hung almost directly overhead, a brilliant-white scimitar against a backdrop of glittering pinpricks. None of the bazillion stars appeared ready or willing to step up and lend a hand, so Victor paced a circuit from the Rovers and their gruesome cargo to the picnic table under the canopy to the rusty Jeep with its snoring occupant. Jumbo sat with his head thrown back, mouth hanging open, and supplied a baritone counterpoint to the high-pitched whine of the insect serenade.

Jumbo's snoring was the only reason he missed the sound of the intruder until a shadow flowed around the rear of the Jeep and tried to stab him in the neck. Victor caught the glitter of metal and the rush of motion from the corner of his eye. He fell as much as sprang backward, barking a harsh grunt of surprise. A burning sensation scored a line across his collarbone, and he twisted away as the attacker's momentum carried him past. The man barked a curse and swept a backhand cut that swished through the air close enough for Victor to smell the steel.

Victor crow-hopped backward to gain some space, but the oily little wisp of smoke kept up the pressure. Moonlight revealed a scrawny black man in a windbreaker—*What the fuck? A windbreaker?*—whipping his knife around in the style of a Japanese chef. A three-headed snake couldn't strike any faster than this guy. If he could clinch the skinny bastard, Victor could squish him like a tube of toothpaste, but hand-to-hand speed wasn't among his superpowers, and the snake kept dancing in and out.

The guy whirled in with a slash that burned across Victor's palm.

"*Chingada tu madre!*" Victor snapped. "Hold still, you little Chihuahua motherfucker!"

"Pettigrew! Back off!" boomed a voice from the night—one that sounded a tad familiar. The scrawny knife fighter oozed out of reach, poised in attack posture.

"Yeager?" Victor squinted at the broad shape looming out of the darkness behind the black man. "Is that you?"

With a few more steps, the shadow resolved into the blunt shape of none other than Abel freaking Yeager. A second later, Victor was engulfed in a bear hug and lifted from his feet.

Yeager pounded Victor's back then put him down. "Goddamn, I'm glad to see you. How'd you... how is it you're here?"

"I—"

"Never mind," Yeager said. "I need to get to a boat. Something fast."

"What—"

"They have Charlie, and I have to catch up to them out at sea. They're going to meet another boat. Will this Jeep run?"

Victor blinked as a crowd of people materialized from the direction of the trail, led by a white guy wearing shorts but no shirt. They looked like refugees from a zombie apocalypse. "Who...? What...?"

The bald man in the tan windbreaker spoke up, his voice as raspy as a ten-inch bastard-cut file. "You know this guy, Yeager? He don't seem too bright."

"Another jarhead. C'mon, Por Que, snap to. Let's get moving. I need to find a harbor and commandeer a boat."

The parade of refugees shuffled closer. Most looked tired out, and Victor noted a frail old lady being carried by a square-jawed fellow with white hair. The chubby shirtless guy in the lead handed an AK-style rifle to the old man with the knife.

Chubby Half-Naked Dude eyeballed Victor but spoke to Yeager. "The Land Rovers are still here, keys in the ignition. The tour guides are dead and stuffed in the back."

"Okay, fine." Yeager raked his hair back with his fingers. He looked at where he'd propped his AK against the side of Jumbo's battered ride, the owner of said vehicle still zonked out, mouth open, cutting wood with a rusty saw. Yeager retrieved the weapon and said to Chubby, "Load everybody up, and let's get down the hill. Dump the bodies if you have to make room."

"Where'd you get the guns?" Victor asked. "And by the way, you look like a bear ate you and shit you down a chimbly." Victor flapped his wounded hand, which burned like everlasting sin, and splattered the black man's windbreaker with drops of blood. "And you, Zorro. Why'd you jump me?"

"I thought you was one of them Chinamen—uh, Chinese."

"I look Chinese to you, hombre?"

Zorro shrugged. "Y'all look the same to me in the dark."

"Shut up, Marines," Yeager ordered. "Por Que, we'll explain on the way. Let's go." He turned to Chubby. "You good, Draper? You can get these people to the nearest town?"

The man named Draper scratched his belly with a thumbnail. "I have no idea where that is, but we'll manage. Go get your wife, Abel."

Victor rapped on the hood of the Jeep, banging his way around the front of the vehicle to the driver's side. "Hey! Jumbo! Wake up!"

The heavy-lidded fisherman snorted and sat up. He wiped the back of his mouth with a bare forearm.

"Jumbo?" Draper asked.

"Dude, hop out!" Victor said. "You need to show these people how to get to the cop shop in Kuana-kaka, or Kabula-kooko, or what the fuck it's called. Throw that shitty AK in the back, Yeager. I'll drive. Just so happens I know where there's a boat with a squid skipper and some good American guns."

Yeager sagged into the passenger seat while Victor tossed out Jumbo's tackle box of six lures, four rusty leaders, and a Ziploc bag of primo weed. When Jumbo scrambled after the baggie of green, leafy substance, Victor took his place behind the wheel.

"Hey, my car!"

"You'll be a hero, Jumbo," Victor said, cranking the ignition key. "Name will be in all the papers, dude." The back of the Jeep bounced, and Victor looked over his shoulder. The black man had climbed in and was settling down for the ride. "Where do you think you're going, Zorro?"

"He's coming with us," Yeager said, scrubbing his eyes with his palms. "Now, find a gear on this bitch and let's go."

SOUTHERN COAST OF MOLOKAI

Monday, 10 May

0002 Local

Charlie Yeager stumbled in the thick sand of the beach and caught herself with her good hand before falling, only to be kicked in the butt and sent sprawling face-first. She bit back a whimper when her throbbing right hand thumped the ground and was squashed by her body. Sand showered her face, and she tasted grit. The pain almost equaled the indignity of being kicked in the rear.

A giant hand lifted her by the belt and set her on her feet. "Keep moving," Kong ordered. Kimo—the other men called him Kimo. "Don't try to slow us down again."

Then stop kicking me! She wanted to say the words, but her jaw remained clenched. A combination of despair, anger, and fear were muddled together and twisted her mind away from finding a solution to her situation. Considering that they were approaching a small fleet of inflatable boats being maneuvered into the water by black-clad soldiers, her situation was headed from desperate to hopeless in a hurry.

From the first moments of leaving the camp with the four Hawaiians, she pictured Abel springing from the bushes, Ramboing all the terrorists, and carrying her to safety. This fantasy played out in various ways, her mind always refusing to dwell on the possibility that he might be killed in the attempt. When the Hawaiians connected with a cadre of their more professional-looking Asian soldiers, the fantasy became more difficult to sustain.

The group had topped a high ridge in the pitch-black night then proceeded downslope through thick, slashing fronds and loose soil that threatened to crumble underfoot. Their path crossed the main hiking trail at one point—Charlie could make out the Park Service steps cut into a slope as they traversed it at an angle.

The men shifted around a lot, making it hard to keep track, but by the time they reached a convoy of high-wheeled vehicles parked under a canopy of trees, she counted at least ten enemy combatants, including Kimo and his bunch of home-grown assholes.

After being shoved into the back seat of an SUV and squished between Kimo and the man he called Hambone, Charlie's hope of a quick rescue sputtered out like the stub of a candle melting away to nothing. The convoy barreled downhill along a game trail barely suited for dirt bikes and mountain goats, and though their speed wasn't anything close to the high end of the speedometer, the SUVs rumbled downhill faster than a man on foot could keep up.

Which meant Abel was far, far behind her when the trucks pulled into the driveway of what appeared to be an abandoned house. Everybody had piled out and double-timed around the back, where a narrow strip of sandy beach lay between the grass of the home's backyard and the rollers of the Pacific Ocean—the same beach upon which she had just stumbled and had her ass kicked for good measure.

The trail would be cold and hard to follow by the time dawn gave Abel enough light to follow her tracks—tracks that would lead across a beach and disappear forever. No tracker in the world could follow a boat across the sea. Cold logic suggested that if she got into a boat, she'd be as good as dead.

Her jumbled thoughts clicked into a coherent picture in the space between one shove in the back and the next. Her life had come to a decision point, and Charlie had never been afraid of making hard choices.

She looked up at the glittering stars. She saw the crescent moon hanging in the sky and felt the sea breeze flutter her blouse. In the space between heartbeats, Charlie said goodbye to everything she had known. David, her son. Abel, her husband. John, the baby. She had to let them all go, for this was it. She wasn't getting out of this alive. She would die on this beach, or the monster, Kimo, would carry her to their waiting boat, rape her, then dump her over the side, dead or alive. She would disappear forever, her body lost to the sea. Abel would never know what became of her.

They were halfway across the beach when her realization coalesced into an action plan. She would rather die then and there than be dragged onto a boat to a bleak and certain future. Charlie broke right and kicked into high gear. Her legs powered her across the sand, kicking up small white puffs with each stride.

She ran for her life.

CHAPTER TWENTY-NINE

Molokai Forest Reserve
Sunday, 9 May
2140 Local Time

"You know where you're going, right?" Yeager asked.

"Dude, quit asking me that. You're making me all nervous and shit." Victor hunched over the Jeep's wheel, squinting at half-remembered landmarks.

He had pushed hard coming out of the backcountry, and the Jeep had taken a beating. The engine temp ran high, and the oil pressure had dropped. There was a strong smell of hot metal and burned motor oil coming from under the hood, along with an ominous knocking that signaled either a crapped-out lifter or damage to something more vital.

Fortunately, the route to the harbor was a pretty straight shot once they reached the main highway and made the left toward Kaunakakai. The Jeep had smoked and rattled along pretty well as they cruised into town, then Victor had slowed, looking for the turnoff to the marina.

"So who is this woman skipper who owns the boat?" Yeager asked.

"You never met Monalisa. You was already off in Fuckmenistan, getting your ass shot at, when I was in flight school. We, uh, had a thing for a while."

Yeager sketched an attempt at a grin. "Alex know you're out playing first mate to an old girlfriend?"

"I... you know, left her a voicemail."

"Brave of you."

Victor shifted in the seat. A glance in the dash-mounted rearview mirror showed that the old man, Winston of the Blade, had wedged himself among the buckets and bails filling Jumbo's cargo space and appeared to be snoozing. His head bobbed loosely with every bounce. Victor resolved to aim for every pothole he could find, just to see how hard he could make Pettigrew's head fly. The slashes on his hand and collarbone still stung like a motherfucker.

"She cool?" Yeager asked. "She gonna be okay with us grabbing her boat and taking off after the bad guys?"

"Man, Monalisa's hard as they come. She should've been a Marine, you know?" Victor spotted a gas station he remembered. They were near the harbor road. "We close, man. It's... gotta... be around... there!"

The tires squalled through a hard right turn. The narrow two-lane road was poorly lit until they reached the finger that extended into the harbor. The sound and smell of the ocean washed over them as they broke out of the gloom and into the open stretch of road. From there, it was a few hundred yards to the berth where the *Guppy* was tied off, parallel to the pier.

The boat appeared dark and deserted, but then a shape moved on the rear deck, and Victor recognized Monalisa, the ever-present mug of coffee steaming in one hand.

She stood as they approached. "You exchanged Jumbo for some more shady characters, I see."

"Worse than that," Victor told her. "I brought the Marines, and we gotta get to a fight, chica."

ABOARD THE *Kekepi*, **Pacific Ocean**
Monday, 10 May

0213 Local

Charlie's thoughts surfaced one by one, like corks floating up from a deep black pool. She became conscious of her world swaying and rolling in a nauseating way, followed by an awareness that she lay facedown on a real bed with real pillows. Though she wasn't under the covers, the warmth of the bedding nestled her in a place of comfort and kept her covered in a blanket of lethargy. She didn't want to move. Movement would bring awareness, and awareness would require action. Movement would bring pain. Throbbing aches radiated at the edge of wakefulness. Jarring any part of her body would result in a penalty she was unwilling to pay.

Not again. That was a strange thought. Why not again? The answer refused to come. She could not remember how she'd come to be in this place.

Charlie's last memory was of being pinned between two hulking men in the back of an SUV as it bounced and bumped down a trail carved out by the white beams of the car's headlights. No... wait. There was a house... on the beach.

A beach...? The memory wouldn't come. As more thoughts gathered, so did the dull ache at her temple. Stickiness tacked her hair to the side of her face. She could feel it when her weight shifted as the boat rode the waves.

She was on a boat! *Duh. Of course.* The motion made sense now. But why did she feel such panic at the idea of being on a boat?

Kimo. He had dragged her from the camp and... somehow gotten her to a ship at sea.

Charlie cracked an eye open... and needn't have bothered. The room was dark. No windows? *Wait, yes.* A single porthole, high on the wall, a pearlescent gray oval cut into a black backdrop. By the dim, watery light, Charlie recognized shapes in the room: a night table with drawers separating twin beds, the opposite bunk empty and neatly made. A gooseneck lamp built into the wall over the night table.

Turning on the light seemed like a good idea. If only she had the energy. Weariness weighted her muscles as though gravity had tripled somehow, making every movement an effort requiring the concentration and willpower of a person she remembered but couldn't summon.

The need to urinate forced her up from her nest. A narrow path between the bunks led her to a small vestibule with a door on the right and a short hall with a washbasin, toilet and shower. Charlie used the toilet without turning on the light. She had no desire to see her face in the mirror over the basin. Rummaging through the drawers proved fruitless—someone had cleaned them out, leaving not even a Q-tip behind.

She tried the door next, and to her surprise, it opened... only to reveal a sleepy-eyed guard with a gun who growled at her in a foreign language. She closed the door and rested her back against it.

Where is Abel...? Cold sweat washed over her face. Charlie shivered as memories cascaded out of the darkened room of her subconscious.

She was on a boat. At sea. Abel was somewhere back on Molokai with no idea where to find her. She was on her own, the captive of a sadist. The parallels to her time in an abandoned convenience-store cooler just a few short years earlier did not escape her—locked in a small, dark space. Waiting for rape.

Charlie slid onto the bed, curling into the still-warm hollow in the covers. That person in the cooler had had the determination and willpower to fight back. To kill her captors and escape. She had dug deep and found a resolve beyond any she believed she possessed. It had taken luck and daring and a willingness to do horrible things to other human beings, but in the end, she had won. Charlie had come home to David and to Abel. It had taken years of love, and not a little counseling, to exorcise the fear and trauma.

That Charlie had disappeared, vanishing somewhere in the long night with her failure to stop Kimo taking Melissa. She'd wound up here, alone at sea, surrounded by evil. Her hand throbbed. The beating of her heart sent bolts of random pain shooting up her wrist and thumped a bass drum in her temple. Air whistled through her swollen sinuses so that even breathing seemed a chore, and nausea threatened to empty the contents of her stomach at the slightest trigger.

Dread crushed the soul of this strange person occupying her flesh. *Not again.*

Of course it was happening again. And this time, she could no more stop it than run from the room, dive overboard, and swim to Tahiti. The Charlie she needed to be wasn't around anymore. Was she ever coming back?

THE *Guppy*, Pacific Ocean
Monday, 10 May
0230 Local

Twin Volvo Penta diesels drove the Cobalt over the Pacific swells at forty-five miles per hour. Monalisa Montgomery claimed she could normally get a tiny bit more out of her, but the seas were running high, and pushing the throttles to the max wouldn't necessarily squeeze any more speed out of the boat. Yeager ground his teeth and clenched his hands to prevent them from shoving the woman out of the way and jamming the throttles fully open.

As it was, the *Guppy* pounded every wave with a hammer blow, forcing Yeager to hold on to a rail with one hand while he studied the touch-screen display in the dash. Monalisa sat at the helm, her pleasant, broad face lit a soft green by the dashboard glow. Pettigrew and Por Que had gone to raid the galley for sandwich fixings. The occasional clanking, banging, and cursing filtered up from below as they were tossed around the small space.

Wind whipped Monalisa's hair in streamers. She yelled over the roaring engines and pointed at an electronic chart display. "We're here. South of Molokai."

"Got it," Yeager said. The *Fair Breezes* had been on the south side of Molokai as well. Victor had filled him in on the fate of the cruise ship, twisting Yeager's knot of anger another notch tighter.

"We'll head due west for forty miles or so then cut west-northwest toward Honolulu. Your guy said to aim for a spot about five nautical miles south-southwest of Nanakuli."

"Any idea what's there?"

Monalisa shrugged a broad shoulder. "Empty sea, as far as I know. Shipping traffic is pretty heavy there."

"The guy Pettigrew questioned said they were after a ship. No idea which one."

"Could be anything from a cruise liner to a cargo ship."

"So no way to know what these fuckers want," Yeager said, half to himself. Pettigrew had told him the kid back at the camp had no idea regarding kind of ship they were after or what they would do once they reached it. All he had was the name of their yacht—the *Kekepi*—and the approximate coordinates of the intercept with their target ship. Kanoa—the purported leader of the Niho Niuhi—had kept the planning for the final strike between him, the huge and ugly Kimo, and a guy named Mr. L, who was some kind of spook. Mr. L had supplied the men, material, and logistic support to make the Niho Niuhi attacks possible.

Pettigrew appeared and handed Yeager a plate with a double-fisted sandwich piled on top and set a travel mug into a cup holder next to him. "Coffee in there. According to your buddy, go easy on it. He says this cutie-pie here makes coffee could send a man to the moon without a rocket ship."

"Cutie-pie?" Monalisa favored them with a half-smile and an arched eyebrow.

"I call it like I see it," Pettigrew said.

"You need glasses, you old salty dog."

"How long?" Yeager asked around a mouthful of bread and sliced turkey.

Monalisa squinted at the display. "Two hours, maybe two and a half. Question is: what do we do when we get there?"

Yeager grunted and washed down his bite of sandwich with a swallow of scalding black coffee. "I'm working on that."

"We could use the radio," Monalisa suggested. "Call the Coast Guard."

Pettigrew shook his head. "Uh-uh. The bad guys hear that transmission—"

"They kill Charlie," Yeager continued. "Dump her overboard and head for open sea. It's why we didn't call before we left Molokai. If they even get a sniff of a US Navy vessel..."

Monalisa fought the helm as a rogue wave pitched the boat into a twist. "And should we split up? Go after the ship they plan to board, assuming we can find it? No offense, Abel, but I'm not willing to risk a mass-casualty event in Honolulu."

"No," Pettigrew said before Yeager could unlock his jaw. "The kid said they would trigger the quote-unquote final strike from the *Kekepi*. Once they position their hijacked ship, the hijackers will exfil and leave it to be blown in place. Whatever that means. And no, the punk didn't know either."

"So taking the *Kekepi* is vital," Monalisa said. "Which begs the question: how do we approach a ship full of terrorist assholes on the open sea, get close enough to board their vessel, and not get blown up in the process?"

Pettigrew scratched his chin and leaned into the bulkhead. "Can we get ahead of them and get to these coordinates before they do?"

"Depends on their speed. I doubt they're hauling ass like we are." She patted the top of the dashboard. "Not many things can outrun my baby here. But I don't know how far ahead they are either. Could be we're already too late."

"They'll see us on radar," Yeager said. "We have to be on an almost parallel course."

"Lots of boats out here," Monalisa told him. She pointed at the blips on the radar sweep. "I'm seeing all kinds of traffic."

"So if we come up on them..." Pettigrew narrowed his eyes and stared at Monalisa, apparently lost in thought. For her part, the lady skipper pushed her hair back and concentrated on driving the boat. There was a loud clang and an extra-loud curse in Spanish from below.

Yeager sat on the vinyl bench seat to the left of the helm and stuffed his face. It had been a long time since he'd eaten anything more than an energy bar, and his hunger had flared back to life at the first bite of sandwich. While he chewed and swallowed food and swigged coffee, he watched Pettigrew. "What are you thinking, old man?"

Pettigrew's eyes glittered. "I think I have an idea how we can get close."

CHAPTER THIRTY

Kekepi, **Pacific Ocean**
Monday, 10 May
0300 Local Time

The *Kekepi* rocked at anchor three miles south of Honolulu. In the salon of the Hatteras 100 Motor Yacht, the Niho Niuhi and Mr. L lounged in deep-cushioned sofas and club chairs. Floor-to-ceiling windows reflected the interior lighting, acting as mirrors to those within. Besides the salon's plush seating, the Hatteras featured mahogany-finished cabinetry and side tables, hardwood decking underfoot, and a fully stocked wet bar. The former owner had been a fan of the San Francisco 49ers and had decorated the walls and shelves with memorabilia, including a signed Joe Montana jersey behind glass—at least, that was where the jersey had been before Kimo had smashed the glass and taken it out.

"A little tight," he complained, shrugging it on.

Kanoa paced the narrow strip of floor between the seating area and the windows, his twinned reflection keeping perfect time with his strides.

"Why did you bring the woman?" he growled at Kimo, not for the first time.

"Because I wanted to," the rough-skinned giant told him. Not for the first time.

"You need to get rid of her."

"In time, bruddah. In time." Kimo's legs stretched out in front of him, and he slumped in the seat, a beer clamped in one hand and a bowl of nuts resting on his belly, for all the world as though settling in to watch a football game on the big screen.

In contrast, Mr. L sat primly with his feet together, hands in his lap, poised on the edge of his chair. "You should relax, Kanoa," said the dapper little spy in his neatly pressed suit. "We are ahead of schedule and the... complications have not thus far disrupted our timetable."

"Man," Kimo rumbled, "you talk like you in a James Bond movie, brah."

Kanoa slashed the air with a hand. "You call twelve dead and six wounded *complications*? Maybe eighteen total available for the *Golden Sun* operation... and hey, brah, where's Alapai?" This last he addressed to Kimo.

"I dunno." The big man slugged a pull off his beer and belched. Peanut crumbs dotted the front of his Joe Montana jersey. "He didn't make the meet at the beach. We left de bruddah a car too. He shoulda come down the mountain after us."

Kanoa ground his teeth. He glared at Kenny and Hambone, both of whom drooped their eyes. "You ever think for a minute maybe these Special Forces guys might've got him? That maybe he rolled on us?"

"Nah, man. What's he know?"

Kanoa paused, trying to think back on which plans the young and eager computer science major had been involved with and which he hadn't. Although Kanoa had tried to compartmentalize the planning so no one person would know too much, he'd been forced to rely on Alapai's computer skills a little too often. Had the kid helped him research the optimal intercept zone for the target ship? Did he know the coordinates for the planned rendezvous with the *Golden Sun*? Kanoa chewed his lip and paced the deck.

"We launch the inflatables in two hours," Mr. L said. "Until then, we are holding at our staging area, well back from the intercept location. Radar will tell us if any Coast Guard or naval vessels are in the area. If your man has given up any intelligence under... duress, then we will know in plenty of time to abort and escape."

"It is not aborting that concerns me," Kanoa growled. "I want to complete this strike."

"As I was about to say," Mr. L continued with the air of one whose patience was not inexhaustible, "if the way is clear, we have plenty of operators to continue as planned. We anticipated casualties, and our numbers are more than sufficient to the task."

Kanoa stopped and stared at his reflection in the window glass. Shadows painted his face in harsh planes. "I just don't like this intervention by these mystery people. They hit us hard. Who are they? Super soldiers?"

Hambone spoke for the first time since coming aboard. "Hawaii is full of haole troops, K-man. One of the reasons we're fighting the occupation, right? Coulda been some Delta guys, y'know, out on a hike. Or SEALs—something like that."

"Fog of war, brah," Kenny said. He spoke less than Hambone.

Kimo lifted a butt cheek and farted his opinion of the matter. He stood and stretched. "Whatever, man. I got better things to do with my time than listen to you ladies bitch. No more rubber-boat rides for me tonight. I'm gonna grab some Z's then maybe plow a red-dirt road. Da kine?"

***THE GUPPY*, Pacific Ocean**
Monday, 10 May
0520 Local

"Doesn't look promising." Monalisa had her eyes glued to binoculars while standing in the cockpit of the *Guppy*. The engines idled as they drifted on moderate seas, waves slapping the sides and the boat bobbing with a motion Yeager's stomach wasn't enjoying.

They had reached the coordinates provided by the kid from the camp more an hour earlier and found a big, fat nothing. Or put another way, they'd found ship traffic of all kinds but nothing that seemed an appealing target for terrorists. A high-stacked cargo carrier had steamed past about thirty minutes before at less than two miles distance, traveling west to east. It had proceeded without incident, sailing into the glow of false dawn and disappearing over the horizon. That was the largest vessel they'd seen.

"What's this one?" Yeager asked. He had long since given up trying to identify any ships smaller than an aircraft carrier by examining distant lights through a wobbling pair of binoculars.

"Fisherman."

Fishing boats spread out from the island and motored away in every direction. Several had passed them without pausing, dropping nets like water wings and chugging hard in the swells. Motor yachts of varying sizes had crisscrossed the water, none bigger than the forty-foot Cobalt and none "acting strange" as Monalisa defined it. They ignored sailboats, both as potential targets and as likely candidates to be the illusive *Kekepi*.

Monalisa monitored the radar and kept one ear tuned to the radio traffic, somehow able to decipher the hash from the scope and the garbled crackling noise from the speaker. Yeager admitted to himself that he would be totally lost if left on his own to try to piece together the picture she tracked in her mind seemingly without effort.

Pettigrew and Victor were both racked out below, following the warrior's dictate to sleep whenever possible. Yeager had nodded off on the bench seat next to the cockpit, but his forty winks had been more like ten, and those were filled with bad dreams. He had given up on sleep and instead downed cup after cup of the skipper's rocket-fuel coffee. At that point, his nerves were a jangled mess, and acid filled his stomach, threatening to burn his windpipe with toxic sludge.

"Who else do we need to check out?"

"There's something big coming up over the horizon. Course would put it headed for Kalaeloa Harbor to the west of Honolulu."

"The *what* harbor?"

"An industrial harbor. Lots of cargo off-loaded there." Monalisa bumped the throttle and sent the Cobalt boring toward the radar contact at a moderate speed. "Let's go check it out."

***KEKEPI*, Pacific Ocean**
Monday, 10 May
0530 Local

Running feet thundered on the deck overhead, jarring Kimo out of a deep sleep. The king-sized bed in the yacht's guest suite was one of the most comfortable he'd slept on in his entire life; seconds after closing his eyes, he'd conked out and snoozed for... *wow*. His watch read five thirty a.m. He'd sacked out for more than two hours.

Heh. Too much exercise last night.

Pounding at the door brought him upright. He scrubbed his eyes and yelled, "What?"

Kanoa stepped into the room and closed the door behind him. "We're about to launch."

"Da kine."

"You're gonna be here with L and four of his guys. Kenny and Hambone too."

"No shit. So?"

Kanoa leaned his back against the door, scratched an ear. "I don't trust him not to leave us swinging, brah. You need to be ready to blow his damn head off if he tries to run, yeah?"

The extraction plan would rely on the Asian spy bringing the *Kekepi* in close to the target ship after the boys had done their job. The inflatables would get the hijack crew off, but they had limited range, so making it to the sub would require the motor yacht.

"You think he'd run off and leave all his guys?" Kimo asked.

"I think he'd run off and leave his mama. This guy's a snake, no two ways."

"You're leaving Kelly, dipshit. What's that make you?"

Kanoa straightened, his fists tightening. "Kelly volunteered," he growled.

"Okay, but..." *What about the woman?* The run out and hijacking would take some time. Getting things set up and the ship in position would take a couple more hours. If he got started after the boats launched, he could maybe have his fun and still have time to take care of the spook if need be. "Yeah. No problem. I gotcha, brah."

"C'mon," Kanoa ordered. "Help us get the boats launched."

"Aye, aye, Skippy."

THE *Guppy*, Pacific Ocean
Monday, 10 May
0540 Local

"Ahhh..." Yeager gawked through the binoculars. "Is that an LNG carrier?"

"Yep," Monalisa said. "Big one too. One of the megacarriers."

The craft resembled a flat-bottomed boat loaded with giant beach balls, except it was nearly as big as a shopping mall. At a distance of three miles, the carrier filled a good portion of the binoculars' field of view. A long dark-blue hull with a blocky superstructure in the rear, the ship carried four moon-sized white domes lined up lengthwise, all connected via a construction of rods and pipes along the top.

"Could be the target," Yeager said. "Can they blow it up?"

Monalisa cut the throttle, and the Cobalt drifted forward on momentum alone. A line appeared between her eyes as she frowned. "I... don't think so. No. Not easily. Trying to remember a briefing from back in the day..." She drummed on the wheel with a quick bongo riff and bit her lip. "Liquid natural gas doesn't blow up so much as it burns really, really hot *if* you can vaporize it and set the vapor on fire. The ships are super-safe, and the containers are engineered against impact or spillage, but..."

"But what?"

"Terrorist attack is one of the worst-case scenarios. If... wait." Monalisa swiveled in her chair and rubbed her temples. "Let's say terrorists hijacked an LNG ship and ran it aground in, like, Honolulu. Maybe Waikiki Bay."

"Uh-huh."

"And let's say they were smart terrorists and knew how to build shaped charges that could penetrate both walls of the liquefied gas container so the tank could boil off its contents in a vapor cloud. Now, the third thing the terrorists would have to do is rig some sort of delayed explosive to light off the vapor cloud. There would be a big fireball, very hot, and a sustained fire near the ship that would burn until the gas ran out." She leveled a serious look at him. "I don't know how much of the city would burn. Not all of it, for sure."

"But they could righteously fuck up a big section of beach-front property, true?"

"Very true. Look at the chart. It's right outside the mouth of the Pearl Harbor's channel. Hitting Pearl could be what your informant meant by 'blow it in place.'"

Informant seemed an overly charitable description of the leaking, damaged terrorist from the camp. After Pettigrew had finished his carving, the youngster had spewed information like a twenty-four-hour news service. Yeager let it pass.

The orange ball of the sun peeked over the horizon, streaking bands of high, thin cirrus clouds with morning light. A gull faced the wind off the starboard bow, frozen in place by the breeze and the perfect alignment of wings and feathers. As Yeager watched, the bird dipped and wheeled away.

"It's this one." Yeager nodded toward the LNG carrier. "Has to be. It's the right coordinates. It's the right kind of potential for mass destruction. I'm feeling it in my gut."

Monalisa regarded him with narrowed eyes. "But what if you're—wait." She snagged the binoculars, focused them directly ahead, and watched for a long count of five then handed Yeager the glasses. "You're a psychic son of a bitch."

Yeager lifted the glasses and panned ahead, following Monalisa's pointing finger. His jaw clenched hard enough to make his teeth hurt when the jiggling view settled on the thing she had seen. Six or seven hundred yards to the west of their position, two inflatable boats skimmed across the surface of the ocean. The details weren't clear by the light of dawn, but he could make out enough to identify numerous people in each boat. The craft arrowed across the open water, headed straight for the LNG carrier.

Yeager tracked back along the line of travel. The breath he'd been holding hissed out. There it was, smaller than a black dot on the flaming orange sea. "You see that on radar?"

After a pause, she said, "Yep. Looks like a ship. About the size of a yacht. Better go wake up the two sleeping beauties."

Yeager nodded, his throat too tight to speak.

CHAPTER THIRTY-ONE

K*ekepi*, **Pacific Ocean**
Monday, 10 May
0622 Local Time

From the plush sofa in the salon aboard the *Kekepi*, the man known as Mr. L typed a short, coded phrase into a heavy-duty laptop. The laptop was attached to an encryption device and satellite antenna that would take the phrase, garble it, compress it further, and squirt it into the ether as a tiny blip of a transmission, virtually undetectable to any listeners who might wish to intercept it. The message would update his commanders—not based in Pyongyang, as he'd led Kanoa to believe—with a status code relaying that the intercept of the LNG carrier was underway.

A flurry of activity would ripple through the small suite of offices housing the Institute for Policy Implementation. Located in an office complex in the Changping District in northwest Beijing, the Institute was a unique experiment of combined operations from several bureaus and divisions, from the Military Intelligence Division, First Bureau, to the PLA's Second Department. It included elements of the PLA's special operations forces—in this case, the troops led by Lieutenant Peng, aka Manu Ho. Rarely known to play well together, the various Chinese military intelligence forces had formed the Institute for Policy Implementation to plan, coordinate, and execute the false-flag operation code named White Swan.

Key to the operation's inception had been Mr. L's recruitment of angry American and potential rebel Kanoa Ino. With the seeds of violent protest present in the form of Kanoa's band of disaffected

Hawaiians, Mr. L's superiors pieced together a joint operation with multiple goals.

Objective one: teach the Americans a lesson regarding their meddling in Taiwan—though Mr. L had little confidence the lesson would sink home, as objective two ensured blame would be deflected onto the demon of the Americans, the hapless North Koreans. Objective three was a bonus, though not insignificant by any means. If "Manu Ho" and the Hawaiians should succeed in capturing the *Golden Sun* and steering it into the channel connecting Pearl Harbor with the open sea, they would weaken the operational capabilities of the US Pacific Fleet for a period of time. Once the boat was placed in the channel, Mr. L would enter a series of keystrokes on his satellite phone and remotely blow the demolition charges planted by Ho's men. This would scuttle the massive LNG carrier in the narrows of the channel, blocking Pearl Harbor like a cork in a bottle, which would deny the US the use of their vital Pacific refit-and-refueling base and severely hamper US naval operations in the Pacific Rim.

Mr. L closed the laptop. Morning sun powered in through the east-facing windows of the salon, forcing him to squint. His stomach complained at his lack of attention to biological concerns—it had been a long night, and the stress of dealing with the barbarians had prevented him from eating. With all of them gone except for the baboon, Kimo Ekewaka, his stomach was putting in a reminder for sustenance.

Kimo Ekewaka. As though thinking about him had conjured the ugly giant, Kimo entered the salon and grunted an acknowledgment as he passed through. Mr. L sneered at the man's back. In his silly sports uniform and black combat pants, the man walked barefoot through the glass doors at the rear of the salon and down the ladder. Headed to the crew quarters and his captive victim, no doubt.

Mr. L shuddered. No matter. Ekewaka and the woman were loose ends that would soon be tied off, along with other Hawaiians.

Once Mr. L had sunk the *Golden Sun*, he would give the order for his men to go down to the crew quarters and gun down both victim and tormentor. The *Kekepi* would head out to sea, leaving Ho and his men to escape via a different route—one unknown to Kanoa and his people, who would be left hanging, martyrs to their idiotic cause. It would interesting to see how the Americans reacted to the evidence and whether they'd have the strength to confront North Korea—

A shout from outside drew his attention.

Mr. L frowned and crossed the salon. He took the companion-way then the ladder that led to the pilothouse. There, a Special Forces commando with knowledge of piloting ships the size of the *Kekepi* was seated at the wheel. Sergeant Wei, if he remembered the man's name correctly.

"What is happening, Sergeant?" Mr. L demanded.

The man pointed off to the starboard side of the ship. "A vessel approaches. A pleasure craft smaller than this one."

KIMO STOPPED BY THE soldier guarding the woman's cabin and jerked a thumb over his shoulder. "Go get some food or sleep, or go fuck yourself some other way."

The soldier recognized the dismissal if not the words. He nodded crisply and trotted away.

Kimo entered the small cabin and stopped, confused for a second by the empty beds. *Where did she—ah, the door to the head is closed.* "Locking yourself in the bathroom won't help, sistah. You might as well come out so I don't get too mad."

Silence.

He tried the handle, which of course was locked. "Fine, we do it the hard way." Kimo reared back and smashed the door with his heel—and rebounded as the door refused to budge. He was cocking his leg to kick it again, the first trickling of anger simmering into his veins, when he noticed the hinges on his side of the door. It opened outward.

"Oh, I'ma gonna take special time with you," he growled.

After pulling a combat knife from a scabbard on his belt, Kimo jammed the point between the latch plate and the door, digging at the spring-loaded bolt where it entered the latch. He jimmied and pried at the gap, the wood crackling as he widened it. Kimo shifted his grip and shoved the blade deeper. He put his weight behind it and heaved.

The door popped open and banged him in the shoulder. He stepped into the head. It was empty.

***KEKEPI*, Pacific Ocean**
Monday, 10 May
0625 Local

Mr. L blinked to confirm the evidence. Sure enough, a white-with-blue-trim yacht motored toward them on a converging course. Sun glinting off the window prevented him seeing inside, but on the foredeck lounged a white woman in a bright-pink two-piece bikini. The woman tottered to her feet and tilted her head back to drain the last few drops from a champagne bottle. As she stood, the top of her suit fell off, revealing her bare breasts. She seemed not to notice or care.

"You got any more bubbly?" The woman's slurred voice came to Mr. L through the open glass doors leading to the narrow strip of deck along the starboard gunwale. She had addressed the question to Private Xiao, who stood just outside the door.

"Go 'way! Go 'way!" Xiao yelled. Per standing orders, he was making an effort to remain covert and held his sidearm at his back, out of sight of the woman.

"Why you bein' so darn orn'ry?" the half-naked woman groused. "We're outta booze. Comprendo savvy that, Charlie?"

"No booze! Go 'way!"

Maybe it was the air of stillness around the woman, as though no other revelers were present on the approaching craft, that raised Mr. L's hackles. Or maybe what bothered him was the fact that he couldn't see past the sun's glare on the smaller yacht's windows. What disturbed him most, he concluded, was the sudden appearance of the boat in the middle of the ocean just moments after they had launched attack teams to hijack a ship. Party girl or not...

"Something's wrong," he said. "Alert your men."

"For naked woman?" Wei's voice carried a trace of a sneer.

"Go 'way!" yelled Xiao from the railing.

The oncoming boat idled closer, its rails only ten meters from the *Kekepi's*.

"Wait, wait, wait." The woman pitched her champagne bottle overboard and reached into the towels strewn about her feet. "I'll trade you a little sumpin', sumpin'..."

"You leave—"

The woman stood with an object in her hand. The towel slid away to reveal a black shotgun with a pistol grip. Mr. L jerked in surprise at the boom when it fired. Private Xiao caught the blast at a distance of less than eight meters, the pellets expanding to a cloud that shattered his chest and flung the private backward into the salon.

At that moment, a figure popped up through an opening atop the smaller yacht's bridge, forward of the radar dome. A thin black man, Mr. L noted dispassionately, with an AK-74. The black man aimed his weapon at the Hatteras, then everything disappeared as Sergeant Wei shoved Mr. L in the side and tackled him to the deck.

Glass blew apart, and bullets *spang*ed off chrome and steel. The angle from the pilothouse to the man's firing position was steep, so the best he could do was annoy them or perhaps get lucky with a ricochet.

Still, it was... deeply concerning to come under such heavy fire when least expecting it. And Mr. L was unarmed. Mr. L stared into at Sergeant Wei's angry eyes as they huddled under the hail of bullets.

"I think the men alerted," Wei said.

YEAGER HELD TIGHT TO the rail as Victor swung the stern of the *Guppy* around to meet the stern of the Hatteras yacht. Both boats featured swim decks at the rear—low water-level platforms that allowed easy boarding for swimmers. Monalisa had warned them that the deck on the Hatteras could be in the raised position, which would make a transition more difficult, so Yeager was happy to see the other yacht's deck was almost on level with their own.

Pettigrew had dropped back to single fire, plinking away at random, more to draw attention forward than to hit anyone. The rush of green sea between the two yachts boiled as Victor feathered the steering jets on and off. Compared to the Hatteras, the *Guppy* was a toy boat in a bathtub. The bigger yacht could eat two of the Cobalt and have a few dinghies as leftovers.

Victor's seamanship wasn't the greatest, and the Cobalt cold-cocked more than kissed the bigger ship. When the two boats banged together with a grind of fiberglass, Monalisa's shout of protest rose over the bark of Pettigrew's firing.

"Sorry, chica!" Victor yelled back.

Yeager hopped onto the bigger yacht and crouched into a firing position, weapon extended. For clearing a tight space, he'd opted to carry Monalisa's Wilson Combat .45 and a pocket full of loaded magazines. There was nothing he hated worse than a bad guy grabbing his rifle barrel as he approached a blind corner. Victor would be close behind with the Ruger M14 to lend superior firepower, along with Pettigrew and his AK.

On each side of the swim platform, ladders led to a higher deck. A closed portal faced him from the middle of the rear bulkhead. He wasn't eager to open a blind door and see what waited on the other side, so he chose the starboard-side ladder and inched his way up.

Yeager scanned the next deck as his eyes cleared the top of the ladder. The stairwell opened onto a covered deck with outdoor seating and a table in the middle of the space. Beyond the seating area, glass doors led deeper into the ship. On the port side, opposite his position, another ladder led to the deck above. The only way forward was through the doors or up the far ladder. The table and chairs would offer a little concealment but zero-minus-zero cover. Somewhere in the bowels of this mega-yacht was his wife, and somewhere else was a terrorist with his finger poised over the button, ready to blow up an LNG carrier off the shore of a densely populated city.

Yeager fired two shots through the glass doors, which left two neat round holes in the glass. Nothing happened for a second, then the world blew apart from the other side of the doors. Automatic rifle fire shattered the glass and *spang*ed off the metal tables and chairs.

Yeager ducked out of sight. *Anytime, Por Que. Any-fucking-time...*

VICTOR JUMPED ONTO the swim deck, and a second later, shots battered the air above him. He ducked and scuttled to the bulkhead, banging his shoulder into the closed portal, where he hunkered down to ensure that nobody shot his ass off.

"Hey, Por Que!" Yeager yelled from the starboard-side ladder. "Could use some suppressive fire. Whenever you're ready!"

Always impatient, Abel Yeager. Nag, nag, nag. "Coming, Lucy! Hold your horses!"

Victor took two steps to port, and the bulkhead door flew open, knocking him backward toward the sloshing green water of the Pacific. Out stepped a Tokyo-eating monster with a face of concrete, wearing a red jersey with a white number 16 emblazoned on it. *Joe Montana zapped by gamma rays and turned into the Thing.* And in case his face didn't scare people to death, the fucker had brought a knife.

Victor backpedaled as the blade swished past his face. His heels found the edge of the swim deck, and when the backstroke came from the giant with the knife, he had no choice. Victor executed a back-buster dive with a half twist, holding the M14 with a death grip.

"Yeager! Watch out!" Then he hit the water.

CHAPTER THIRTY-TWO

Kimo watched the Hispanic dude fly off the back of the boat and hit the water with a splash. The man held a rifle in one hand, and it would only take him a couple of seconds of recovery from being dunked in the water before he could shoot. Kimo only had a knife. He didn't think he'd need a gun on a yacht.

Where had the guy come from? Who was he yelling at? There was a boat next to them. It rocked him when the sterns banged together. He heard a woman cursing.

More gunfire rattled from above and behind him, as if somebody was firing from the salon onto the rear deck with the picnic table. A black man in a tan windbreaker appeared at the rear of the other yacht. Kimo registered the AK and dived back into the crew companionway as the man fired. Rounds chased him, some hitting the open door with dull thunks.

"Who the fuck are you guys?" he yelled from his back.

A double thud vibrated through the deck—probably the black guy jumping on board the *Kekepi*. Kimo scrambled down the narrow companionway and up the stairs leading to the salon level. The door at the top opened out onto the picnic deck, and from there, he could bolt right, heading into the salon and back to the room where he'd left his guns.

At the top, the stairway terminated in a human-sized closet next to the salon, with a door that swung out. Kimo cracked it open and peeked through. *Crap.*

Both sliding glass doors into the salon were blown out, and half an acre of broken glass littered the deck. Kimo wiggled his bare toes and winced. Running across the open space, even for a short distance, would shred his feet and leave him damn near crippled. And that was assuming the trigger-happy son of a bitch guarding the salon didn't mow him down.

Nope. It was better to face anyone who decided to come up the stairs from the crew quarters. In that situation, a knife wouldn't be a bad thing to have in a gunfight. The stairs curved right, which meant a right-handed shooter would be in a bad position to bring his weapon to bear. He would be exposed and his weapon pinned against the inside wall as he climbed.

Kimo settled down to await events.

YEAGER DUCKED BACK down the ladder as the glass doors exploded outward, shattered by automatic weapons' fire. He crouched against the wooden treads, which were coated with a clear nonslip resin that smelled of salt spray and seaweed.

"Abel! Watch out!" Victor yelled from below.

An instant later, Pettigrew appeared at the stern of the *Guppy* and raked the swim deck of the Hatteras yacht with a burst from his AK. Yeager eased back down the ladder and found Victor in the sea, doing the sidestroke one-handed, rifle held overhead.

"Hold up." Pettigrew leaped onto the deck and held up a palm to Yeager. He'd exchanged his automatic rifle for the Mossberg pump shotgun. "One of 'em went in here."

Here turned out to be the hatch that Yeager had decided not to storm earlier. As he watched, the hatch swung shut, pulled by the motion of the ship or by air currents. Yeager went to help Victor, but his muscular pal had already scrambled out of the ocean and gotten to his feet, dripping large quantities of seawater.

"You okay?" Yeager asked.

"I ain't fucking dead," Victor groused. "Second time today somebody come at me with a knife."

Monalisa throttled up the *Guppy's* engines and moved the Cobalt away, per the plan. They wanted some space, both to prevent a counterattack and to preserve their exfil in case things went to shit—though Yeager didn't plan to exfil without Charlie. One way or another, he wasn't leaving this boat without his wife.

"Pettigrew," he said, "guard the back door. Por Que, take the port ladder. When you get to the top, lay down covering fire into the room past the glass doors. I'll assault it after you cut loose. Don't shoot me."

Victor swiped water off his face. "Don't tempt me."

Pettigrew nodded and moved to the blind side of the hatch. Those who opened the door would have to exit fully, exposing themselves to his shotgun before they could engage him.

Yeager told Pettigrew, "If it ain't one of us or a redheaded woman, kill it. Ready? Let's roll."

CHARLIE LAY IN A COFFIN—WORSE than a coffin. Tight, dusty, cramped, smelly, you name it—the under-bunk storage compartment had all those discomforts and more. She had discovered the storage space under the bunk while poking around the cabin for a weapon. Running the length of the bunk, the storage space was accessed by lifting the bunk like a lid. In it were clean sheets, towels, socks, and underwear. It also contained personal mementos of the crewman who had last used the bunk: photo albums, books, a tablet computer—with a dead battery—and some Japanese manga porn.

What had happened to the crewmember? Dead, she guessed.

Stuffing the contents into every available space took several minutes of one-handed effort. Climbing inside the compartment and lowering the bunk on top of her took an act of will. Claustrophobia torqued her nerves to the snapping point. Her nose itched, and she wanted to sneeze.

And then Kimo stomped in and started tearing the place up. Charlie clamped down hard to avoid wetting herself. Given time, she had no doubt Kimo would find her hiding place, and there was no latch or lock on the inside that would prevent him from ripping her out of it. Wooden support slats on the bed's underside were nailed or glued tight to the lid. She dug at them with the fingertips of her un-injured hand but could find no purchase. Holding the lid closed was not an option.

So she hid. And cursed herself for her helplessness. Charlie listened carefully from the tight, dark space as Kimo addressed the locked bathroom door. She'd pressed the pushbutton lock and closed the door prior to hiding—a delaying tactic, nothing more. A faint smile broke through her despair when she heard the giant trying to kick down the door, which opened outward.

"What the fuck?" growled Kimo's dismayed voice.

Thumping footsteps vibrated the deck. Gunshots rattled from somewhere on the ship. Kimo's footsteps pounded out of the room and away.

She heard some shouting and then possibly some lowered voices, but it was hard to tell. More gunshots. Was someone attacking the ship, or had the terrorists fallen out with each other?

Hope you die first, Kimo.

Charlie put her palm against the lid and hesitated. "Come on," she whispered. "Get a grip."

Shoving the lid open, Charlie winced at the relatively bright light. The cabin was empty. More importantly, the door to the room swung open, revealing the unguarded hallway.

KEKEPI, **Pacific Ocean**
Monday, 10 May
0630 Local

Yeager pounded up the starboard ladder again and waited for Por Que to reach a firing position on the other side. The Ruger was a semiautomatic, but Victor could crank a semi almost as fast as someone firing full auto. He rapped out fifteen rounds of .308 like a drum solo in a marching band, punching out more chunks of glass from the shattered salon doors. Hopefully, the defenders inside would be feeling some heat and getting under cover.

If not, I'm a dead man.

At round number ten, Yeager vaulted the top step and charged the gaping hole in the plate-glass doors. He dived and rolled behind a sofa. A hot lead bullet burned a line under his armpit. He ignored it.

More rounds popped holes in the leather side of the sofa just above his head. *Leather means concealment, not cover. Check.* Yeager wriggled left, toward the sofa's back side, away from where he'd landed. He had the fleeting impression of a single shooter crouched behind a wet bar, almost dead center against the far wall of the salon.

"Covering!" Yeager yelled and popped up. He fired at the shooter's position, clacking off all eight rounds in a concussive roar of sound and fury. The man ducked down an instant before the wet bar began splintering from impacts of full-metal-jacket ammo. Yeager shifted aim partway through emptying the magazine and smashed some liquor bottles on the shelves behind the bar.

"Got it!" Victor shouted as he came in behind Yeager and ducked right, setting up behind an armchair and training his rifle downrange. He took over the covering fire as Yeager swapped mags and toggled the slide release. The lone shooter made a break for the far door, and Yeager snapped off a shot that had the man spinning to the deck, clutching at his leg.

"I got this," Yeager said when Victor started to his feet. Yeager stepped forward for a better angle and fired twice more, both rounds punching the black-clad soldier in the chest. Gun smoke drifted on the air, its burnt metal tang harsh in Yeager's lungs. His ears rang, but he was used to that—he'd sometimes wonder what was wrong when his ears weren't ringing and his nose wasn't inhaling powder smoke.

"Only one door," Victor said. He'd swapped magazines during the lull. Yeager did the same once Victor had finished.

The door through which the commando had tried to exit was on the starboard side, near the windows lining the salon. Beyond the windows, the *Guppy* was silhouetted against a fiery sunrise. A bulkhead blocked most of Yeager's view of what lay beyond the door. Victor squinted over the rifle's open sights.

"You see anything?" Yeager asked.

"Nada for squat. Dark on the other side. Unfriendly, huh?"

A shotgun boomed from somewhere near the stern.

"Pettigrew!" Yeager was spinning when motion from the far side caught his eye. He froze for an instant, half-turned, his instincts caught between the threat to Pettigrew and the motion from the forward part of the ship. He recognized the spherical object lofting into the salon an instant after Por Que.

"Grenade!" Victor yelled.

WINSTON PETTIGREW JUMPED in his socks when the hatch flew open. He blinked, and his brain short-circuited. *Good guy or bad guy? Shoot or don't shoot?* By the time it clicked—*Bad guy, shoot now!*—a big motherfucker in shorts and a red jersey had grabbed the Mossberg's barrel.

Pettigrew jerked the trigger, and the shot went high and wide. The big man ripped the shotgun from him with one hand and tossed it to the deck behind him. The other hand held a shining steel combat knife that nearly took Pettigrew's head off on the first swing. He bent backward and avoided the blade, though he could've sworn it shaved off a few stray beard hairs as it went by.

More twisting and belly dancing in a wide circle bought him some distance, though not much. The swim deck was about the size of a small kitchen and slippery with sloshing water. He circled around the knife-wielding giant, ducking one swipe and twisting around another. Then the shotgun was behind him, though he had no chance of reaching it before the big man poked a big hole in Pettigrew's hide and made him some kind of dead.

A boom shuddered through the boat, but Pettigrew had no time to worry about that. He avoided two more swings of the giant's short sword with moves that taxed his brittle joints to the breaking point. His spine crackled like popcorn.

The giant laughed when Pettigrew whipped out Little Bessie. "What is it with you old fucks? First that big mofo, and now you. They let you outta da home today?"

The heat rose up under Pettigrew's collar. "You killed Osterchuk? The white guy in the Hawaiian shirt, back at the camp?"

"Snapped da fool's neck." Godzilla snapped his fingers. "Just like that."

"Shit, you gonna die now, boy."

The monster laughed. "Sure, old man. Bring it on."

Pettigrew dropped into a knife-fighter's crouch. Godzilla was a slasher, not a stabber, which meant he was both untrained and clumsy. On the flip side, he had the wingspan of a 747, so he could sweep that big blade like a scythe, and there was only so much ducking Pettigrew could do before he'd be driven overboard or slashed in two.

Godzilla encouraged him with a *come on* gesture, grinning, as if daring Pettigrew to take the first shot. *Well, okay, then.* Pettigrew darted in, feinted high, and stabbed low. Bessie flickered in and out of the giant's thigh, slick as two frogs fucking, and Pettigrew danced back, ducking under the tree limb swinging from his left. He left a slash on the underside of the big man's arm just for good measure.

"Goddamn you, little fucker!" Godzilla stepped out of reach and examined the blood slicking his forearm. "You fucked up my Montana jersey." Apparently, he hadn't even felt the stab wound in his thigh.

Sweat dripped off Pettigrew's eyebrows and burned his eyes. His breath came hoarse, and he wanted a cigarette in the worst kind of way. The rising sun burned the surface of the sea to a warm gold. The yacht swayed a little on the swells, rocking, soft as a lullaby. A good day for a cocktail on the sundeck—not so good for a knife-fighting monster.

The giant bull-rushed him, and Pettigrew went low again. This time, he rolled in a ball and dived past Godzilla's knees. Flick-flick—another slash was added, this one to Godzilla's calf. Pettigrew rolled to his feet in time to catch a face full of fist as Godzilla spun and swung with his off hand. The punch clipped his cheek and rocked his lights out for a half second.

And a half-second in a knife fight was all it took. Steel glittered, and Godzilla slashed him. Hard. It didn't hurt at first, but he was cut badly—that much he knew.

That slash was followed by another fist, which tagged him squarely on the chin. Pettigrew's world exploded, and the deck hit him in the back. The lights went out.

CHAPTER THIRTY-THREE

Kekepi, **Pacific Ocean**
Monday, 10 May
0630 Local Time

Mr. L huddled in the relative safety of the pilothouse while Sergeant Wei and Privates Jun and Minzhe fought the attackers in the salon. His mind struggled to cope with this development. Who were the attackers? They appeared to be *civilians*, but that was ridiculous. Mr. L had lived in the US and knew that, despite the silly Hollywood propaganda films about ragtag citizens defeating trained armies, civilians did not fight back against the military. Hawaii was not some crazy, lawless place like Texas. Hawaii had strict gun laws.

They could have been the same group that had plagued Manu Ho and the Hawaiians on Molokai, but Mr. L couldn't see how they would have followed the commandos across the ocean. CIA, then? A branch of military intelligence? But the black man had looked... old. And the woman had bared her breasts. *Who goes into battle half-naked, with grandparents?*

A grenade cracked inside the ship, shuddering the walls of the pilothouse. He had confidence in Wei and his men. They were hard, well-trained men. And yet... the attackers, though small in number, seemed determined.

Mr. L clutched his pistol and considered his own death. Capture was not an option. He had no illusions that, if captured, he could resist torture. Sooner or later, everyone broke. He had seen the training videos, and even though most Americans peed themselves at the thought of inflicting such indignity on another, there were more than enough realists in their military and clandestine services who wouldn't hesitate to do whatever it took to break him.

Small-arms fire thundered from the dining room. The dining area separated the salon from the forward section, which included the pilothouse—an area accessed by an open staircase—and the galley. If he cared to, Mr. L could peek down the stairs and observe Wei and the others defending the narrow passage along the starboard side, which joined the salon with the dining area. He did not care to.

Escape from the yacht was not an option either. The *Kekepi* was their escape. They needed the Hatteras to carry them far out to sea, where the submarine waited to pick them up and torpedo the yacht. All remaining evidence, including the charts and plans—which were lying out *in the salon!*—would sink to the bottom of the sea.

Mr. L slapped his forehead and cursed in Chinese. His laptop and all the documentation the Americans would need to piece together his responsibility remained in the salon, where he had foolishly left it. The computer was encrypted and had built-in fail-safes to destroy the hard drive if anyone tampered with it, but the Americans were extremely good at computer forensics and code breaking. Even the paper documents in his portfolio might reveal enough to defeat the carefully constructed false-flag operation and lead them back to China instead of North Korea.

Disaster. Even suicide was not an option, at least not until he secured the laptop. But for the moment, he had to complete the mission. Mr. L removed the encrypted satellite phone from an inner jacket pocket and keyed a speed-dial number.

The phone burbled in his ear, ringing five times before Lieutenant Peng answered. "*Shi*?"

"Have you reached the channel?"

"Yes."

"Are the charges placed?"

"Yes."

"*All* the charges?" Mr. L asked.

"Yes."

Unknown to the Hawaiians, Peng and his men had placed specially designed breaching-and-detonation charges on the LNG containers. When Mr. L keyed the detonation sequence, not only would the ship sink and block the channel, but the globes containing liquid natural gas would also be ripped open and the escaping vapor triggered to create a massive conflagration. A large section of Pearl Harbor would be turned to ash.

Mr. L continued, "The *Kekepi* is under attack by a... small force of irregulars. Return at once. Leave the Hawaiians to pilot the ship. I will blow the charges in five minutes. That's how long you have to get clear. Understood?"

"Ahh... *shi*. We can be back in ten to fifteen minutes."

"Make it sooner." Mr. L ended the call and tucked away the phone. He checked the chamber on the North Korean CZ 75 knockoff pistol, drew a deep breath, and settled on his haunches. His thumb moved over the keypad and dialed the detonation sequence then paused over the send key.

The *Golden Sun* was a prophetic name. Honolulu would soon see a new golden sun arise in their harbor.

THE GRENADE *tink*ed off a bust of Bill Walsh and bounced under a red, white, and gold armchair. Yeager dropped behind his new favorite sofa and clamped his hands over his ears. The detonation punched him like God's angry fist. Glass along both sides of the salon blew out, and a giant foot stomped his brain flat. Shrapnel blew chunks from the leather sofa, and something hot jabbed Yeager in the ribs, though the sensation came to him via airmail from a distant country.

Automatic-weapon fire raked the room, which he dimly sensed through the broken film images flashing in his brain.

Pock-pock-pock!

That was Victor's Ruger. Somehow, Por Que was still in the game. White smoke drifted along the floor in wisps.

Metallic taste in his mouth. Wetness under his nose. Blood dripping on the carpet.

Weapon? Wilson Combat in his fist. Hammer back. Safety off.

Yeager's consciousness returned the way an old computer booted up. His reflexes recovered, and his muscles regained connectivity with his brain. His head rang with a high-pitched whine, but he could function.

Directly ahead of him was the bulkhead with the wet bar. To the right of that was the corridor held by the defenders. Behind and to the right somewhere, Por Que was keeping the enemy from extending into the salon.

They had caught Yeager and Victor by surprise with that first grenade but had been too slow to follow up. Had they charged in right away, Yeager would be dead and Victor overwhelmed. Somehow, Por Que had saved his ass again by reacting quickly and driving back the aggressors, allowing him time to recover.

Get back in the fight, dummy. Yeager belly-crawled to the wet bar and levered himself upright. He edged toward the corridor. He paused at the corner then glanced back and noted Por Que, sheltered behind a splintered mahogany coffee table tipped on its side, and raised an eyebrow. He received a thumbs-up from Por Que.

They knew the drill without needing to discuss it. Yeager would lay down cover fire, and Victor would advance. Yeager would change mags, and Victor would return the favor, pinning the enemy until Yeager was ready to assault the corridor. The last part was the hardest: get close enough to the enemy to inflict casualties without getting killed.

Yeager assessed the odds and didn't like the result. Charging a narrow corridor in the face of enemy guns was a suicide mission. He wouldn't make three steps before being shot to shit. Yeager cursed and slapped a palm against the wall. His way forward was blocked, and he still had no idea whether Charlie was on the far side of the defenders, somewhere else on the ship, or...

No. There is no third option. She's here somewhere. Yeager scrubbed his face in the crook of an elbow. *Think, Yeager. Take the time to think it through, and do the smart thing. You have a few minutes, so use them.*

WINSTON PETTIGREW OPENED his eyes to the grinning face of a big ugly bastard bending over him with a knife. His head ached, and a line of fire scorched his chest. He was lying in a puddle of seawater. No. Make that blood. And the guy standing over him...?

Oh. Godzilla. Well, fuck.

Godzilla knelt on Pettigrew's knife arm and pushed his head back to the deck with one meaty hand. Pettigrew's right arm creaked under the weight and threatened to break. But he had bigger problems. Six inches of shining steel scythed toward his neck.

"Goodbye, old man," Godzilla said.

The point of the blade touched his throat.

"Hey, asshole!" The comment came from a voice behind Godzilla. Pettigrew twisted his head, but he couldn't see, his view blocked by six tons of Samoan. It had sounded like... a woman's voice?

Godzilla spun around, though he kept his knee on Pettigrew's arm. Pettigrew grinned despite the pain. Charlie Yeager stood on the far side of the deck, in muddy shorts and dingy tank top. Legs scratched. Copper hair matted and grimy. She held the Mossberg in an awkward grip, left-handed, with the muzzle braced across her forearm. Her right hand was swollen, purple and yellow, and twisted.

She was the most beautiful woman Winston Pettigrew had ever seen.

"Hello, Mizz Yeager," Pettigrew wheezed. "Your husband's been looking for you."

CHARLOTTE YEAGER HELD the pump-action shotgun on Kimo and suddenly realized she had no idea whether the chamber was loaded or empty. Shotguns were not her favorite type of firearm—she had occasionally gone trap shooting with Dad in the long-distant past and had used an over-under then. Her experience with pump guns was limited. There was a pump release somewhere near the rear of the trigger guard, as best she could remember, and loading the chamber with a live shell required depressing the tiny button, pulling back the pump, then ramming it forward. On the gun she had fired, a button at the *front* of the trigger guard controlled the gun's safety.

Oh, happy day. It was all meant to be operated *right-handed.*

"Red wants to play, huh?" Kimo leered at her from across the deck, where he knelt by Winston, whose tan windbreaker was soaked red.

Kimo stood. A knife dangled from his massive hand. He twirled it around his fingers in a fancy movie-stunt sleight of hand.

Your husband's looking for you, Winston had said. How was that even possible? Could he be here, on the boat?

Kimo stepped forward, and Charlie pulled the shotgun's trigger. *Click.*

"Abel!" she shrieked. She fumbled around the grip, fingers seeking the release button as Kimo took another step. He was between her and the hatch. Winston appeared dazed. His blood tinged the seawater slopping over the swim deck.

"You need to jack it back." Kimo pantomimed pumping a shotgun. "You know how to jack it, right?"

She risked a glance and found the button next to the trigger guard, right where it was supposed to be. After clicking it up with her thumb, Charlie jammed back on the pump, which she pinched in the crook of her elbow. The chamber clacked open, and a bright-red shell spun away to fall into the sea with a soft plop.

"There you go." Kimo was within reach. He seemed to be encouraging her, but his grin was mocking, sneering. "Now push it back up."

Charlie panted, her face hot and dripping with sweat. Her heart thundered, and she tasted copper on her tongue. The giant loomed over her, cast in silhouette, his shape eclipsing the low morning sun. Slick with sweat, the pump slipped out of her elbow when she tried pushing it forward. The weight of the shotgun pulled at her left hand, unsupported, the muzzle wobbling toward the deck.

"No, no," Kimo told her. "Don't drop it. Here, want me to—*huhn*!"

Charlie glanced up in time to see Kimo's mouth open and a scream of such hideous horror pour out that it washed her with terror. At his feet, Winston Pettigrew cackled.

"Take that, Godzilla motherfucker." Pettigrew's extended arm held a knife, its blade buried to the hilt—as best she could tell—between Kimo's ass cheeks.

The giant stood on his tiptoes, lips pinched, eyes bulging. Charlie snagged the pump in the crook of her elbow again, this time muscling it forward until it clattered home and locked a fresh shell in the chamber. She didn't waste time on speeches or fighting words. She tucked the Mossberg under Kimo's chin and pulled the trigger.

Winston sagged out of the way as Kimo toppled. He choked out a laugh and grinned at her with reddened teeth. "I believe that feller done lost his mind," he rasped then flopped on his back and closed his eyes.

"ABEL!"

Yeager snapped his head around. That was Charlie's voice coming from somewhere behind them, back toward the swim deck. A dark object sailed past his ear.

What was...? Oh hell.

The grenade bounced off the side of the shredded armchair blown up by the first grenade and rolled to a stop at Yeager's feet.

David Buchanan Yeager—Charlie's son who had taken Yeager's last name after Abel and Charlie were married—played soccer. The twelve-year-old approached the game with the same intensity with which he tackled everything. He gave one hundred percent and practiced daily. Yeager had been roped into front-yard practice sessions even though he booted the ball like a pregnant yak. David ran rings around him while Yeager flayed and stomped at the bouncing sphere.

But something must have stuck—muscle memory. By reflexive habit, Yeager side-kicked the grenade, launching a perfect shot back down the corridor. The detonation slammed through the gap a heartbeat after his sweeping foot had shot the metal ball back the way it had come. Smoke billowed from the hole, followed by a shriek of pain.

Victor raised a fist and screamed, "Goooaaalll!"

Yeager hesitated. Tactically, the right course of action would be to follow the detonation with an assault and attack the stunned defenders before they recovered. But Charlie's voice had called him. She sounded desperate. Hurt. She needed him.

But going back would leave an enemy at his rear, one who might recover at any second and overwhelm them with numbers.

Victor's shout broke him free. "Go! I got Charlie."

Yeager screamed his frustration and charged the hall. A commando lay sprawled in a ragged heap on the deck, his body torn as though run over by a threshing machine. Another knelt against a square high-top dining table, holding his face with one hand. Beyond the table, an Asian guy dressed in a neat suit and tie lay stunned, his mouth gaping.

Yeager stepped up and coldly shot the kneeling man in the head. He crossed to the bloody heap and added two more insurance shots. The man in the suit had regained some control and was groping for a satellite phone on the deck.

Yeager kicked it away. "Hey, you." Yeager snagged the survivor by his tie and dragged him to his feet.

The man blinked and focused. "I tell you nothing."

Yeager punched him in the face. Hard. The man's head snapped back, and his eyes fluttered. He gaped at Yeager as blood ran into his mouth from a squashed nose. Tears flooded his eyes. Yeager hit him again, and the man's eyes rolled back. He passed out.

CHAPTER THIRTY-FOUR

G*uppy*, **Pacific Ocean**
Monday, 10 May
0643 Local Time

Monalisa Montgomery stood at the *Guppy*'s helm and rested her binoculars against the rail one-handed and held the radio mic with the other. After the first blast of her shotgun—which had incidentally been the first human she had killed by any means, and her stomach still wasn't sure how she felt about that—they'd had no need for concealment.

With the attack in full swing, she was free to radio for help. "Mayday, mayday, mayday. Any Coast Guard or US Navy vessel, this is the *Guppy* with urgent traffic."

Windows exploded from the Hatteras, and Monalisa ducked instinctively. The radio crackled and spat. A scratchy baritone said, "*Guppy* this is the Coast Guard command, Honolulu Station. State your emergency."

State your emergency. Now, there was a task. She had any number of emergencies, all of which needed stating and all of which needed to be believed by the powers that be.

"Coast Guard command, *Guppy*. There is a hijacked LNG carrier"—she glanced at the GPS and read off coordinates—"in the Pearl Harbor channel. I believe these to be the same terrorist group that has attacked other targets in and around the Hawaiian Islands. I am retired Master-at-Arms Monalisa Montgomery, US Navy, and this is not a hoax."

There was radio silence, then, "*Guppy*, Coast Guard. Go to Channel 21."

Another explosion rocked the Hatteras, and shards of debris pattered the water. Monalisa flinched again, though she held the *Guppy* at one hundred yards, and none of the shrapnel came close. After switching channels, she spent the next ten minutes arguing with an ascending scale of Coastie officers, each one more suspicious than the last.

"Look! Just check it out!" Monalisa yelled at the latest example of military efficiency on the other end of the line. "A goddamn floating bomb is in the channel leading to Pearl Harbor. Don't you think you might want to fucking stop it?"

"Young lady," Admiral Dimwit said, "there is no need for that kind of language on the radio. A cutter is already en route, and we'll be checking your story. In the meantime, be aware that your transmission has been triangulated, and if your story fails to check out, there will be consequences."

"Fine. I don't care. Just get your ass out here before—" Her finger released the transmit button. She dropped the mic to hold the binoculars steady with both hands. Focusing, the lenses snapped to the image of an inflatable powering over the water. The inflatable carried a number of men. And they were making a beeline toward the *Kekepi*.

YEAGER SWAPPED MAGS on the run—more of a shambling shuffle than a run. Fatigue weighted his legs with concrete. Adrenaline could only take a person so far, and Yeager had used up an industrial-sized supply of it in the past forty-plus hours. The well was dry.

He passed through the salon and ducked through the blown-out doorframes at the rear. Glass crunched underfoot, making more noise than a tractor in a field of dry wheat. If Pettigrew was down, and an enemy held the swim deck, then Yeager's presence had just been announced with a brass band.

So be it. He might as well make some noise. "Charlie!" Yeager crabbed toward the port ladder leading down to the swim deck, pistol extended in a two-handed grip. "Where are you?"

A long silence passed, followed by, "Abel? Is that you?"

A sluice of relief washed through Yeager, and he staggered to one knee. Glass stabbed through his jeans, and he hardly registered the discomfort. His throat had closed, and he had to try twice to force the words out.

"Charlie?" It came out so weak he could barely hear it himself. Yeager drew a breath and tried again, louder. "Charlie?"

His wife appeared at the bottom of the ladder, and God's fist squeezed Yeager's heart so hard he was sure it stopped beating. His eyes watered, and breathing through the dry knot in his throat became a chore.

Charlie held herself awkwardly, one arm cradled tightly to her body. She had been battered and bruised, it looked like, but she was alive. Her blue eyes were red rimmed, and tears spilled down her cheeks. The look on her face mirrored the emotions tearing through him.

"I... I..." Words refused to form.

"Abel. Oh God." She drew a shaky breath. "Winston's hurt bad. We need to get him to a hospital."

THROUGH THE WOBBLY binoculars, Monalisa counted eight men in the inflatable boat, wearing black fatigues and carrying AK-style rifles. She studied the group for a long time before convincing herself they weren't allies coming to the rescue. No, these were terrorists, returning to their lair, either as part of the plan or in reaction to the assault.

She estimated the inflatable was sixty seconds from crossing her bow and less than two minutes to the hundred-foot yacht. A force that size would quickly overwhelm the three-man rescue squad.

She switched her focus back to the Hatteras and caught a glimpse of Victor escorting a man in a suit past the blown-out windows along the starboard side, the man walking like a prisoner with his hands interlaced behind his head. He appeared oblivious to the threat.

Monalisa cranked the Volvo Pentas to life, and the Cobalt rumbled with contained power. The feel of the big diesels charged up her spine like a crackle of electricity. As much as she loved her sailboat and the challenge of mastering wind and wave, the *Guppy's* power thrilled her in ways she cared not to admit aloud.

"Sorry, Thad," she muttered. "I'm going to scratch the paint a bit."

Thirty seconds out. Monalisa eyed the closing gap with a sailor's intuition and pinned an intercept point in her mind's eye. She had no targeting computer to calculate speed and trajectory, so this would be pure seat-of-the-pants guesstimation and prayer. The inflatable was much more nimble than the motor yacht. If she missed, they would run circles around her, either reach the Hatteras unimpeded or shoot her full of holes, then continue their mission. Though perhaps the noise would give Victor and the guys a heads-up.

Fifteen seconds. *Blow the horn?* The sound would definitely alert the boys to trouble, but it would also alert the bad guys that the Cobalt was a threat. If they vectored away or started evasive maneuvers, her chance at a clean intercept would be blown. Then it would be back to a firefight.

Ten seconds. Monalisa caressed the throttle and waited. Three... two... one... *now!*

She shoved the throttles full forward, and the Pentas roared. The Cobalt's tail dropped, and the forty-footer powered ahead. Water churned and frothed behind her. The *Guppy* slapped the waves, bang-bang-bang, and the diesels bellowed. Monalisa screamed with them, howling a war cry of her own.

All the faces in the inflatable turned in her direction. The man at the tiller gawped for a moment—Monalisa could see the perfect O of his mouth—then pushed the control handle hard to starboard. The rubber boat swerved away, curving sideways and smacking a wave hard enough to tip the boat high. For a second, Monalisa thought the thing would go over completely—*Problem solved, yay, let's all go have a beer*. But no, the craft flopped back down and powered for open sea. Gunfire ripped out from the inflatable, rapping the *Guppy's* hull.

The men in the boat gaped at her in the last second before they disappeared under the yacht's prow. She felt a thud, and the Cobalt stumbled for a second, then it leaped ahead. Squealing, scraping noises came from the hull.

She hoped to God she was right and that the guys weren't a bunch of SEALs out for a cruise. Monalisa cut back the throttle and steered the *Guppy* in a wide circle to get a look at her handiwork. The inflatable was dying. It sank stern first, being dragged under by the weight of its outboard, half-deflated and with only the prow holding enough air to keep it from sinking completely.

A couple of heads popped up, then two more. A fifth man floated, face down and limp. Red froth and debris marked the collision site, evidence of where her screws had churned through the inflatable and the men aboard her.

Sickness clenched her belly, and she fought back an urge to upchuck. *Oh God. Did I do the right thing? I've gone from killing one man today to killing a bunch.*

And the four survivors? She certainly couldn't take them aboard, which her instincts were driving her to do. Four hostile terrorists? They'd tear her apart.

The men had all swum to the floating half of the rubber boat, where they clung to it. As she idled closer, one of them cursed her in an Asian tongue and shook his fist. Monalisa held the *Guppy* at thirty yards from the foundering inflatable and paused there long enough to throw out four life vests and an inflatable ring.

"There!" she yelled. "Best I can do for now. I'll call the Coast Guard to come get you."

Whether they understood or not, she didn't know. Packing away her guilt for later—where Monalisa was sure it would come out and twist her in knots—she kicked the *Guppy's* throttles back up and headed for the Hatteras.

"I hope this nightmare is over soon," she said to herself.

CHAPTER THIRTY-FIVE

Yeager didn't want to try moving Pettigrew to the *Guppy*, so when Monalisa idled up alongside the *Kekepi*, he asked her if she could drive the bigger yacht and get them into Honolulu, "STAT-fucking-fast." The former Navy master-at-arms nodded and set about anchoring and shutting down the Cobalt. Yeager ducked back into the crew quarters where Charlie had said she'd been held earlier.

Pettigrew lay on one bunk, swaddled in blankets except where red-stained towels wrapped his midsection. The slice across his torso traveled diagonally from under his left nipple all the way across his diaphragm. Shallow at first, the cut deepened, splitting open skin and muscle. He had lost a lot of blood. Charlie sat on the bed next to him, keeping pressure on the wound.

Looking damp and drawn, the old man cracked an eye when Yeager stepped into the cabin. "Don't suppose you got a butt?" he wheezed.

Yeager put a hand on his wife's shoulder. "I know you're hurtin', babe, but can you hold here a bit? I need to clear the rest of the boat and make sure there's no lurkers."

She cast a tired smile his way and touched his hand with her cheek. "I got this. Just be careful. And if you find some ibuprofen, bring the bottle."

The engines rumbled to life, and Yeager had to catch himself as the boat started moving under his feet. He held Charlie's shoulder a second longer, trying to impart as much strength, or draw as much love, as possible from that simple touch. All he wanted to do was sit and rock her in his arms.

But there was work to do. It was a big boat, and it took a lot of clearing. Yeager was dragging by the time he reached the salon, where he found Victor seated on the torn-up sofa. The muscular Latino was bent over the coffee table—also splintered and shot up—and had several charts and diagrams spread out in front of him. The Asian man in the suit sat in an armchair, trussed with thick-braided rope like a heroine tied to the railroad tracks. He glared daggers at Yeager, though the effect lacked power, considering the bloody snot bubbling at the man's nostrils.

"Hey, El Toro," Victor said. "Charlie okay?"

"Yeah." Yeager slumped to the sofa next to his friend. "Yeah. I guess. Her hand is broke all to shit, and Pettigrew's holding on by a thread. The boat's clear, though. No more bad guys."

"Not so fast, hombre." Victor stabbed a dirty finger on the chart in front of him. "We got big trouble here."

"Talk to me."

"We know these assholes snatched a liquid gas carrier, right?"

"Uh-huh."

"And Monalisa said the Coast Guard is sending a cutter to check it out."

"Good. What's the problem?"

Victor leaned back, rubbed his eyes. "Well, ain't no cutter made gonna stop a chip that size, homes, if it don't wanna stop. They'll brush that little boat off like a fly. So this big chip is gonna keep on goin'."

Yeager had noticed that Victor's low-rider gang-banger accent had magically cleared up when Dr. Alex came into the picture. Now he appeared to be regressing.

"So the Coast Guard sends a bigger chip—I mean ship," Yeager countered.

Victor wagged his head no. "It'll take too much time, dude. By the time the Coasties pull their finger out, Mr. Big Fucking Chip is in the channel to Pearl." He poked a finger at the chart. "See here, this narrow cut? Back in '41, when the Japanese sneak attacked, one of the battleship skippers—I forget which one, not the *Arizona*—ran his ship aground to keep it from blocking the channel. The water's maybe a hundred feet there, so—"

"So if they scuttle the LNG carrier there, it blocks Pearl Harbor."

"It blocks Pearl Harbor."

"Cuts off the base from any navy ships coming or going," Yeager said.

"Fucks up the squids big-time."

"And," Yeager added, "if they blow the gas tanks, somehow set 'em on fire..."

"They burn a whole buncha people all to death, dude."

"So what do we do?" Yeager's exhaustion pinned him to the sofa. Just moving would require an act of willpower. "I don't have another ship assault left in me."

Victor scratched his chin. He held up his cell phone. "Let me see if I can make a call." His thumb swiped a few times then stabbed. He held the phone to his ear. "Hey, Butch, it's your old pal, Victor... no, the other old pal Victor, smartass. Listen up, man. You ready to be a hero?"

THE *Kekepi* had been allowed emergency clearance to dock at Aloha Tower, and Monalisa powered the yacht like a Jet Ski into Honolulu Harbor. They were met by a trauma team who jammed Winston Pettigrew full of plasma and transported him to the hospital where, by request, Dr. Alexandra Lopez waited with a surgical staff to receive him.

Charlie and Yeager went in another ambulance, leaving Victor and Monalisa to deal with a large number of hard-faced men in suits and others in military uniforms.

Yeager watched the news on the hospital room TV while the doctors took Charlie in for X-rays. According to reports, the Coast Guard had confirmed the hijacking of the *Golden Sun*, and the navy had acted on "credible intelligence" of a severe threat to national security and public safety. A team of navy special operations personnel had retaken the *Golden Sun*, inflicting 100 percent casualties on the Hawaiian terrorists. Tugs had pushed the LNG carrier out of the channel, where demolition technicians would board and disarm the explosive devices.

Yeager lost the thread of the report, and his eyes glazed over. Seconds later, he blacked out.

HONOLULU, OAHU
Tuesday, 11 May
1945 Local
Thirty-Six Hours after Taking the *Kekepi*

Victor found Dr. Alex Lopez in room 364 at the bedside of scrawny gray-haired Winston Pettigrew. The old vet's bed was lifted to a reclining position, and tubes extended from various points on his body to machines and bags and to the bathroom sink, as near as Victor could determine.

"You're not dead, dude," Victor chirped.

"With this angel looking out for me? How could I die?" Pettigrew's voice came out as though squeezed through a rusty tube, but he had a rogue's twinkle in his eye. "When I get outta this bed, I'm gonna give you a run for her hand."

"And some people"—Alex shot Victor a dark-eyed glower—"better do some explaining real soon if they ever want to see my hand or any other part of me again."

"What?" Victor touched his chest. "What'd I do, *querida*?"

The Latina woman put her hands on her hips and squared off with a glare. "Don' you *querida* me, Victor Ruiz. Running off into the jungle without telling me, getting shot at again, getting... getting..." Alex launched into Spanish and proceeded to describe, with many adjectives and colorful idioms, how stupid and thoughtless he had been over the past three days. By the third chapter, second verse, she was in his face, poking a finger in his chest. "And who is this woman? Huh? This woman with the boat who you just happened to know?"

"A friend, sweetheart, j-just a friend."

"A friend with boobs, yes? A friend you don't tell me about, whose number is still in your phone!"

Victor felt sweat drip down his collar. He appealed to Winston with a look, but the old man just spread his palms and wheezed, "Flowers, chocolate, and make-up sex. That's my only advice."

Alex showed every inclination of continuing her rant, so Victor did the only thing he could think of. He grabbed her by the shoulders, looked her in the eyes, and said, "Will you marry me?"

"I—what did you say?"

"Will you marry me?" His heart hadn't hammered half this hard while ducking grenades on the *Kekepi*. He thought it would slam right out of his chest.

The anger drained away from Alex's face, replaced by shock. In a small voice, she asked, "Are you... are you serious right now?"

"All the way serious, my love. Marry me."

"I..." Tears welled from her dark eyes. "I... of course I will!" The last part was muffled by her face buried in his chest.

Winston said, "That works too. Hey, anybody got a cigarette?"

HONOLULU, OAHU
Tuesday, 11 May
2320 Local

Thunder jerked Yeager from a heavy sleep. He caught himself an instant before rolling to the floor in reaction to being under fire. He lay under a thin blanket on a couch next to the window in Charlie's hospital room. Rain sheeted the glass, and lightning flickered through the half-drawn blinds.

His wife slept on the bed with an IV fluid dripping away. Her breathing was deep and regular, mouth hanging slightly open. Bandages wrapped her head, covering a scalp wound where some asshole had clocked her with a hard object, probably a gun butt. A heavy cast covered her right hand. She'd held it up to him before going to sleep and said with a crooked smile, "Looks like I won't be learning the piano anytime soon."

Anger clamped his belly at the sight. He wished he could revive the monster—now headless—who had done this to her and kill him all over again. His failure to protect her and keep her safe ate at him. Acid burned his throat. He pulled from his pocket a damp roll of antacid tablets and chewed two of them.

Earlier that day, he had been driven out to Marine Corps Base Hawaii and met Victor's friend Butch. The Marine officer had escorted Victor and Yeager to a hangar just off the flight line. The place was pristine, so clean the floor shone. Two flag-wrapped coffins on stands waited inside.

Yeager's footsteps echoed on the polished floor as he approached Betty Pyle, who sat in a chair next to her husband's coffin, her hand upon it. A handkerchief was twisted around the other. "I'm so sorry, Betty."

"Don't you for a minute, Abel Yeager." The woman's reddened gaze pinned him. "Ted lived as a Marine and died as a Marine, serving his country. I suspect Ted went out a happy man, helping his brothers, defending his people. He wouldn't have wanted an ounce of sympathy for doing his duty."

"He was..." Yeager's voice was unaccountably hoarse. He cleared his throat. "He was a good man."

"Damn right he was," Betty Pyle had said. Then she'd hugged him. "They both were."

Lightning flared, and the hospital window rattled at the following rumble of thunder. Yeager flipped the blanket off and checked on his wife. She appeared to be resting comfortably, so he resisted the urge to touch her face.

Danny Osterchuk, dead. Jan Osterchuk, missing, presumed dead. Ted Pyle, gone. Lu Kim. Melissa and Austin from California. Countless other lives destroyed. Why?

"We think," Butch had told them in confidence, "the Chinese are trying to teach us a lesson about messing with Taiwan."

"The Chinese?" Victor barked. "What the hell?"

"What's gonna happen?" Yeager asked.

Butch had shrugged, palms up. "Above my pay grade, gentlemen." He slapped Victor on the shoulder and shook Yeager's hand. "Semper Fi, boys."

Yeager stood watch over his wife in a darkened hotel room and listened to the rain and wind beat at the window. "I'm never leaving you again," he whispered. "Semper Fi, honey."

HONOLULU, OAHU
  Wednesday, 12 May
  0506 Local

His ringing cell phone pulled Victor up from a deep, contented dream of riding horses and camping somewhere in the high mountains. Alex was there, but oddly, so was Jumbo, the stoned Jeep driver.

Alex mumbled in her sleep and rolled over as Victor fumbled the phone to his ear.

"Dude, whoever this is, it's fucking early, man."

The voice on the other end of the sat phone connection was American. Midwestern, if Victor had to guess, though he wasn't good with accents of native English speakers. Born in McAllen, Texas, Victor's formative years were spent in a Spanish-speaking household. English sounded to him like a bunch of pots and pans clanging together.

"I'm looking for Victor Ruiz," the man said. "Is this Victor Ruiz?"

"Who're you?" Victor said. Giving away information was against his religion.

"Thomas McGuffey, United States consulate's office." He paused. "In Hermosillo."

"Hokay, Señor McGruff. Wachoo waan?" Victor laid on his dumb-Mexican routine whenever he dealt with gringos of the government persuasion. He was one tick away from going all *no-hablo-ingles* on McGuffey of the US consulate. In Hermosillo.

"Ahhh, if this is Victor Ruiz, I'm trying to find out if you know a Milton Quattlebaum."

Victor blinked. The name stirred a distant bell. It didn't so much ring it as brush up against it and gave the clapper a wiggle. "No, I don' thin' so."

"Well, he says he knows you—oh, wait." There was another pause, filled by the hiss of an open line. "He said to tell you, 'It's Cujo.' Do you know Mr. Cujo?"

"Cujo?" Victor blurted without pausing for thought. "He's dead. Or, I mean, thass wha' I heard, anyway."

According to Yeager, Cujo had flown his plane into a mountain above the village of Rascón. When he crashed, Cujo was flying into a firefight with a highly modified rocket-firing technically illegal aircraft, and he was blowing the shit out of Mexican citizens—bad drug-cartel citizens, but citizens nonetheless. That made Victor want to keep his friendship with Cujo at an arm's length.

"No, he's not dead," McGuffey was saying. "He's in a prison—Federal Prison Number Eleven to be precise. In Hermosillo."

"Mm."

McGuffey paused again as if waiting for more. When it didn't come, he went on. "Mr. Quattlebaum is charged with terrorism."

"That sounds really bad."

Victor had a vague memory that Cujo's real name was something German, but hearing McGuffey say "Quattlebaum" was like someone saying, "a fermented beverage made from hops" instead of beer.

"It is bad," McGuffey said.

"What's it to me?"

"Uh, excuse me?"

"What's it to me?" Victor repeated. What the American consulate—and by extension, the Mexican police forces—knew about his personal role in the little bang-bang at San Felipe de Christo would go a long way toward how he approached Cujo's situation. If they were clueless who was involved in the firefight, well and good—Victor could go straight at the problem. On the other hand, if they suspected one tremendously handsome, muscular Mexican of Texas descent—and his butt-ugly jarhead friend—of being involved... well, then, something more devious would be required. Even if Cujo, Yeager, and Victor had saved priests and orphans from certain death, their methodology had been rather... destructive.

McGuffey, at least, acted as if he had no idea of Victor's role in stamping the shit out of Grupo Verdugo. "Mr. Quattlebaum reached out to the consulate for assistance. The most we could do, we told him, was help him find an attorney. Instead, Mr. Quattlebaum asked us to locate you." Papers rattled in the background, and McGuffey's voice changed to a reading tone. "He said, 'Victor Ruiz is a friend from the old days. He'll get me a lawyer.'"

"He didn't say nothing else?"

"No, that's pretty much it."

Good for you, Cujo. "Well. Okay, then."

"Okay what?"

"Okay, I guess I will go see this Mr. Quattlebaum, who I hardly know and can barely remember, and help him find a lawyer."

"Great, thank you." McGuffey sighed the way a bureaucrat did when he'd successfully handed off an assignment. "Any message I should pass along to Mr. Quattlebaum?"

"Sure," Victor said. "Tell him Yeager and Por Que are on the way."

Also by Scott Bell

An Abel Yeager Novel
Yeager's Law
Yeager's Mission
Yeager's Getaway

Standalone
Working Stiffs

Watch for more at snapshooter4hire.com.

About the Author

Scott Bell has over 25 years of experience protecting the assets of retail companies. He holds a degree in Criminal Justice from North Texas State University.

With the kids grown and time on his hands, Scott turned back to his first love—writing. His short stories have been published in The Western Online, Cast of Wonders, and in the anthology, Desolation.

When he's not writing, Scott is on the eternal quest to answer the question: What would John Wayne do?

Read more at snapshooter4hire.com.

About the Publisher

Dear Reader,

We hope you enjoyed this book. Please consider leaving a review on your favorite book site.

Visit https://RedAdeptPublishing.com to see our entire catalogue.

Don't forget to subscribe to our monthly newsletter to be notified of future releases and special sales.